LUNAR CYCLE BOOK 3

LUNA'S LAMENT

露娜的悲歌

DAVID COLBY

THINKING INK PRESS
CAMPBELL, CALIFORNIA

Published by Thinking Ink Press
P.O. Box 1411, Campbell, California, 95009
First printing, 2020

Print edition ISBN 978-1-942480-24-2

Ebook edition ISBN 978-1-942480-25-9

Printed in the United States of America.

Project Credits

Cover art: Sandi Billingsley

Cover layout and Ebook Interior layout: Streetlight Graphics

Lunar Cycle branding: Nathan Vargas

Editors: Aaron Sikes, Anthony Francis, Betsy Miller

Copy Editor: Gayle Schultz

Early Reader: Tessa Miller

Chinese Language Editor: Roger Que

Interior layout: Betsy Miller

DEDICATION

To the random musers.

"In our tenure on this planet we've accumulated dangerous evolutionary baggage—propensities for aggression and ritual, submission to leaders, hostility to outsiders—all of which puts our survival in some doubt."

Carl Sagan (1934-1996)

CHAPTER 1
TWEEN CHOP

6/25/2068

Republic of Deseret, NAU

T-Minus L-Day: 43

"Today, we are going to teach you eighteen silent ways to kill a man."

Of the many things that I could call Selection out on, I could (at the very least) say this one single positive thing: they don't *fahn leong jian* about what they're teaching you. I sat up and paid attention—not that I really had a choice, not in the VR sessions, where you weren't just required to attend, your brain was hooked in and pumped with neurotropic drugs. And let me tell you: the fact you can't not think about the instruction helped.

It helped a lot.

Our instructor for this little tween chop seminar was a gray-skinned transie that looked like he had come right out of a Bollywood slasher film: machined lines ran along his joints and his arms were made of matte-black carbon composites, molded into the crude shapes of muscle and joints. He summoned a virtual bad guy and tapped him twice on the shoulder.

The bad guy—dressed in Loonie yellow and black—half-turned to see who was bothering him before our instructor smashed his face in with the mother of all sucker punches. It was fairly silent—nothing more than a soft crunch—and the man fell, his face dutifully simulated with a crumpled jaw and scattered teeth.

It seemed silly, but that was the Selection motto: simplicity breeds success. Why bother with kidney strikes or eye gouging or fancy kung fu when you have a 1000 PSI harder-than-steel piston for an arm? Of course, that was just one of eighteen "silent ways" that our instructor had to show us. By the time he was done, I was feeling a little green around my virtual gills, drugs or no drugs. The Class Two Cyberlimb wasn't just strong and tough, it was also flexible. Joints could bend in ways they never could with a human arm, as demonstrated when the instructor grabbed a virtual bad guy by the head and spun him three hundred and sixty degrees with his articulated wrist. That kind of thing upped your lethality from scary-good to suit-soiling terrifying because most of the process of winning a fight was based on an intense understanding of how people moved and how to move them right.

Well, move them wrong.

From the point of view of their bones, internal organs, nerves, blood vessels and so on.

"Zhao. You're up."

I felt my focus shift. My brain felt like someone was reaching in and twisting the knobs, twiddling the dials, tapping the touchscreens. It was just the drug mixture shifting around, but it made me go from a floating point of focus to a me: Drusilla Zhao. Teenage Spacer. Veteran marine.

On the spot.

"Demonstrate," the instructor said, his half-illusory shadow body melting in the VR. Reality closed around me and suddenly I was there. My limbs felt heavy and metal and there was a Loonie standing right across from me. I really hoped that the disconnection between limb and mind was just a function of VR and not an accurate simulation of what it was like to have these things.

I looked at the Loonie. And I thought of everyone I'd lost.

Once the show was over, we all got dumped straight out of the VR. Total time, subjective, three hours. Total time, actual—that is, recorded by clocks in the real world, not by brains hopped up on neuros—was something close to three minutes. That's why they called them "tween chop" seminars: you could hit them up between your meal and your physical training and not even miss a beat.

Didn't even need to clean the blood or bits of brain off your hands.

With every new tween chop lesson, I was reminded of an earlier training run I had gone through—and that kind of reminder made me wonder what the hells I was doing here. I'd gone through this mill once before—and now, here I was, going through it again. And why?

Because in the S3TA—the Space Special Service, Transhuman Arm—I'd get to kill Loonies. Loonies had kicked off the first war in space by flying a shuttle into the unfinished space elevator—the elevator that my parents had worked on for their whole adult lives. Their ashes were mixed in with the ashes of a few million other people in Kenya, where the elevator deorbited and smashed into the ground like a city-smasher nuke.

And yet, if that had been it, I might still ...

I shook my head. Trying to focus on the lessons that had been seared into my thoughts—trying to keep everything straight in the swirling rush of coming down from neurotropics. Focusing ... focusing ... focusing on how to kill Loonies. It made everything feel slightly less raw when the neuros finished draining—though less raw wasn't saying much. I still felt like I had a hole punched through my chest.

So I tried to force my brain to settle into the present, tilting my head up and down, back and forth, all to overload any feeling of pain with visual stimulation. I was in a gray, plastic tube and felt hot, the VR shunts blazing against my skin. I still lurked in the tube for just long enough to be considered slacking, at least by the vicious standards of Selection.

Why?

Well, because outside of this *feh feh pi goh* tube was ...

The world. And the world was a terrible, terrible place. That thought wasn't helped by the raw fury and terror of Deseret winter, which could flay a man to ice shards faster than a vacuum. It also didn't help that we were outsiders in this place, staying only because the Chinese-American Alliance had the military wherewithal to make the Mormons do whatever they wanted, and because the CAA had been plastered from orbit since the beginning of last month, when the war had taken the last shred of my future from me. That was the real reason the world was a terrible place.

In the tube, I felt too hot, too cramped, and there was not enough air.

But at least the gray plastic hid the ghosts.

And so ... I waited. I waited until the nanosecond after slacking.

I opened the tube from the inside, shaking and quaking from the VR dumpshock and my own nerves. Selection didn't ease you out, like commercial VR systems always did. Dumping you out produced a load of pleasant neurological symptoms, such as muscle tremors, low blood pressure, dizziness, fainting spells. That kind of thing. But if you couldn't hack dumpshock, then you couldn't hack Selection.

My bare feet hit compacted dirt and I rubbed my shoulders, catching some glances from Alvarez, his face and barrel chest showing he was from the southernmost parts of the North American Union under the Alliance's jurisdiction. His forehead furrowed, pulling his scars into new constellations of ugly as he sent me a look that combined irritation and psychopathic rage. Or maybe it was lust, I couldn't tell when it came from him and, more importantly, I didn't care.

"L-l-look somewhere else, Lightfoot," I muttered, rubbing my shoulders to try and get the post-VR-dump shivers out of my system. Being the youngest girl in Selection was its own special kind of hell, made all the worse by being stuck in this freezing cold, dirty, low-tech, backward hellhole full of religious nutcases. "Or I might practice on you."

Technically impossible, as none of us had been augmented beyond what we had come in with. Alvarez had stepped on a land mine during a police action in Brazil or something, so his left leg was all chrome and metal. He, like me, was among the one-in-a-million combinations of decorated combat soldier who also had a *jing tian dwohn di* immunity to Cybernetic Psychosomatic Rejection Syndrome and its many delightful side effects. Dissociative personality disorder, for example, and going on through intense body dysmorphia, schizophrenia, megalomania, and psychosis, to name a few.

At least, Alvarez and I hoped we were immune.

He smirked. "Hey, I don't see you sometimes, PR."

He whacked my shoulder and padded off toward the stairs that led from the basement with the rigs to the mess hall. You wouldn't think a man with a foot made of synthetic parts could be so quiet. Other candidates walked past, some of them talking, most of them not. They were all cut from different cloth.

Selection plucked from across two continents and most of the orbital arena, so they had all kinds. Bulky guys, skinny guys, girls with more scars than I have hair, and so on. There weren't any other Spacers though, not naturally born ones like me. And none of them had a nickname like mine.

See, the DIs here, unlike the DIs I had to deal with up in space, loved their sardonic nicknames. Alvarez steps on a mine, they call him Lightfoot.

I do one high profile stunt, mostly by dumb luck and my even dumber decision-making process, and the entire Chinese-American Alliance press (and what passed for Deseret press, for that matter) glommed onto my story and started shouting it from the rooftops. So, I got to be called PR. Well, hey, it could have been worse. They could have called me Media-Whore.

The mess hall sat in a building designed to look remarkably like a Mormon hut. Packed earth, no electricity, no running water, no nothing. Now, see, the Salt Lake Arcology held all the normal citizens of Deseret, insofar as such a thing could exist. When they peacefully seceded from the Chinese-American Alliance, they'd also splintered their own selves. Some, more used to modern amenities than others, went to the arcology. Others ...

Others built their own towns, following their own interpretation of their holy book. And our Selection training facility had been built right into one, subtly, over the course of a few weeks. These are the kinds of things you had to do when the enemy has orbital superiority on you and is willing to throw rocks at anything that looks military. That thought caused a flash of pain in my mind.

I put it out of my head, stepped through the door, and headed inside the mess hall. It looked just as impoverished as the outside, with metal tables and chairs and a guy ladling out food from a big old pot in the corner, heated by a fire. A wood-burning fire.

And I had thought that Sarah's cabin was primitive. My heart ached at that thought, and I kept my face dead, totally dead.

Our commander watched us and I watched her out of the corner of my eye as I got in line. Colonel Mary Singh, formerly Lt. Colonel Mary Singh, had been a bit odd when I had first met her on a VTOL from Quebec to Shanghai. I knew enough now to know just what she might have under her skin. That was enough to know how very afraid of her I should be. I forced myself to not wonder about her career. Her past. How she'd ended up in S3TA with a body mostly made out of killing machines. Instead, I tried to focus on what was important right now.

I got my chop, shoving my hand through a scanner held out by the cook. The scanner looked totally out of place in this hut, but since we weren't in line of sight from orbit, it didn't matter. The tracking chip they'd slipped into me at the start of Selection was scanned. The scanner dinged and the spoon ladled out a hunk of slop, perfectly balanced for my projected nutrient requirements. We'd had some washouts from that, people who were too used to eating slightly too much. I didn't have trouble with it. Standard procedure for space.

I took a table besides Chin and Lee. There were like a million Lees in the CAA, and exactly three had ended up in Selection. The one sitting beside me was younger than Alvarez but still a few years older than me. He looked up at me and got right to the point. "Got any smokes?"

"No." I didn't pause in my eating.

"Shit."

"Got any infosec?" I asked, glancing at him sidelong.

He snorted. "Oh, so, you expect some computer time for free? Do I look like a Maoist?"

"No, but I can get you some smokes." I grinned. It, like many of my expressions, was halfhearted. "I know a guy."

"She's talking about me," Gloria said over her shoulder.

"I said I know a guy." I glanced over my shoulder at Gloria. She smirked. She had her hair at the longest allowed length, tied into a tight bun that drew her face taut. The blond was an injection, her skin was space black. And that was the blackest black I knew words for. It was also exquisite in a way that made me feel a sharp knife-twist of utterly illogical guilt.

"Exactly," she said. "I'll give you smokes if you spot me for this night's watch."

I side-eyed her. Gloria …

Gloria and I …

My heart didn't know whether to speed up, slow down, or stab my lungs and commit suicide like a Japanese Samurai. But still, taking watch for her meant both infosec and making things easier for her. That cinched it.

"Deal." I pursed my lips. Gloria grinned and slipped me a battered box of crappy smokes, thoughtfully smuggled into camp by some gentiles that visited the town to trade with the locals. The Selection's stance on smokes, infosec, and trading watches was pretty strict: if we got caught, we'd be sent through CAPE. And not the wimpy kind of CAPE that I'd gone through in the Marines, no, but the Selection's idea of CAPE. The kind that could actually kill you. Not that it was likely to kill you if you were inhumanly attentive to detail, brutally strong, and lucky. Easy.

But they also expected us to do it—be sneaky, that is. Slipping stuff past them was a sign of "clever" minds, and the S3TA wanted the sneakiest killing machines they could make. So they left holes in their security. Except for when they didn't.

Lee pushed a pebble of gray plastic along the packed earth of the floor. I slipped it into my shoe with one of my toes, eating as fast as I could. I managed to get it out of my shoe before we hit the night run, thank the gods, and it settled into my pocket as we ran, following our training instructor, whose legs whirred and clicked as he jogged backward, his torso held perfectly level.

"Get the lead in!" he shouted. "Come on, come on, come on, show me you mean business, you flats."

I gritted my teeth and thought of what infosec could buy. And I tried to feel both eager and not eager and guilty and not guilty, logic be damned.

We got back when we were bone-tired and half-frozen. As hot as Deseret could get in the day, it got so much colder at night, and the pseudo-winter triggered by the destruction of the orbital climate satellites made it so much worse. We stood beside our beds for inspection. Our training instructor walked along the row, examining our feet and hands and everything. You'd think they would not care so much, as our limbs were all going to be gone when Selection was done. But the way it was explained to me was thus: we went through physical hell less to build muscle and more to train our nerves, so they could adapt to our cyberlimbs once we had them.

And, more than that, it washed people out. People quit when they could not hack it, or they got kicked out by being stupid or unlucky or both. Two people—Singer and Hung—had fallen off a training platform and broken their spines. They were in Beijing getting their nerves knit back together, all expenses paid. I wasn't sure if I envied them.

Once we were inspected, the lights slammed out and I slipped into my coveralls. I picked up my flashlight and started my fire watch. Gloria stayed in bed. Thankfully, the gray skies that had been threatening cleared, giving us an unobstructed view of the night sky and the full moon. I sighed slowly, my head surrounded by an illusory and temporary atmosphere as my breath condensed. The fog dissipated and I remained staring up at the moon.

Luna.

You'd never think it'd be so ugly. I hadn't thought the moon was ugly until almost a year ago. Maybe I was transferring some of my anger toward the people who lived there. But if there had never been the moon … then, well, the Earth would have sunk into a new dark age in 2034. No moon, no lunar regolith. No Helium-3. No fusion reactors. No way to support a planet-sprawling civilization, not one hooked on fossil fuels, for so long.

I shook my head and went back to patrolling. I was technically supposed to report any people shacking up—against the rules down here, a nasty change from my time in the Marines. I just tapped their bed when I noticed, so they'd know to be quieter, and went on walking, going from the inside to the outside to the inside.

Eventually—finally—my shift ended. I crashed and didn't dream. That was a kindness.

>+<

Three days later, I got to spend my infosec. I slipped the pebble into the secure lock on one of the armory closet doors. The armory didn't hold anything more lethal than practice rifles and a few stunner-guns the instructors could use. Right now, we were at chop, but some things were more important than chop.

Gloria slipped in after me, and before I could say anything I was against the wall and her lips were on mine. I grabbed her hands and she pushed her hips against me. I trembled and my knees felt weak.

I ... was so godsdamned horny that I was going cross-eyed. Gloria's mouth drew back. She had a fierce bite to her kiss, more ...

I desperately tried to not think of Sarah. It didn't work. I started to cry. Gloria slid her arms around me, comforting. I whispered, "I'm sorry, I'm sorry ..."

She whispered soft nothings in my ear. My hands tightened on her. And then I kissed her again, through the tears, desperate to feel something that wasn't deadness and nothingness and sorrow.

The infosec, which had shut down the security systems of the armory, gave us time to burn away the world in physical training that didn't hurt. Oh, no ...

It didn't hurt at all.

Until it was over.

I sprawled on my back, one arm over my head, feeling the weight of Gloria's head on my stomach. The hurt came with the closeness. My eyes closed.

"So, PR," Gloria murmured into my skin, her voice soft and her breath warm. "What are you brooding about now?"

"Life," I said.

"Heh." Gloria didn't really laugh. She just said the word "heh." Like a verbal punctuation. Her lips glided along the lines of my abs. She nuzzled me slowly, then brought out: "Ever tried lightening up?"

"Yeah," I said. "Then everyone I loved died."

Gloria was silent for a bit. "Changing the subject. What are the odds you think that someone's got a bug in this room and they let us slip through the firewall as a test?"

I was silent for a moment. "Depressingly likely."

Gloria pushed herself up, her hair falling around her face. She tossed it back with a flip, then smacked my belly. "Come on, PR. Let's get dressed before they stop testing us and start drumming us out."

Watching her dress made the hurt different. It didn't make it go away.

I should be here with Sarah, not with a near-stranger. What did I know about Gloria? Beyond her warmth, and the corded muscle of her arm, and the feeling of her lips on mine. But ... the only thing worse than watching her dress and aching for what wasn't there was not watching her dress and aching twice over. For Sarah and for a loss of contact.

I'd gone celibate for, like, a distressingly long time for a Spacer.

Then I got a shot, and now I was alone and, holy shit, I was thinking about getting laid when Sarah was dead. I put my head in my hands and my shoulders started to shake. Embarrassment warred with self-horror and I tried to stop the sobs, to choke them off. But Gloria just sat down and slipped her arm around my shoulders. She squeezed me against her and I kept on crying and crying and crying.

>+<

The next day, we kept our distance.

That was why I took a roundabout route to the sim-units, weaving my way around the back of a building that I'd normally pass in front. I was crunching through shin-high sooty snow that had brushed up against the back of the primitive house when I realized that going this way was just as obvious as if I had walked arm in arm with Gloria. But it was too late.

Far too late.

I stopped. I had a clear view from the back of the house to the headquarters building, which looked like every other hovel.

Outside of that, underneath a copse of scrawny, shitty trees, was Mary Singh. She was leaning against a tree and chatting with a woman in black. The woman in black had no rank insignia, no clear indication of service, and the kind of face that'd vanish the instant you took your eyes off it. A small, circular drone hovered next to her.

It was armed. My skin prickled as I remembered the buzzing police drones from the courthouse shootout. This one looked about two decades more advanced. The tiny nubs along the forward disk shape had been beaten into my head during the tween chop seminars. Seeker darts. Each one was a tiny rocket with enough Delta-V to zip across half a kilometer and hit you where their laser targeting sensors said you were weak. Their payloads were small micro-charges tipped with drills.

The idea was they'd hit, and that'd hurt. Then the drills dug in, and that hurt. Then the micro-charges went off under your skin and turned your organs into jelly.

I froze, though I knew it was pointless.

The two women saw me. Mary smiled. She shimmered and vanished with a faint ripple—like an optical illusion. I blinked stupidly, shocked that she had done it despite having seen the exact same freaking thing in Shanghai.

The other woman, the one in black, smiled.

She lifted her hand—and, for a terrifying moment, I thought she was going to plant a targeting laser on my forehead. Instead, her hand formed an "O" with the pointer finger and thumb, her other fingers fanning out. She tapped the middle finger to her forehead, then swept her hand toward me in a mocking salute.

"Be seeing you, Drusilla," she called, her voice carrying across the crisp air.

Then she and the drone pulled the same vanishing act.

I was still shivering when I crawled into the sim-unit.

"You okay, PR?" Alvarez asked, pausing as he finished socketing his leg in.

"Fuck off."

CHAPTER 2
WEIGHT

7/6/2068

Republic of Deseret, NAU

T-Minus L-Day: 39

Selection, at least up until this point, had a very specific rhythm to it, and that rhythm was weight. In orbit, weight was a Peel word. When someone—a Peel—pointed at something and went "how much does that weigh?" you knew to mock them endlessly, and hope that no one ever noticed when you screwed up and used the word yourself. The right word to use was mass. Mass didn't change. It didn't matter if you were on Mars or Earth or the surface of the freaking sun: twenty-five kilograms is always twenty-five kilograms.

By the time my third week of Selection had ground by, I knew that that was a *feh feh pi goh*. Twenty-five kilos didn't feel like twenty-five kilos after running in the snow, up the foothills, along the mountain paths, past the arcologies. Twenty-five kilos didn't feel like a twenty-five kilos at all. And all along the way, we had to keep ourselves going. See, the instructors went out with us the first two times. First, to show us the right way, then again, to show us the wrong way.

Then they showed us the Selection way: they gave us a compass—a freaking magnetic compass, not even a GPS locator—and a cloth map and told us to go from point A to point B, wearing our full kit (which, in case it hasn't been made abundantly clear, is twenty-five kilograms of ammo, rations, weapons, armor, and assorted gear). And we went off in silence. Absolute silence. No shouting instructors, not anymore.

Do you get the difference between that and basic training up in space?

It was just you, the cloth map, the compass, and the weight. Nothing to force you to keep going but your own self. No one for you to blame as the weight got heavier and heavier and heavier and your head whispered: "What kind of stupid idiot are you? How can you be so shortsighted and pigheaded and ..."

Usually, my brain went into deeper, more complex and nuanced deconstructions of my various failings. The first, and clearest, was not keeping Sarah safe. Why had I let her come across the sea to see me? Why hadn't I gotten her a better home? She was my girlfriend and I had let her stay in a slum. I'd let her die under a billion tons of rubble at the bottom of a ruined megacity. No, even better: why not just imagine that I never met her in the first place? A thousand scenarios blew past me, flaring and glowing with various amounts of probability. Some were even possible: I could have told Sarah to stay at her farm, that her mother needed her. Some were just silly.

All of them reiterated the same idea, though.

I was pathetic. I was stupid. I was weak.

They all begged me to stop.

That was why I was here, really. That was why I was in Selection—despite the psychopaths in it, despite the difficulty, despite everything. I was here because in Selection ... I wouldn't stop. I wouldn't stop, because if I did, I would be in the Marine Corps again. I knew that the regular Marines would be going in hard sometime in the future.

But the Space Special Service, Transhuman Arm, would be going in first. And they would be going in harder.

And I was not going to let that get away from me. I refused.

Part of me boggled at that thought.

What has the war done to you?

And yet, without the war, I'd have never even thought of talking to Jillian. That was the kind of thing that I thought about when I wasn't beating up on myself, the things I considered while jogging down a lonely, muddy, ice-cold path in the back-woods of Deseret. I would have never talked to Jillian, or David. I'd never have known Chuck or Liam or Jones. Liam's charms. David's quiet strength. They would have been as important to me as the politics of the South American Confederation.

Of course, without the war, they'd never have died. They'd still be alive. Sarah would still be alive.

And it would all cycle back to the sins my mind went over, flowing in on itself like a sump-recycler, burning hot and angry and bitter.

That fire was what made me want to get to point B first.

I never did.

I usually ended up near last, and in my defense, Earther gravity is hard on the bones. I'd spent most of my life taking injections to keep my muscles from atrophying, my bones from becoming brittle and as easily snapped as a DI's temper. Even that hadn't been enough, not really, so I'd also spent a good part of my "free" time running, lifting weights, and generally trying to trick my body into thinking that it lived in one gravity, when really, it was closer to one third.

It also didn't help that as far as girls went, I was a bit smaller than most. I was also younger than the rest of Selection. You'd think that'd be enough to kick me out on physical grounds alone, but so long as I hacked it psychologically and at least came somewhere close to finishing up the challenges they put toward us, I knew for a fact that Selection didn't give a flying *da shiong la se la ch'wohn tian.*

It didn't matter my arms were skinny, my legs were short, or my wind short-lived at best when compared to the slabs of muscle that made up half of Selection. Those muscles were good enough for the Air Force, the Space Corps, the surface Navy, even the godsdamned Marines. Not here. Here, you could go beyond the muscle and become something bigger and better.

You could cut out the weakness.

So, I kept arriving last or near to last, and I kept jogging and they kept letting me stay here.

And then came the last Friday of this stage. Not that I had known this was the last Friday, or that there were multiple stages. They'd kept us in the dark during training up in orbit, and more than that, my training had been cut in half to rush some barely competent troops out the airlock. The only warning I got was, once I got dumped out of the tween chop seminar before breakfast, instead of breakfast, I got a rucksack.

"Report to the airpad in five minutes," the instructor said.

I took my rucksack and ran—along with the rest of the potential S3TA members—to our bunk room. Once there, I started jamming everything that I owned—my clothes and my shoes and a frame loaded with a picture of Sarah I couldn't bear to look at—into my ruck and chucked it over my shoulder.

Gloria muttered to me, "Figure they're going to fly us somewhere worse?"

I snorted, shaking my head.

What could be worse than this place?

Then she asked: "Think we could find privacy?"

I looked at her, thought, then shrugged. Gloria smiled at me and shrugged back, as if to say: well, what can you do?

And despite the fact it twisted a knife in my guts, I smiled back. I'm not sure I can get across the sick, twisty feeling of smiling at Gloria. Because she made me happy. Well, happier. But that momentary flare of "not miserable" came with a swell of renewed guilt.

Never stopped me.

The VTOL waiting for us on the snow-covered landing strip was one of the big cargo-haulers with extending wings that could get a huge glide-on, and more than that, glittered with solar panels to help run the engines. Once the cargo-haulers hit a certain altitude, they could fly continuously. At least, until some part of the engine jammed or the plane vibrated itself to pieces. But, still, weeks and weeks of continuous flying had to count for something.

Despite the futuretech, the idea of having to continually push against a gravity well, to use air and airfoils to keep yourself from smashing into the ground, struck me as quaint as hell. The VTOL was classic military: stretched cargo webbing instead of chairs, with our rucks slung under our legs and tucked up agaist the walls. The only concession to the century or so of technological advancement between now and the first cargo planes adapted to military use was the smart-fabric that made up the webbing, which adjusted its grip on us to keep our bodies secure and steady. I wondered if the webbing would work in high-G maneuvers.

Course, this lumbering crate was never getting near space.

I got sat next to Alvarez, but he immediately went to sleep, a trick he'd learned sometime in his years in the force. His bulk started to spread out, straps or no straps, so soon I was hemmed in by an arm, a knee, and the omnipresent manstink. Ugh. I managed to catch Gloria's eyes and she mimed shooting herself in the head, the smart webbing clinging to her arm like a funerary shroud. I smiled/guilted again, then looked out the window as the VTOL lifted up and out of the camp.

I craned my head hard so I could watch the camp dwindle, the snow buffeting around and cutting my visual acuity down to nothing. The acceleration pushed me to the side and I breathed in and out and did my little hand gestures. My PTSD had been beaten savagely by a combination of somatic exercises and targeted drugs ... but it still reared its ugly head from time to time. Defanged, it gummed at me, trying to get the same reaction. Less during training, but that might have been because all my old impulses were not useless relics, but actually useful feelings to have.

The plane rocked and shuddered and I almost threw up a few times. I used to think that throwing up was the worst thing in the world. I knew better now. Getting shot, deafened, beaten, and seeing your friends die around you had a way of fixing that attitude. Still, I clenched my jaws and tried to keep my stomach down.

Alvarez kept snoring. Bastard.

Eventually, I slept too. I had a few dreams—faint memories, really, of running endlessly down corridors toward the distant sound of gunfire—and when I woke, the VTOL's wings were whining and folding back into the main body, the vertical engines taking over as we started to approach a swath of ocean with a single glittering steel island in the middle of it. This wasn't what I was expecting. Selection was run for the blackest of black ops units: the S3TA, an organization that most of the CAA didn't even know existed. Those that saw them in action usually didn't understand their acronym. I suppose rumors floated around out there, but I had never heard of them, and none mentioned any details of Selection.

Now, I was learning another chunk of truth. We were land-ing on what looked like a secret island base right out of an old spy fic. We drew closer and I could see out of the pitted window of the VTOL: it was an offshore oil rig, one of the old, old, old models that still sat and rusted their lives away in the big, blue sea. It reminded me of the plastic recyc-center that I'd visited a few months ago.

Great. Way to start off on an ominous note.

The VTOL landed and we grabbed our rucks and hustled off to find Colonel Singh waiting for us. How she had gotten here first, I had no idea, and I figured that anything was possible. She might have been in the passenger seat up with the autopilot, or she might have just teleported through sheer force of will. Who knows? She was standing on a pipeline that ran along the side of the rusty floor. I looked at the floor and shifted my weight just so as I stepped out with the rest of Selection. Earth gravity always felt too damn heavy for me, but right now, it felt deadly. I could easily see the floor turning into a jagged pit of stabby tetanus, like a medieval mace.

"Welcome to Section Two." Colonel Singh spoke with the standard S3TA tone of voice: neither happy nor sad, angry or disinterested. Plain. Unmodulated. It didn't sound like it should be creepy in theory, but hearing it always made my spine crawl. "You have all demonstrated your somatic capacities. Even if your bodies are not up to the physical tasks, your minds are. Now, you will demonstrate your reflexes, intuitive grasp of three-dimensional spaces, and your ability to assimilate these abilities. Seventy-five percent of you will not pass this part of Selection."

I didn't glance away from her, but I just knew everyone around me was thinking: Not Me.

Or, hells, maybe I was giving them too little credit. I was pretty sure I'd be able to pass this. Hells, they were called the

Space Special Services for a reason, and I was the only Spacer in the group. That had to count for something. Right?

Still, Singh led us across the top of the oil rig. We got to a squat, ugly, industrial-looking protrusion that stuck out of the side of the rig. It looked like it was right out of the dark ages. Like the kind of thing Hitler or Stalin or some other 20th century warlord would fight over. We went inside and were forced into a single file. Inside, the salty smell of the air—almost overpowering—was mixed with this oily, rusty stench that made me wish my lungs were metal too. I was near the front, slotted in behind one of our Lees. He didn't slow down, but around his back, I could see a light. The light got stronger and stronger and, quite suddenly, we stepped from the old and into the new. The corridor expanded into a metallic room that looked minted within the past decade, full of computers and technicians and supplies. Singh gestured five people into an elevator, and I got to wait as the elevator went down. When it finally came back up, I got to step in myself.

The elevator door was solid metal, no glass. Nothing to watch but Alvarez's back. Still, we went down and down and down. When we stepped off, we were in a pressurized area. The cues were obvious—the walls were curved, for one thing—and I just knew we had to be under the water.

I noticed something else too: the other group of would-be-Selection members had been ushered off. A moment later, a man—wearing a plain black uniform—came to our room through a hatchway. He gestured us along, and we followed him.

"I suppose this is the deadzone test," Alvarez muttered.

I glanced at him, even as we ducked underneath the hatchway.

Alvarez grinned. "PR, some of us have been around a bit longer. I've heard rumors about this … you know the Atlantic still has a lot of deadzones, right?"

I nodded. The Slump—hell, even the pre-Slump period—had created huge deadzones in the oceans. Artificial oxygenation and deacidification had been a big industry right after the Slump, even during the end of it. Oceanic reconstruction continued, but people still thought that we'd never manage to get back what we had before. Deadzones were proof of that: swaths of ocean without life, deadened by, well, take your pick. Heat. Acid. Plastics. The list went on.

"So, what, they chuck us out into the deadzone and say go fish?"

"Yup."

We got to the end of the line—a barracks, but for some reason, this place felt like the wall before a firing squad. I took in the whole room as fast as I could to try and get to the bottom of my gut reaction. It looked like a berth and an armory, all at once. Cots for sleeping, armory tables spread about with the tools and pieces of the trade. Tech-pens for making smart-fabric squirm and roll around, sealant and soldering tools. Several doors that looked like airlocks were hanging out in the back. Ominous. There were spacesuits waiting for us, and once everyone was gathered around, we got chucked into a spacesuit training course.

That was it. The spacesuits. The feeling of foreboding faded as I remembered we were on the Earth. Not in orbit. Not in space. Spacesuits didn't mean we had a thin skin between atmo and cold, killing vacuum.

Thus relieved, I paid attention with my body and let my brain fall asleep. Oh, I didn't completely slack off, these kinds of things always had tips and bits of advice that were good to hear. And I didn't find anything worth tearing my hair out over:

the instructor led us through all the basic points on spacesuit design and donning. And then we drilled on them. I got a feeling we'd be drilling on them for a while …

Either way, I enjoyed the mental vacation.

And I got ready to have the other shoe drop.

>+<

The shoe dropped a week later. After essentially throwing tech-manuals at us and giving us a few instructional seminars on spacesuit handling, we were given a week to "acclimate." No one told us what we were acclimating for, so rumors got more common than trolls on an unmoderated Lag-Net forum. We were going to be put out into the deadzone to fight each other. We were going to be shoved out into the deadzone and forced to survive the next two weeks without any supplies but what we could scrounge. We were going to be escorted into the deadzone by a giant robot and shot, then our corpses would be reanimated by fancy black-tech and used as zombie soldiers.

Hey, put a load of wanna-be Special Forces into a small room, make them train on a single piece of kit—even if the kit in question was the most complex and compact one designed by humanity in the history of the world—and give them no new information, and the rumors get weird. Still, I tried to make myself focus to a laser-sharp degree and take in every detail about the suit in question. It was hard, harder than I liked to admit. But, after almost two decades of being trained on spacesuits, first in virtual reality, then drills, then in an airlock with the air vented, then at war, spacesuits were my skin. I knew spacesuits better than I knew how to tie shoes. I knew spacesuits better than I knew Gloria's erogenous zones.

Against that smug knowledge, that instinct to conserve energy by being lazy, rechecking information felt as useful and sensible as eating paste. But—and I had a really great appreciation of this—what you felt and what was really true usually had almost nothing to do with one another. A gnarly existential problem, if I had the time to think about it. Instead, I forced myself through drills I had run since I was six and tried to only slightly troll the opinion pool about what waited out the airlock.

"So."

That was Gloria's primary way of starting a conversation. If she didn't just grope me, which I didn't mind so much. It usually let us skip the awkward build up and get right to the part where my brain stopped working overtime for a bit of bliss. But when she hadn't found a time to pounce while I was alone, she'd just tool up with a "So" or a "Sup."

It was just her style.

I glanced at her. She was sitting at the armory table in front of me, rechecking her left glove. One of our handlers was walking up and down the middle of the room, ready to give any answer to any question. That was Selection's style. They didn't teach past a certain point, they just waited for us to ask. And people did ask ... but watching them amused me, because they were trying to ask and not ask at the same time. We knew that someone had to be judging us, so asking questions would be hanging a big old sign on our head saying: drum out of the service.

Ai Yah.

Was this training program designed to make us all paranoid? Well, of course it was, Dru; way to ask a silly question. Maybe I should just *toh shung* and go home, join the Marines and get biological fingers.

Still, Gloria continued to speak. "What do you think is waiting for us out there?"

"A pack of genetically engineered sharks made out of the failed members of previous S3TA teams."

Gloria snorted, and if she had been drinking something, it'd have gone out her nose. As it was, she popped and dry swallowed one of our food pills. We'd been upgraded—yay—from gruel to pills. The upside was pills had no taste. The downside was they, like the pills I'd popped in space, had no roughage and treated your digestive tract like a punching bag. She drank a shot of water.

"I think whatever it is, we should stick together."

"Oh?"

She grinned. "Well, you're a badass. A pipsqueak, yes. But badass. Also, you have amazing tits, and a belly I can do shots off and—"

"Please. Stop ... describing me." My cheeks were burning. Not with embarrassment—being told I had a belly flat enough to do shots off was rather gratifying, it made all the pain that Basic had put me through kind of worth it if you avoided thinking about the dead friends and lost hopes. No, my cheeks burned from shame. Shame about cheating on a girlfriend. A girlfriend who had been dead for real time weeks ... subjective months. Yeah. See why I liked it more when we cut to the physicality? "So, once we're out of the airlock, find me. We can discuss this out there."

Gloria nodded and went back to the armory. I watched her go and shook my head.

The sessions in VR screwed with my perception of time—but what screwed with it even more was the fact that I knew I was going into battle. If I had any illusions about my mortality, Jillian had proved it. You could survive space, you could survive the Forge, but then any asshole with a gun could just ...

So it was logical to grab onto anything that flared bright and shone at you with warmth and comfort and ... and love. Even if it was sweaty, grind your nipples together, gasp and leave fingernail marks on their back love. What Earthers—the stuck up puritans—would call lust-love or even just sin.

And I was glad I did it.

But ... but ... but ...

Was it totally psycho that the guilt made the orgasms better? What was wrong with me?

Having zero answers and no psytech on hand to ask, I shook my head again and went back to work.

When we went to sleep that night—after popping our dinner pills, of course—I stayed awake a bit longer than I should have and for once I wasn't thinking about Sarah. Something had been bugging me about the suits. It hadn't quite sunk home when we'd just been handling bits and pieces and elements of the suit. But now that we'd practiced donning drills, it leaped out to me, clear as day. The weight was wrong. They had extra weights put here and there. Additional mass in a spacesuit didn't make sense, not when every kilogram you had to push around could cost more than my first year of backpay.

That kept me up, thinking and tossing and turning.

It turned out that I wasn't the only one staying awake a bit later than normal.

"How *w'rin bu lai whai w'rin bu jwo*," Alvarez's voice growled out of the darkness. Underneath it, I heard a faint slurping, burbling noise. "They're flooding the godsdamn room!"

CHAPTER 3: WATER

7/13/2068

Atlantic Ocean, Undisclosed Location

T-Minus L-Day: 32

I put my feet into the water. It was bone-chilling, death-bringing, toe-freezing off cold. *"Joo fuen chse!"* I swore, jerking my feet out of the water. I stood on my bed as Alvarez strode through the water and slammed his hand into the light control, eschewing military discipline for the moment. The lights winked on, revealing that the hatchway out of the room was closed and the lock-light glowed a bright red. Our suits were where we had left them, and I chewed on my lip, opening up old canker sores as I looked down at the ankle-deep water.

Gloria and other members of Selection waded through water. All of them except for one of our Lees, who remained frozen on his bed.

"Come on!" Gloria and I shouted at the same time. I glanced at her, but she was focused on gesturing at Lee. He remained stock-still, looking at the water. His left hand was metallic and gleaming, and I heard that he'd lost it in a lake. Well, something had triggered him. Me, I was just glad that water was so completely out of my experience that I didn't feel any of my panic reflexes pushing in.

Gloria waded across the way to Lee, dragging him off the bed and shoving him into his locker. "Get this on, *Bao Bai.*"

Lee started fumbling into his suit while I surged to my locker. The old childhood song came to mind. *Feet First, don't be worst, Feet First, and you won't burst.*

I made sure to sit on the bed and swing my feet up and out of the water before donning my boots.

They'd keep the water out.

My toes were still wet, but that was better than nothing. I rolled up the skinsuit, tapping its hardness to max before slipping my support bladders underneath one armpit, then the other. Gloves, then shoulders, chest piece and backpack. My helmet clacked on, first of the group. I looked around, quickly. Alvarez, the big dope, had gone helmet first and was struggling to get things to attach to it. I sloshed through the water—now thigh-high, it wasn't filling as fast as I had feared—and grabbed his helmet, holding it straight.

I shouted through the faceplate. "Come on, Lightfoot, get the damn thing on."

Alvarez attached his helmet and then smacked my shoulder, a signal that he wasn't panicking anymore. Across the room, Lee had frozen up again and now Gloria had to shout at him.

"GET THE LEAD IN! COME ON!"

Other members of Selection had already gotten to the airlocks and cycled them. Bastards. Gloria and Lee and I got to an airlock that Alvarez held open for us.

I shot Alvarez a look, even as Lee and Gloria got into the lock.

Alvarez leaned forward and his ugly mug filled the faceplate as we made out. "Making out" was Spacer slang, so of course it was sex crazy. The basic idea is you touch faceplates together and shout. The voice rings through the glass, even if you're sur-rounded by hard vaccum. Unlike lots of other communication techniques in space, you couldn't listen in on that.

"You'll stop bullets for me, PR. I'm sticking with you." He grinned. I think he was joking.

The door closed and the airlock cycled. Water filled it and the outer door burst open, revealing the infinite blackness of the deadzone outside.

Gloria stepped out first and activated her headlamps. I fol-lowed. Lee behind me. Alvarez came out last. We fell and fell and fell, until we lightly touched down on the ocean floor. Our headlamps illuminated a dim space around us ... gray-silted landscape, lost almost immediately in the darkness around us. Moving felt slow and sluggish, and I realized that explained the weights.

We were approximating Lunar gravity. I tried it, bouncing and shifting from foot to foot, as Gloria tapped the side of her helmet. She was testing our frequencies, while Lee stood stock-still and Alvarez looked around and around. No other mem-bers of Selection had landed nearby, but I could pick out their headlamps.

"Does this work?" Gloria asked.

"Got you, girl," I said, finding that my bouncing gait almost exactly matched the movement on the Moon. The only differ-ence was there was pressure pushing against me from the water, but still, it was remarkably close.

That's when the sledgehammer hit my shoulder.

In the moments between sailing from foot to foot to being on my back, I could see—frozen in my eyes—the tunnel of water ripped open by the projectile. Then all I saw was silty water flowing around my faceplate.

"Get down!" Alvarez shouted.

I tried moving my arm, groaning loudly as other shouts of alarm—and a series of faint *thrums* that ran through my suit and made my bones quake—came over the comline.

Then Lee filled my faceplate.

"You okay?" he asked, making out with me to avoid filling the channel.

"Yeah, I just feel like I've been hit by a horse ..." I sat up, rubbing my shoulder. There wasn't any penetration, but gods-be-damned, that had felt like it should have.

"Horse? *Gǒupì.* How would you know what being kicked by a horse feels like, PR?" Alvarez asked.

"*Qù nǐ mā de,* Alvarez," I said, not wanting to go into the painful happy memories of Sarah's farm.

I looked around, trying to get a feel for the situation, but silt continued to filter through the water. Lee's helmet light was off. I switched mine off as well and snapped my faceplate forward. The infrared cameras whirred to life, and there were Lee, Gloria, Alvarez, all glowing green and orange and red—the suit masked their prosthetics, which would have been a few ticks hotter and colder, depending on the area. Of course, my visual range was maybe two feet in front of my face, and I got absolutely nothing beyond their heat signatures. I started dialing through the light frequencies and—

Shit!

I'd hit the UV cameras, which had broadened my visual range up past blue. And, fancy that, there was a UV light shining out there, tracking back to something dim and occluded by the water. It targeted another member of Selection who hadn't switched to UV yet. Wham! He got hit right in the belly and folded up. He didn't move, but his groans sounded over the speakers. His suit started to flash on the radio freqs, a signal that caused our suits' computers to slap a HUD symbol over him: DEAD.

Because life was an unending parade of horribly blunt metaphors, I could see the UV light that would kill us, but not the actual source of the weapons fire. Too much silt, too much *dark* down here at the bottom of the Atlantic. I could guess, though: there was some pillbox out there with an automated turret sitting on it, just itching to blow us away.

I noticed that my star-mates had all gotten the same idea I did. Alvarez gestured, quickly, indicating that Gloria and Lee should go left, he'd take the right. I wondered—for maybe five seconds—why he didn't use his radio coms, but I noticed that a few other knots of Selection teams were still chatting, sending information back and forth and the turret was taking potshots at them more often.

Tracking radio? Possibly. We were also hearing confirmation from other ad hoc squads that more turrets were taking shots at them.

Fantastic.

I started moving, wincing at first, then gaining more momentum, bouncing behind Alvarez. The lunar-esque landscape of the deep blue sea wasn't totally accurate. There were, for one thing, not nearly enough craters. For another thing, rock formations rose up as a surprise, stark and sudden out of the gloom. Alvarez got behind one just before a tunnel of water slammed into it and exploded a haze of white stuff. I got behind it a moment later and waved my hand in my face.

I pushed my face against his. "What is this stuff?"

"Reef, I think."

I looked from him to the rock outcropping. I'll be damned. It was solidified reef ... dead reef. Another thing you wouldn't find on the Moon. Not unless something went really wrong during a dome invasion.

Then we got a single radio flash from Gloria, a quick squeal of notes and tones that sounded out, roughly, to "in position." I signaled back, which earned me a shower of projectiles from the hypothetical turret. I hunkered down and noticed that Alvarez had bounded out to the left. I waited for the projectiles to pause and for the UV light to swing away. It didn't. It kept pinned on me and every few seconds, another projectile would slap into reef, silt, or cut by overhead. Of course I got stuck under fire. Just my luck.

Finally, the UV light swept away from me.

I bounded out of cover. That was really the only word for it: bounding from foot to foot, bounce bounce bounce. Despite almost thirty years of practice and struggle, the Loonies had never found a better way to walk around on Luna. So, I used it, even if it made me feel just a little bit like a traitor. The gun turret loomed out of the darkness, illuminated by my suit's optics. It looked like it had been thrown together and dropped out of some old cautionary tale, plucked right out of the American Civil War. Fully droned and loaded with what looked like canisters of compressed air.

Gloria was coming from the left. Alvarez, from the right. That left me right in the middle, with the UV searchlight swinging around to pin me. What blocked UVs? Well, I figured that a longshot was better than none. I bounded forward again, then dropped and hit the ground at a right angle, leaning backward as best I could. My heels dug into the silt and a cloud exploded around me. My back hit the ground and more silt rushed up, turning the water into chalk. I actually saw—shooting over my head, right past my faceplate—one of those tunnels of displaced water, distorting the silt into a wild flurry of particulates and smog. It was downright beautiful, if eerie, illuminated in false colors and advanced optics.

Then Alvarez grunted, over the radio, and Gloria shouted, "Clear!"

I got to my feet and stepped carefully out of the cloud, trailing bits of silt and dribbles of whitish muck. The turret had been taken apart rather alarmingly quickly. Wires had been pulled, containers slashed open, and the whole barrel assembly was bent sideways. Gloria slid her knife back into the knuckle slot that it rested on and Alvarez looked at me sidelong.

"So, uh, is that all you're good for, PR? Getting shot and distracting people with guns?"

"Someone has to do it. Might as well be me."

He snorted.

More "clears" were filtering through our radio networks. Within twenty minutes, we had the half-circle perimeter that we'd been dumped into secured, with six turrets taken down, and nine people "killed," maybe fifteen "wounded." A black, orb-shaped submarine—flitting around like a grim reaper UFO—came and picked up the people who had been "killed." Singh came out as well, wearing the strangest looking spacesuit I had ever seen. The chest piece and face cover seemed fine, but her arms and legs were open to the vacuum (well, ocean), letting them move more freely. Even a skintight suit had some give and push that, clearly, limited what a cyber-limb could do.

She landed and spoke on the general frequency. "You have managed to disable six relatively stupid, nonlethal turrets. Those of you who died, you are out of the program. Those of you who were wounded and pushed on, good job, you're in. I'm uploading the map and mission briefing to your HUDs. You will be assembled into squads. You will accomplish your mission briefing using your trained skills and your teamwork. After this point, your enemies will be using live ammo. By continuing, you will have acknowledged this fact and will forfeit any legal right to seek grievances against the CAA or the S3TA."

My eyes bugged. It felt like my head was being sucked through a pinprick hole in a high-pressure environment. They'd *kill* us? For failing a training program? What was this, Panem? I looked at Gloria and Alvarez and Lee. They looked at me, and at each other. Their faces were blank, and I realized …

If I gave up, I'd be leaving them behind. To face the death-traps that the CAA Special Forces would throw at them. To leave them down here at the bottom of this ocean hellhole? *Ai Yah Tien Ah*, there was no way I'd do that. And they were all thinking the exact same damn thing. Not a single person said no.

And in the back of my brain, a tiny little voice raised a point that I couldn't quite argue down.

If I died … so what?

No, really. Who'd get sad? Who'd miss me? Gloria, for about fifteen seconds before she found someone warm and soft and willing to lock hips and lips? I shook my head behind my helmet, trying to get the voice to shut up. Shut up. I wasn't going to die. I had too many Loonies to kill.

So much better, that tiny voice whispered.

The submarine whirred off and I tapped my wrist computer to bring my HUD up. The objectives gave us a few scant swaths of information: there were four bases, each one protected by an uncertain number of drones and turrets, all lethally armed and armored. There were supply drops and a few bits of information about terrain and patrol areas. The squadrons were given bases to hit, and times to hit them by. I was slotted with Alvarez, Lee, and Gloria.

Yeah. Like that was a coincidence.

"All right," Alvarez said, tapping his glove to invite us all to a shared AR space. Soon, we were all looking at an image of a map built by consensus. "We need to hit Base Three."

He pointed at it. It highlighted, a glowing dot on the map.

"Need more intelligence," Gloria said.

"And guns." That was me.

Lee nodded, silently.

"Okay," Alvarez said, pointing at Gloria. I wondered—for a second—if I should make a grab for leadership. Then Alvarez laid out his plan. "You and Lee, hit the supply dump and bring everything to here." He tapped an area. "PR and I will be scouting out the base from there. If we're not there—or if we're there and riddled with holes—fall back." He pointed again. "If we're there, then we'll organize the hit, but if we're dead, you're in charge and need to take out the base. Got it?"

Gloria bobbed her head behind her helmet. "Don't get full of holes."

"I won't." Alvarez gestured. "Come on."

Once we started bounding away, he added, "Hand gestures from here on out, helmut-lights off."

I nodded and tapped my helmet. Off went the lights and we went to pure passive optics. Our visualization went from pretty good to, well, absolutely shit. Still, I soon fell into the rhythm, the rolling gait of a long-term Loonie walk. And, hey, I had a reason to thank the somatic workouts that we'd been put through in the first section of Selection: my thighs didn't start burning until we were halfway there.

The landscape that loomed past was weird and depressing. Reef corpses. Bones. Metal fragments. I had begun to notice how dark and cold this place was. There wasn't even the glimmer of Earthlight, like there would be on Luna. The water-sky was as black as washed out starlight and the ground was depicted in shadows and false colors—splotchy and more alien than Alpha Centauri's exoplanets. After about an hour, we came onto a rising part of the ground. Here, Alvarez signed—quick and nimble, his fingers flashing—and went belly first. I went down too. We waited until the silt had settled, then crawled forward. It was agonizingly slow and so godsdamned alien that I took a moment to marvel at it. Crawling, pushed down by gravity and traction. Slurping through the silt and sand, keeping ourselves from being seen using cover and earth.

Nothing like fighting in space, where the horizon went from here to Proxima, where cover was using the Earth to hide from a laser fired from a million kilometers away.

We got to the crest. Alvarez and I looked out. The base was as obvious as hell, shining with UV light and other active sensor equipment. There were five circular drones, the size and shapes of the camera drones I'd seen on dry land, back in Shanghai. They moved in bubbles of frothing water, making it hard to square away what they had. We couldn't risk active sensors to try and cut through the froth, but waiting just a bit revealed the answer: when they got to the end of their patrol-route, they paused for a bit before turning to the next patrol-route, creating an irregular rectangular around the base itself.

They were armed with underwater adapted guns. Obviously.

Alvarez scrawled words in the silt near my faceplate: *Semi-Automatic*?

I waited, examining the drone, my image amps pushed to the maximum that was safe.

After at least four "stops," I felt sure of my answer. I crossed out the "semi" and Alvarez bobbed his head. He'd come to the same conclusion. So, the drones were armed with automatic weapons; their shapes were right and the gun mechanisms (at least the parts we could see) corroborated the idea. Considering how an internal ammunition storage unit could load rounds until the stars burned out, we couldn't count on them having a short battlefield endurance.

Alvarez had already moved on. His finger etched in the silt, not risking the radio. Good man. The base appeared in crude etchings: a circle, with three dots where the turrets were located. A dotted line served for the track that the drones were following. Alvarez leaned forward and mashed his faceplate into mine. You know, I'm all in favor of making out, both in the slangy sense and in the real world, lip locking, spit sharing sense. But Alvarez wasn't even attractive to *straight* girls, gods. I tried to focus on his words and not his pug-dog-meets-blender face.

Too bad his words involved us all getting shot at.

"All right, once Lee and Gloria get here, we split up the guns and do a quick takedown of the drones. Once they're down, we've got immobile targets to deal with."

I nodded.

And so, we waited, watching for any changes. The drones seemed pretty dumb ... but that could just be because the environment down here was stupidly bad for most good sensing equipment, save sonar, and they weren't pinging us like crazy, and ... moreover, I wasn't entirely sure if our soft, squishy bodies could even be picked up on active sonar, and us making out wasn't enough noise to pick up on passive.

Hopefully.

Lee and Gloria arrived like ghosts behind us, lugging with them two large, sleek, rectangular crates. They laid them out in the muck behind the rise that we were sheltering on, and we slipped back a bit, careful to not kick up too much debris. It felt agonizing to move so slow and so careful, but I forced myself to remember that we weren't just playing around out here ...

Lee and Gloria opened the crates, flipping some toggles. The crates, thankfully, didn't have any air in them to give up a spray of bubbles. Instead, we got foam packaging and four caseless, hydro-adapted rifles. I'd been drilled on these in space—then in Selection, during tween chop seminars. They were XM-88s, designed for modularity. The firing chamber—normally loaded for caseless 5.56—had been replaced with an underwater chamber. The ammunition came in smaller magazines, because they couldn't go caseless when you were firing inch long steel darts.

I loaded my XM-88. Alvarez got our attention, made a few gestures—simultaneous shot, on his radio ping.

We got up on the rise. The drones hummed past again and again. And I realized, there was one minor problem with this plan. We didn't know the ranges on the turrets. Still, this was better than any idea I had …

I tapped on my XM-88's UV painter, laying a laser on one of the drones. My visor illuminated stabbing lasers from my squad mates. We were all drawn on different targets. The drones stopped, ready for their next jaunt.

"Take 'em."

We all fired once. Our guns didn't make bangs or even pops. They *hissed*. Gasses from the ignition bubbles from vents mounted on the firing chambers. Darts ripped through the water and slammed into drones, into each one's center of mass. Turns out their armor wasn't that thick, and four of the drones started to float to the ground in tiny bits and pieces. The last drone got hit by Alvarez who fired a second shot faster than the rest of us.

The turrets swept around to our direction. They started firing back, launching freaking spikes that made our darts feel very phallically insignificant. A dart whistled right by my head, a closing tunnel of water shaking my vision. We opened up. Darts shredded one turret, two.

The last fired again and Alvarez swore, rolling to the side. The spike missed him—barely—and I smirked. My last shot picked off the turret's pressurized firing chamber. I remained on my belly, but out of the corner of my eye, I saw Alvarez switching to active sensors.

"Looks clear. Who wants to go first?"

No one suggested anything.

"Ai yah," I muttered. "I'll do it. Cover me."

I released my empty magazine, slapped in a new one, then vaulted over the side of the rise. I fell down and landed, my knees taking the impact with ease. I swept my rifle back and forth, and bounded toward the base while trying not to feel like an absolute jackass for bouncing like a bunny when soldiers were supposed to move in economic, rapid motions.

I got to the base, hopped onto the top, and whacked the turret with the butt of my rifle.

"It's good!" I radioed back to my squad.

They came on over. We started picking over the base, using every single piece of optical equipment we had to paint a picture of just what we'd fought to grab. It looked like the start of a hubcap (which I'd gotten to see lots of in Shanghai), sunk into the ground and mounted with the turrets. There weren't any openings, but there were plenty of places to screw and unscrew. Gloria got to work on those, and soon we had the "base" opened up just a bit more to reveal the guts within.

"It's all standard," Gloria radioed, her hand holding up a chunk of metal as she looked into red and black and green wires inside the turret's guts. "Just radio transmitters, optical cables, everything you'd imagine in an automated base."

"That can't be it," Alvarez muttered.

"Why not?" I asked. Lee was scanning his optics back and forth, then shifting to cover another quadrant. Alvarez glanced around in a less methodical, but no less attentive, way.

"They said we might die. That wouldn't have killed a *soldier.*"

"Hey, I was in the Army." Gloria swung the panel shut.

Alvarez didn't respond. Instead, he stepped off the base.

Lee popped off a shot and shouted at the same time. "Tangos, As PMO!"

As per my orientation. That was more useful in space, when you could orient in any direction. Still, I dropped to a knee and turned and—

There were the oncoming drones. I didn't count them, not immediately, instead I took aim and fired in a single, numbered motion. Two drones exploded to bits, while the survivors—four, the count was clear by then—returned fire. Their needle-bullets stitched through the water, carving out tunnels that I could trace from their sleek, disk shaped bodies to—

Gloria grunted, falling backward, red expanding in the water around her. She started to skid back down the side of the base, her gun floating to the side. Alvarez hit the deck and Lee spun his body around, remaining in a crouched position as he fired at the drones swooping overhead. A third drone exploded.

Alvarez got to Gloria and I adopted the same posture as Lee. The drones had stopped and were about to swing around. No time to think no time to think. No time to think.

I fired. He fired.

The drones exploded and their bits started to fall to the ground.

"Gloria's bleeding pretty bad, Alvarez said—glancing up from Gloria.

"No shit," she snapped, reaching up with one hand.

I clung to the logic: if she was hurt, but she could still swear, then it was not that bad. I refused to let it *be* anything but that bad. I refused. Not again. Not again.

I moved to help, but Alvarez snapped, "Maintain security with Lee."

It sounded logical. It was logical. It made me want to bite my own fingers off. Lee, though, proved himself to be at least five times more logical than me … he'd set himself up to cover an approach and dug himself into the silty sea floor, heaping up at least some cover.

I did the same thing, pushing up some ground. It wasn't enough to really stop anything, but it gave me a great stoop to rest my rifle on ... even in "Lunar" gravity, a gun could get annoying to hold forever. I mean, I could hold a gun for hours without wavering, but just because I could do something didn't mean I wanted to do it. Just because I could lose ...

I'd start wondering about a curse on your lips right now. A kiss of death, hmmm?

Shut up. Shut up shut up shutupshutup.

I shook my head inside my helmet and realized I was almost crying. I clamped down on the impulse.

"All right," Alvarez said. "Which way did the drones come from?"

"This way." Lee gestured.

"Okay," Alvarez said. "Disperse, five meters spread, we're going that way. Optics on passive."

I glanced over my shoulder at him, trying to give him an "are you kidding me?" look. Unfortunately that was kind of impossible when you wore a face-covering spacesuit and Alvarez didn't give a single shit. I stood and hoped Alvarez had a plan. If he didn't have a plan, I'd have to come up with one—unless his plan involved leaving Gloria behind. *No*, I thought. *Marines don't leave Marines behind. Alvarez was in the Marines. He won't leave her behind.* Alvarez didn't. He slung Gloria over his back, moving with a bounce bounce bounce. She floated semi-limply, but her shoulder had been bound up tight in sealing wrap.

Lee pulled ahead of us.

And as I bounced and kept my eyes open and my ears— what little good they'd do—peeled, I tried to figure out what might happen next. Every radio signal we put out could be picked up by someone, anyone, who was listening. So, that left asking Alvarez right out. Being my de facto CO, his job was to get on my ass for breaking regs. I couldn't even ask if Gloria was okay.

But when I looked back, she gave me a thumbs-up.

I smiled. Somehow.

Some thought led to a guess: Alvarez was trying to track down and take down the drone's main base.

Lee held up a hand, then made the sign for "sighting" ahead. We dropped down. Gloria slid off Alvarez's back, but then she got to her knees, signing in two simple gestures that she could move and fight.

We dug in …

And two suited figures advanced on us.

They wore the same cut, the same design, as our suits.

"Squad Three?" Alvarez radioed.

"Jesus Christ!" A drawling voice that set my teeth on edge bounced back. The two figures had stopped dead, snapping their guns up to cover the sudden voice—though, of course, they didn't have their active optics on either. "Lightfoot?"

"Yeah." Alvarez stood, slowly, from where he'd dropped down. "What happened to your friends, Applejack?"

"Don't call me that, I'm not in the fuckin' mood." Smith sounded irritated and tired. "Two drones popped out of the ground and took down Yung and Lee … our Lee. Zir and I are all that's left."

"Did you take your base down?" Alvarez asked.

"You kidding?" Smith asked. "The drones spotted us before we even got close—"

"Of course." Alvarez sighed, turning to face us. "PR, you've got a finely-honed sense of cynicism. What does your cynic meter say about this?"

"We're not getting out till every base is down." I sighed, shaking my head slowly. My eyes closed.

This was going to be a special kind of fun.

>+<

By the time we made it to the next base, Gloria seemed to be alive more due to sheer concentrated willpower than anything else. She muttered obscenities in increasingly slurred Mandarin and Spanish and every other language she'd picked up in her career as we took recon in our stupidly by-the-numbers way. There wasn't any other choice. And, maybe once this was all done and over with, I could even think it was a good idea.

In the moment, I had a hard time thinking about anything except how Gloria was bleeding out. And not even on the battlefield. This was a godsdamned training exercise. This was a godsdamned waste of time. I was the one who was supposed to be bleeding to death.

I realized I should have been keeping my eyes on Alvarez and the base we were supposed to take out. It looked like it had beefed up its defenses, compared to the other bases. Because Selection hated us and wanted us to die.

I had just considering going AWOL and taking my damn chances on finding Canada on foot when Alvarez gestured and my peripheral vision and Pavlov-trained brain kicked me into motion before I even thought about it.

I snapped my gun up and took potshots at drones. The mobiles went down fast. It was the turrets that started really screwing us up: they fired those huge darts that we were all overly familiar with by this point. A dart took a huge hunk out of the cover I'd slipped behind and I swore, realizing that my ammo had run dry when I poked the barrel around the corner and tried to fire at the turret. The trigger didn't budge.

I ducked down and started to reload, while Alvarez barked out orders over the PA. No sense in being stealthy anymore, I guess.

"Hey, hey, Dru ..." Gloria spoke, her voice reedy over the radio.

"Yeah?" I shifted over to her. She looked pale through the face mask of her suit, and her hand was still splayed against her belly. My heart turned over.

"So, you ... you were ... going to tell me about your girlfriend one day, right?"

"Yeah." I clenched my jaw.

"All right, I just wanted you to know ... I don't ... I don't want to know anymore."

I glanced away from Gloria. Alvarez, Lee, Applejack, and company had taken down two of the turrets and as I watched, the last one was going down under a spread of needles, streaking in from our flanking positions.

"What makes you say that?" I asked, bemused and scared and a little annoyed for some stupid reason. She had been the one who had asked, when we had had our first real "couple" conversation. She had asked, and I had clammed up. It was too painful to think about, let alone speak about. Gloria had understood. She had held me as I cried. And now she was dropping it?

At least she's talking! my brain chimed in.

"Been married five times." Gloria closed her eyes, gritting her teeth. "Twice to boys, once to a girl, then to a boy and a girl ..."

"At the same time?" I asked, confusion winning out over anything.

"Heh." She grimaced. "It is fun. Only one died. The rest, I just left. I just let go ..." She gulped. "It was letting go of Juan that was the ... that was the hardest ..."

"Yeah, well, you better hold on." I put my hand on her shoulder, not sure if it was worth detangling her delirium. The thought raced through my head for like the fifth time. This was just training. This was just *practice.* "You better hold on, Gloria, so you can walk away from me. I'll even throw crockery at you and call you a heartless bitch and everything! I lost one girlfriend, I don't want to miss that chance."

She chuckled, and her voice came through dazed. "This means ... we'd have to get married first."

I shook my head. If she was talking this much, it had to mean she wasn't going out. Right? Right. Even if she was talking craziness.

"Sure. Fine. Whatever."

The radios flared with a broadband transmission, one that wasn't coming from any of us. It was nothing but a set of coordinates.

>+<

Gloria was strung between Alvarez and me, with Lee and Applejack leading the way. We came to the coordinates—each of us ready for something to shoot us in the back—and found a sleek submarine waiting for us.

I set Gloria down, as Alvarez patted her helmet, gently. "See, Gloria," he said. "I told you. They've spent too much money to let us all die down here."

Something started buzzing through the water. My limbs went numb and I had half a second to puzzle about it.

A familiar sensation ... a memory.

I was falling.

Unconsciousness.

Chapter 4: REDACTED

X/XX/XXXX

XXXXXX XX XXXXXX

XXXXXXX

I was floating in nothingness.

Yellowy light surrounded me and I remembered. A VR loading screen. The part before your in-game avatar appears and you just float, a mass of amorphous information. But there were words whispering in and out, at the back of my hearing.

If I had bones, they would have buzzed.

slegnA nellaF oF hselF ehT

slegnA nellaF oF hselF ehT

slegnA nellaF oF hselF ehT

I didn't understand.

"But you don't have to understand."

My eyes fluttered open and I saw a woman. She was pure Han and dressed all in black, with a voice that didn't have a single accent to it. No tone, no regional sound, nothing. It was like a newscaster's voice, only more so, unnervingly so. I was lying back in a chair and she was smiling.

Her finger tapped my forehead. "If it takes ..."

"If it takes, then we didn't waste several million credits." Another voice—every word in harsh, Californian English—spoke. "Put her under and let's go to Stage Three."

A finger tapped my forehead again.

Her finger.

"Simply remember ..." Her voice was soft as I felt something close around my scalp. A VR harness. I realized—through the haze of VR dumpshock and the confusion of going from dream to dream—that I should struggle and found that my wrists had been tied down."

You have tasted the
    flesh of
        fal
            len

angels

I blink. There's this weird muffled feeling in my head—like someone's put a pillow where my brains used to be. I slowly furrow my brow and then just as slowly, I lift up my head. I was lying on a table. When had I been lying on a table? I look out at something vast and blue and glittering and recognize it as an ocean. The sky is blue, too, and the two horizons of sea and sky meet at some infinite point.

I'm in a house as white as a space station—reflective and cool, even with a blistering sun overhead. There isn't a cloud in the sky. Birds wheel by overhead, cawing softly. The air smells rich and unnatural, thick with salts and out of control biosystems.

Smells like nature.

I stand up and notice that I'm dressed in a white gown that doesn't feel like anything. My hands go to the fabric and I crinkle it between my fingers.

"It's not quite perfect, I know," a voice says from *ahead* of me. Between blinks, a man is standing by the balcony. Also, there *is* a balcony. Before, it was just a room. Now, I'm on a balcony, and the man is looking out to sea. He looks pure Punjabi. Except I have no idea how I know that. Lightly browned skin, a well-trimmed beard, a turban that's the same blue as the sky.

"Where am I?" I ask.

"I'm sorry, Dru," the man says. "It feels dirty to do this. I wish I ..." He trails off, then chuckles. "I hope, at least, my associate doesn't bother you too much."

"Your ... associate?" I asked.

"You'll meet him later." He squeezes my shoulder. "And you'll know me when you know him."

My brow furrows.

Faint memories crawl in the back of my mind. I've *heard* this voice before. I've heard it before. The man looks out to the sea.

His voice is soft. "For now, this is all I can do. One moment of peace."

He falls silent and I feel like ...

Like saying something would be the same sort of stupid as putting a pinhole in a spacesuit. So, instead, I take hold of the railing and I look out at the blueness. Fish flit by in huge, impossible swarms. A dolphin leaps out of the water, then lands back in. The beach is pure white and the trees that grow from craggy, rocky cliffs that surround the beach like the arms of a lover are gnarled and old. Like time. It feels ancient, this place. Ancient and *quiet*. I feel the breeze on my face and my eyes close and I drink in this quiet.

"Where am I?" I ask. *Déjà vu* crawls along my scalp. Had I asked that before?

"A VR sim." He sounds wistful. "We still have the genetic records of the dolphins, but a lot of those fish are gone now.

They're not coming back." He pauses. "And I won't be, either. It won't be safe."

I nod, then looked down at the oceans. They juxtaposed with faint memories of trudging through deadness—and an ache hit me in my gut. "We really hosed this planet, didn't we?"

The man snorted. "Less people than you'd think, Drusilla Zhao. Less people than you'd think." He clapped his hand on my back. "Remember that, okay?"

I smiled at the genial Punjabi man. A name was on my lips. But then he was gone and the balcony was empty.

And I spent some time there, leaning on my elbows, feeling the sea breeze against my face.

Just watching.

For some reason, I wanted to cry and cry and cry, and I had no idea why.

And slowly, inch by inch ...

I started to slide out of VR.

My arms came to life. My toes. My fingers. My heart. My sense of gravity. Then the VR helmet slid away and I saw the woman in black, smiling at me. I knew her. I'd seen her. I'd heard her voice. *Be seeing you, Drusilla.* My skin was soaked with sweat and my heart *hammered.* I could feel my nerves throbbing in time with that pulse—a *beat beat beat beat* of agony along every single part of my body. Faint memories warred in my mind, and the juxtaposition made me want to scream.

"Good job, Lance Corporal. You passed."

"If ..." My voice came out raspy and raw. Like I'd been screaming and screaming and screaming. My lips were chapped. I was painfully thirsty. And yet, I had a sudden flash. A fear. A *terror* of drowning. "What did ... you do to me?"

I felt ...

What had they *done* to me?

"What we had to do." She caressed my thigh, as if I was *meat*. "We'll put you back together. But right now, you have to give us consent."

I goggled at her.

Consent?

She looked back, bland as ever. I shook my head.

>+<

Consent? The word echoed in my mind. I tried to remember what it was I had been *doing*. "What did you do to me?" I asked, again. Why was my voice so raspy? Gods, I was thirsty. My brow furrowed and my eyes half closed.

"What we had to do," she said. Her fingers were sliding along my thigh—as if I was *meat*. I shuddered convulsively. "We'll put you back together. But right now, you have to give us consent."

The way her words hung in the air made it sound like she was waiting to see *something*. Was this a test? A godsdamned test? After *all* of this? I gritted my teeth and rasped out the words before I could ...

Forget again.

"I. Did not come. This far. To give up. Now."

She nodded.

Something hissed into my arm.

And once again, blackness swallowed my body. As I fell, a single thought flickered through my head.

What had they done to me?

Chapter 4: New

7/3/2068

Hong Kong, China

T-Minus L-Day: 11

I woke up for the first time in pieces.

I was on a bed and someone leaned over me. For a moment, I thought it was the woman in black, but it wasn't. It was a man, with blond hair and slanted eyes. He looked into my eyes and shone a bright light in them.

"The overlays are working?"

"Uh, we're getting near total communication."

"Spark her."

I felt a finger that wasn't a finger curl up. It was like getting shocked—but the shock had come from inside. Deep inside. And nothing *actually* curled in on itself. There was no tensing of muscle. There was just a spark.

"Seeing confirmed psychosomatic feedback loops in the computational area. She's good."

That seemed to satisfy the man with blond hair.

"Put her under again, then."

I fell asleep all at once.

I woke up for the first time with an arm. A woman was leaning over me, and held a tool normally used for cutting into spaceship hulls. Electrical light crackled and a smell like burning hair met my nose. I made a mewling noise. Something *hurt*.

"Hey, we got an SFU 50."

"It's always the arms, isn't it? Hit her with another dosage."

"We're nearing the redline, doctor."

The doctor sighs. "Will she remember any of this?"

"No." The other voice is brutal.

"Then hold her down."

I am held down.

Nothingness.

>+<

I woke up for the first time, this time to a warm room and faint bleeping noises. I recognized those: heart monitors and biofeedback devices. But something felt right. Something felt distinctly *right* about me, which was a change of pace so shocking that it was nearly as discombobulating as waking up with a migraine would have been. My arms shifted up, so that I could see them. It was a weird motion, for just a few seconds. Like ... they looked normal. But rather than *lifting* my arms, I had thought: *I want to see my arms.*

And up they had come. An eerie inverse of the normal way things worked. I shook my head and glared at my fingers. Wriggling them around felt normal. I lowered my arms. That felt normal. Okay. I lifted my arms again and noticed a very tiny *seam* along the edge of my wrist. My brow furrowed. I focused and turned my wrist. Instead of turning the forearm too—as was normal—my wrist just started to rotate like the drill bit on a screw. It went around and around and around and *around*. I kept pushing on, marveling at how this not only didn't feel painful, oh no, it didn't even feel *weird*. I guess that's what months of training before getting implants gets you. I didn't miss the crawling, awful feeling that my cybernetic fingers had gotten me in my first tour.

I stopped with my palm facing the right way.

Okay, I thought. *What the fuck?*

The last thing I remembered was being at the bottom of the freaking Atlantic ocean. Now, here I was, with …

I wiggled my fingers. I bent them backward until they touched the back of my knuckles, winced, and put them back to normal with a thought. I sat up, and the sheet covering me slid down, revealing that I was just wearing a sports bra. This made it easy for me to trace my arm all the way to my shoulder. As I craned my head and moved my hands, I heard a few faint *clicks*, which I ignored. Instead, I focused on examining every inch of my skin. I wasn't frantic to find seams. I was just *curious*. That feeling of rightness persisted, and my skin looked totally normal—no more seams. When I checked my wrist again, the seam I had seen there was gone. It seemed that my body had *settled* into the right position.

A knock came on the door.

"Yeah?" My voice felt normal, but there was something weird at the back of my throat. Like a lump, small enough to not be overly worrying, but big enough to be distracting. I felt a sudden itch back there, and resisted the urge to stick my hand in my throat to feel it.

The door opened and in came a doctor. He was an improbably blond Chinese man I'd never seen before, holding a tablet and a stylus. He whipped them both up and checked something off for me, then started reading from the tablet.

"Lance Corporal Drusilla Zhao, you have been equipped with two Class 2 cyberlimbs, two Class 3 cyberlegs, a Mark 4 respiration system, augmented reality interfaces, internal duction computational systems, wired reflexes, carbonized bones, gastrointestinal modifications, active camouflage, vacuum sealing, medi-stasis, and a palm-light." He tapped the tablet again, then looked up at me. "How do you feel?"

I licked my lips, thinking. My head was all ... fuzzy. My brow furrowed and I tried to piece together how I'd *gotten* here. Nothing. "W-Wait," I said, holding up my hand. My cybernetic hand.

The doctor pursed his lips, looking at me like I'd just taken his entire plan for the day and thrown it out the window. But my grin was hard to repress.

"I made it?" I asked, voice *quivering*.

His pursed lips turned into a smile as genuine as any I'd ever seen in my life. He laughed. "Yes, Lance Corporal. You made it. The surgery and anesthetic tends to mess up short-term memory formation during the process. And you did *not* want to be awake for a lot of the, uh, procedure."

I chuckled. Even if you did think about it, it wasn't actually very funny. Which was why I was planning to never *ever* think about how I'd gotten cybernetic *skin*.

"Now." The doctor clasped his hands before him, clipping the stylus to the side. His grin grew playful. "How do you feel?"

I thought about it for a bit, looking down at my hand. I touched fingertips to palm. "Mostly human," I admitted.

"That'll change." He tapped the stylus again.

A sharp pain shot through my head, right at the back of my eyeballs, like my brain had decided that they were hogging too much attention and stabbed them in the optic nerve. My vision hazed, then came back into even sharper focus. A shimmering outline surrounded the doctor, starting out like a vague glow before it snapped to form a solid yellowy line. Similar glows surrounded all the other objects around me, until they were highlighted as well. Images appeared around them, names and information.

Dr. Huge Chung III
Security Clearance: Omega
Tablet: Mk4 IMB Smart-touch Duratablet (4 day battery life.)

I closed my eyes and the images faded.

"You can alter your augmented reality filters through a process known as ducting," he said. "Think the word *options* in your mind."

I opened my eyes and did just that. Just imagining the word didn't work ... I had to actually think it out, like I was going to say it, but just didn't open my mouth and push the air out. A box appeared in the left side of my vision, full of settings and, well, options. I got the hang of it fast, biting my lip as I thought words like, "Color Highlight, Green" and "Information Display: Eye Focus."

Soon, I'd whittled down the mist of augmented reality. Now, I'd only get extra information for things I looked at for a few seconds, and the outlines were only for people, not every single object in the world. All this thinking was actually making my head feel ... hot. Tense, like there was a VR rig in my brain that was running at max speed.

Which, to be fair, there actually was. After a fashion.

I slid my hands through my hair and sighed while Dr. Chung the Third tucked his tablet under one arm.

"All right," he said. "Now that you've acclimated somewhat to the AR inputs, we'll move on to the next part of the orientation." His lips split into a wide grin. "And I think you're going to like it."

"Doc?" That feeling of rightness had evaporated. No. No. That wasn't the right word. My body still felt smooth and precise and well-oiled. In fact, it was finally *hitting* me what the rightness was. It was a sudden absence. It was a lack of minor aches, tiny pains, all the minutiae you pick up when you go through Basic. Or, well, Selection in this case. Figuring that out made the rightness fade into the background.

Which meant I could get right back to being morose. Especially when promised something I was going to *like*. Seeing my expression, Dr. Chung gestured with both hands, like an eager member of the Crèche.

"Stand up."

I shifted, so that my legs slid out from under the sheet. I was wearing a pair of sports panties too. Well, at least I was being modest here. I put my feet on the ground and stood. I felt my balance go all off, then center. I shifted, bending my knees, then bounced up. I bounced from foot to foot and started to grin despite my best efforts at cynical dourness.

My legs felt like *springs*.

"Duct the word Cheetah."

I did. My legs whirred, the flesh opening up and revealing the metal underneath. I felt queasy, then confused as my legs went from feet to … fins. Curved fins of some kind of sproingy metal. The fleshy bits and lots of the metal had slid up into my thighs, which were now a bit thicker than before, and I definitely looked like a horror movie monster.

I didn't *feel* like a movie monster. I felt like … like I wasn't sure. The rightness and my cynicism were mixing together with a new, third ingredient: *excitement*. How could I not be freaking excited, to see my legs whir and shift and click like multi-function smart machines? I started to move from leg to leg, feeling the way that the fins and the knees both bounced. It was like being at a third of a G.

Dr. Chung the Third stepped out of the way and gestured to the door. He smiled. "The track is down the corridor."

I looked at him curiously and took a step. I almost fell flat on my face, my legs slipping along the ground funnily. I held out my arms … and then took another step. And another step. My legs sprang and felt so freaking weird that I almost didn't notice that I was hurtling down the corridor, a shimmering arrow appearing before me, guiding me to a specific door, which opened up to reveal a gym. And a track.

I felt like a rocket spotting a refueling station.

I ran onto the track and started to sprint with my fin-legs. I tried to slow my forward progress by slamming one fin-leg down perpendicular to myself. This made me skid to a stop. I tensed, spread my arms, then moved into a running position. The track stretched out before me, looping around and around in this small room.

So. Let's see what I was supposed to like so much. I set my face, set my feet (fins?) and then took off like a rocket. I pounded forward, my legs absorbing the impact and sending me jetting forward with every single step. I almost swept my legs out from under me as I took the turn way harder and way faster than I thought. But as I slipped, I felt something in my stomach and my brain whirr and instantly *knew* exactly how to fling out an arm to shift my center of mass there so that I—

My eyes widened as my legs worked almost automatically, sprinting along the curve of the track's wall before I righted myself, running down from the wall to the ground, then forward again. Joy bubbled up from my thighs to my belly to my head as I hit a straightaway and picked up speed again. I grinned and started to run faster and faster. A thought brought up my speed on the AR interface as I hit the next corner. Holy shit.

Fifty kilometers an hour. And I wasn't even feeling *tired.* My arms pounded and my legs bounced and it was *all* worth it. Every. Single. Part. The wind blew through my hair and along my body and everything moved right. That wonderful feeling of rightness flowed like the wind and I couldn't help it. I laughed and I almost cried as I ran and ran and ran, watching the kilometers tick higher and higher, taking the corners tighter and tighter.

[*Whoa there, slow down.*]

I skidded to a stop, my legs whirring and clicking, the fins sliding up and the feet sliding down. I looked around, curiously.

[*Over here, PR.*]

An indicator appeared in the left edge of my vision—a freaking arrow, like this was a video game—and I spun around to face the person who had spoken in my mind. It was Colonel Mary Singh. She wasn't smiling. But then again, she never smiled.

I saluted.

She saluted back. [*At ease.*]

"Permission to speak freely, ma'am?"

[*Use transducting. You have radio transceivers in your ears and transmitters in your vocal cords.*] She inclined her head. [*It's a good habit to get into.*]

I nodded, then tried ... thinking my words at her. Nothing. I closed my eyes and thought harder. I knew it wasn't telepathy, but I still felt like a New Age idiot. I thought and thought and then boom.

[*How's fish?*]

[*Try again.*]

I coughed.

[*How's this?*]

[*Better.*] She ducked her head forward and then started to step around me on the track. [*From here on out, you're not quite in the same place that you used to be.*]

I grinned, starting to get a hang of this. I focused and felt my curved fin-legs whirr and click into place. I bounced on them. I could still feel the wind on my face and on my shoulders and arms.

[*Sir?*] I ducted.

[No sirs, not now.] Singh smiled and I almost faceplanted in shock. *[Come with me, I need to show you something.]*

I focused and my legs collapsed and folded and became regular human legs again. Yeah. I got this. It felt like each time I shifted my legs, it got faster. Easier. Less distracting. I followed her, my bare feet slapping on the ground like flesh. We moved like freaking predators and I felt taller. Maybe I was taller, I didn't actually know. AR ghosted up and cut through that I was actually about the same height. Stupid illusion-shattering computers.

We came to a room adjoined to the gym. It looked a bit like someone had taken an old industrial area, like what Sarah's father had spent his whole life taking down, and just plopped it into the middle of this futuretech facility. There were brick walls and bits of metal, tangled-up cars and rusted barbed wire. The floor was strewn with gravel and someone had set the wallpaper to show an outdoor sky. It smelled like rust and failing life support and for once, that smell didn't trigger me. Though I was getting a serious case of temporal whiplash, seeing the juxtaposition.

Singh stepped over to the doorway. Leaning against open space—the wallpaper was that good—was a sledgehammer. She picked it up one-handed and chucked it at me. I caught it with both hands and found it was maybe a quarter of a kilo. I hefted it and my AR readings came in. The thing weighed ten kilos. Well, 9.52 kilos, but I almost dropped it.

Singh grinned. *[That's the big step,]* she ducted. *[That's what separates a human from a transhuman. Anyone can live with limitations. The trick, for us, is to love the lack of them.]*

I gulped. This ... to be honest, after growing up with movies like *Terminator* (the remake) and *The Mumbai Slasher*, hearing that kind of thing sounded like something the bad guy would say before being defeated by the plucky humans.

I kept looking at the sledgehammer, hefting it in my arms, then bouncing it on my palms. It slapped faux-flesh and sounded like a meaty slap slap slap.

[So, the first thing is what the shrinks explain as psychosomatic stress relief via the exploration of primal deconstructive urges.]

[You got that in Cantonese?] I ducted back with a grin. It was weird, the humming voice in my head was starting to feel normal.

[Dru smash.]

I had never in the whole of the history of the universe imagined that a superior officer—let alone one with almost sixty years of combat experience—would call me by my first name. I grinned at her and then stepped over to the brick wall. I held the sledge up like a baseball bat ... and swung it. Hard. The head slammed into the bricks and dust filled the air. My AR kicked on and scanned through the dust, painting a greenish outline where the wall remained. A jagged hunk the size of my torso had gone bye-bye.

I laughed, out loud. *[HAH!]*

"Go nuts! That's an order!" Singh's voice sounded like a firework, bursting in my head. I spun on my heel and the sledge ripped through the wall. Bricks that survived went tumbling, and dust filled the air. My mouth closed itself and I didn't need to breathe. I felt no coughing, no hacking, no nothing. Instead, an indicator showing my internal CO_2 filters popped on. I breathed without breathing. I grinned fierce and ran straight at the busted, broken-down car.

"YEAAAAHHH!" I shouted like I was in an old vid-game. I bounced, my legs driving into the ground and sending me hurtling up, almost into the freaking ceiling. Crash alarms blared in my ears and indicators flashed around my eyes, but I remained focused.

The sledge slammed into the engine block. The chassis of the car flipped into the air and flew over my head. Something clicked on in my brain and everything went slow as molasses. I counted the flecks of rust in the air.

The car slammed into the wall, tearing a great big rip in the wallpaper sky that left behind exposed gray metal and a squeal of a dent. I winced. *[I don't envy whoever has to buff that out …]*

[All right, try out your active camo.]

I focused and thought the word that my AR interface told me to think: Predator. My skin shimmered and vanished. I looked at my hands and saw only a rippling distortion. I laughed, under my breath. I did feel like a predator, a stalking hunter. Singh, though, just laughed under her breath.

[You don't even know what a Predator is, do you?]

I walked around a wall and noticed her eyes followed my every motion. I must be more obvious than I thought.

[Old movie alien.]

[Ah, good … kids these days don't usually know their film history.]

[Blame my … my old friend, sir.]

It didn't hurt as much now.

Singh smirked. *[Something you should know …]* She turned to the wallpaper and some of it shifted into a mirror. I saw a faint distortion where I stood, but in the light levels of the room, it was actually pretty hard to spot.

But there was one thing that kind of sort of stood right out like a *f'n zse*. My eyeballs. They both sat right where they should be, eerie and creepy as hell.

[Right … I forgot how eyes worked for a second there,] I ducted, a bit sheepishly.

Singh shook her head. *[Now, why don't you try out your arms?]*

[Yes, sir!] I grinned as my active camo slipped off my skin like an electronic cloak. My skin wasn't really skin anymore. I tried to not think about how that had to have been applied … but my brain went and did it anyway. They'd hacked off my arms and legs, peeled my skin away, replaced my lungs, shoved a new heart in, and basically turned my bones into diamonds with injections and chem treatments. Then, they'd slapped a new, specially grown skin back onto my body, teased my nerves to integrate with it and with artificial bundles of faux-nerves, which tied everything into a single artificial whole.

Considering all that …

I actually felt pretty good.

And when I figured out how to extend the arm-blade, I felt even better.

>+<

A hood yanked off my head. Light flowed through slats of a wooden hovel, and the air was humid and hot, like a slap to the face. I groaned and looked around. A vague shape walked back and forth, around my body. I was tied to a chair, a harsh metal one. My wrists felt sore, like they'd been tied that way for a while.

Great.

Fantastic, even.

I tried to gulp and my throat seized up like it had become the Gobi desert when I wasn't watching. I coughed and slid my tongue along lips, finding them cut up and sandpapered.

The pacing form didn't stop pacing. He … it looked and moved like a he, didn't say anything. Were they waiting for something?

I tried to think through what was happening …

But …

There had been the submarine. Then …

I jerked awake all at once, gasping heavily. Gloria was looking down into my eyes, her palms on my shoulders. Pinning me down. The bed under us squeaked slightly. That was one of the downsides of being augmented to hell and back: we were both a bit heavier than we used to be. Enough that a bed could be almost louder than we were during ... uh ...

Fine motor skill and acrobatic practice.

Yeah.

I blinked away my confusion and my fear and slowly settled back.

Gloria shook her head, her grin wicked. "Do I even want to know?" Her voice was husky. My fake skin wasn't slick with sweat, but I still tingled in the warm night air gusting through the window in our little room. I reached up, caressing Gloria's neck, feeling her with my fingertips. I looked into her eyes, feeling my heart rate slow.

"Mmmnope," I mumbled.

Gloria laid herself back down on me. One advantage of skin tough enough to tank low caliber projectiles? Your girl could just lay on you. Sprawl across you, hug you tight, squeeze you and nuzzle you and make the night less dark. I cupped the back of Gloria's head and looked up at the metallic ceiling of our room.

Selection was the tryouts.

Not training.

Everyone who had survived the ocean training hell—and that included Gloria, the memory of the blood and the muffled *thunk* of the bullet hitting her making me squeeze her just a bit more—had been sent to a new training facility. This one was in the middle of Hong Kong, and it was still far enough away from Xin-Shanghai that I didn't want to cry myself to sleep every night.

Well, almost every night.

Gloria mumbled into my ear. "Can't sleep either?"

"Not even a little," I said.

Gloria bit me. *[Come on. Let's do some studying, PR.]* Her voice ducted into my head and I swear to the gods I'm not lying, but her ducted voice tickled the part of my brain that controlled libido. Either it was a mistake in my brain surgery, or ...

Gloria got up. Lithe. Beautiful. I watched her stand and tried to suss out if I *felt* felt for her, or if it was just wanting to drag her into bed and lick every inch of her body. And a voice that wasn't quite my own internal thoughts muttered in my head: *Does it matter?*

And you know what?

No. It didn't.

Gloria walked over to the desk—the room had once been a four-person bunk room, but some helpful soul had cut some of the beds out and replaced them with desks in the decades between the Slump and now. She sat her naked ass down and I admired the way the neons and sky lights of Hong Kong shining through the windwo glowed along her dusky skin.

Hong Kong, circa 2068, was a city exploding (in a good way). There were now five distinct Hong Kongs. Old Kong sprawled on the coast and the Hong Kong island, which had pretty much become the exact same thing. The five other districts were sprawls of carbon composites and aeroplast and other fancy meta-materials that could float on water. There was New Kong, South Kong, Under Kong, and finally, Fort Kong, which had been thrown up during the hazy first days of the amalgamation when the *USS Obama* had moored off the coast to provide air support during the entirely fictional Second Sino/Russian police action.

"Get over here, PR," Gloria said, crooking a finger. I forced myself out of bed, stretching and yawning.

I sat down next to her and we started to get out our files on the Sino/Russian police action from 2028. Which, again, never happened. Sure, we were reading classified technical and tactical briefings on the precursor to the S3TA: the PLA:SFO and the JSF:HTART cooperation, organized under the EOB, with oversight from the DOD and the PLA's CPC. Sure, we had actual footage of the event and actual casualty lists ... but it had *never happened.*

"I know some people on the Internet who would feel really validated by all of this." Gloria's voice was husky in my ear. I groaned.

"Trying to focus, Gloria," I said. But thanks to her little nibble, I read the same sentence, like, six times in a row without it actually imparting a single iota of useful information. Gloria, thankfully, went back to reading—this part of the document was about the technical specifications of the *USS Obama* and how it had been adapted after the police action.

The whole damn ship had been rooted in place and rebuilt into the beating heart of this facility. It had been the last of the great big aircraft carriers, before they had become too expensive and too rarely used to be worth the men and materials. It had shipped out with five thousand men and women onboard, three nuclear reactors (one a generator, two breeders) and enough heavy weapons, munitions, and smart bombs to turn half of Europe, Russia, and Africa into smoldering craterlands.

Now, it was one of the CAA's primary military seaports. And, wonder of wonders, it hadn't been rodded yet.

Maybe that was because every attempt was being made to make the whole thing look like nothing more than a sleepy, unguarded post. Which, incidentally, meant they actually made it into a sleepy, unguarded post.

It was hard to feel like I was meeting my potential here, on a cruddy forty-year-old aircraft carrier cum (uhhh, not that kind) floating nuclear power station, bunked in rooms that had been used to store the generation between my grandparents and my parents as they sailed around the world. The last, dying gasps of the American Empire. I could look underneath my bed and see a scribble: *The Center Cannot Hold*. It had been carved into the deck and hidden by a footlocker for who knows how long ...

It was like I was sitting in a room that was still waiting, with bated breath, for the end of the world. I could feel that creepy, crawling feeling come back. The same sensation I'd had when I woke up, chased away by closeness and warmth.

It helped even less that our *scintillating* reading material was hardcopy. That is, it was paper.

Yes.

Paper. Not even smart paper or tech paper or projection paper. No, it was just regular old run-of-the-mill completely non-electronic paper. The worst part wasn't the lack of a search function, actually. See, the mnemonic augmentation was the most finicky pieces of *luh suh* that had been shoved into my frontal lobes. The idea was you focused and *tagged* a recent memory to be backed up into a little computer file. But because that file shouldn't be completely overflowed with thoughts and ideas, they made that "tagging" thought one of the trickiest works of ducting in the universe.

So, when we studied on tactical reports, we used highlighters to mark what we needed to remember. And do you know what an oldtech highlighter *smells* like?

How w'rin bu lai, whai w'rin bu jwo!

"Ugh, kill me," I muttered after an hour of reading. Gloria, who had been quietly sitting next to me, snorted.

"Dru, I managed to survive at the bottom of the Atlantic with the next best thing to a sucking chest wound," Gloria said, her voice teasing. She switched to ducting. *[You can survive some homework. <3]*

I glared at the file. On from tech-specs to a linked report talking about an engagement between Russian paranationals armed with "combined force arms and light munitions" and two members of the Chinese special forces while the Americans provided technical and long-ranged support. I was supposed to study the failures, the successes, and talk intelligently about why and how they'd happened, and how to apply the lessons learned to a new generation of warfare.

Okay.

Sounds fun, right?

Except it all comes out like this: *SFO UNIT 1, 2nd Lt. Shi Du-fa and 1st Lt. Gao Zhao advanced 3 meters, taking light fire from Sector B-4 (refer to figure 1.1a). 2nd Lt. Du-Fa returned fire and overland support was called in from HART-COM, provided by JSF UNIT 44, JSF-F 221, piloted by ...*

And so on. Letter salad was a danger—and considering lasers and sandcasters, a fairly minor one—in any military branch. Didn't make wading through it any fun. But, considering all the things I had to deal with, bitching about reading seemed like an even bigger waste of time.

That fact didn't stop me from mentally complaining. But, then again, mentally complaining was better than the alternatives. Maybe it had something to do with what I had felt back in the hospital, the need for revenge and blood and snapping necks. Maybe it had something to do with the fact that I was sitting on the most advanced buttocks in the freaking world, and instead of doing all the super-soldier shit I had trained and bled and almost died for, I was reading *paperwork.*

[You're leaking.]

I closed my eyes. Because thinking and talking had a lot in common, ducting by accident could happen. Down here, everyone made fun of you mercilessly, sexual relationship notwithstanding. Mostly because if you leak in the field ... well, anyone with even remotely good detection gear might pick it up. Ducting was usually carried on local wi-fi in encrypted channels, simply for the convinence. A wi-fi network could bounce around corners, unlike tightbeaming, which required you to have a line of sight laser-link with your buddies. But there was also a radio antenna stuck in my head, so I could duct using a radio. Which had the downside of being easier to pick up and ... well ... that was what led to *leaking* in the first place.

And I'd been doing so *well*.

I rubbed my eyes with my palms and ducted back at Gloria, *[Sorry ... you getting anywhere in this alphabet soup?]*

She bumped her hip against me and smirked. *[Nope.]*

I shook my head and flipped through another few pages. I tried to not think about how surreal it was to be reading this file which could have been dropped right out of a historical drama, while I was sitting here with arms and legs that felt and acted like they had come out of the far future. Future-shock was the kind of thing my parents would have said ... I shook my head, burying the old pain. Which, unfortunately, led me straight to feeling the new pain.

[Leaking again.]

Damn it!

[I heard that.]

I turned my head, leaned forward, and bit down on Gloria's neck, muffling my growl with her toughened skin. I ducted, hot and fast. *[Maybe if you stopped bitching at me constantly.]*

"Maybe you should stop thinking about everything so much." Gloria chuckled. She completely no sold my bite. Which was part of why I'd done it. "You know how I don't leak? Yeah, I do that by being focused. I don't wonder about my parents or how much I want to kill Loonies or any of the other thousand and one things that cross your mind." She smirked, slightly, looping her arm around my back to pet my head.

I released her neck with my teeth and nuzzled up against her, my eyes closing. For the past year, thinking was the only way I'd stayed sane. Thinking kept me from going crazy in space, on the ground, and while people were pointing guns at my face. Now I just had to ...

Gloria's finger twined through my hair and tugged hard enough to jerk my nose away from the faint dimple I'd left.

[Seriously, do I need to get out a wrench?] Her voice was playful.

[To do what? Tighten my screws?] I smiled up at her. But deep in my gut, a tiny worm wriggled. I clamped it down, feeling a rushing horror exploding behind my smile, which became masklike and hard in that instant. The last thing in the *universe* I wanted to leak was ...

Was ...

Thinking that this was *fake*. This was just me, crawling up against someone else because ...

[No, to beat you to death so I can get some work done.] Gloria kissed me. Fierce. Assertive. I melted against her, my eyes closing. Then she was pushing me back with a finger on my forehead. *[Now, get back to reading. Or I really will kill you.]*

I narrowed my eyes as if I couldn't quite tell if she was being serious or not. It broke down and I grinned as Gloria collapsed into a series of verbal and electronic giggles and that tiny little worm subsided. I shook my head and went through everything I'd been taught about leaking. Diagnostics, internal reflection, thoughts focused toward myself ... not of the world. My biometrics flowed past my vision and I felt them as I read them. Heart rate, breathing ...

There we go.

I wasn't Buddhist, but I'd tried meditating a few times in the Crèche, just for fun. Turns out that meditation for fun didn't work at all but I found myself slipping into the old thought pattern like it was a glove. But it had been good groundwork: meditation was pretty similar to what S3TA wanted you to do to get your implants under control.

I opened my eyes, smiled, and went back to reading.

Focused.

The trick to understanding special operations was that they were *special*. There was no set procedure that they used again and again because warfare kept changing. These documents we read were the beginning of what our instructors called "drone warfare," when telepresence and miniaturization put enough firepower into a Frisbee to tilt engagements one way or another. Then the enemy had adapted, drones were jammed, hacked into, or generally put out of business and things moved into transhuman warfare, where the technology was focused on improving soldiers themselves, not just their kit.

It was funny, reading these dry, terse reports about military activities ... it was like hearing the dullest, most uninteresting person ever tell you about the nightmare of the Great Leap Forward or the first AIDS Crisis. After a few minutes of forcing yourself to feel sick at the stories of infanticide and starvation and governments laughing at dying people, you just started to hear statistics.

It reminded me, in a grim and twisted way, of the time right after the Disaster, when I'd still been trying to—

[It starts with an L—]

I bit Gloria again. And this time, I *chewed*.

Chapter 5: Smoke

7/10/2068

Hong Kong, China

T-Minus L-Day: 4

[Smoke 'em.]

For a moment, everything slowed down. The tango I had in my sights was going about fifty KPH, with a pretty hefty crosswind. My AR and my instincts worked in tandem, to put a bullet right …

There.

My PK-404 coughed and tried to buck, but I held it stock-still. Four other coughs went off at the same time from five other places, and five other bullets struck. The five tangos dropped and their jeep slewed out of control for a few feet, the auto-brakes kicking into effect and the AI bringing it to a smooth stop. We all moved out of cover, our active camo making us look like ghosts.

Ghosts with guns.

Something was wrong.

No time to think. Alvarez—indicated by a few symbols over-laid on my AR—went to the front of the jeep and tugged one of the bodies out. I hurried to keep up, moving to grab my target and hauling him off as well. I overshot a bit and the body went flying into the river we had been hiding by. Alvarez shot me a duct: *[Careful, PR.]*

Gloria and Lee took the back seats.

[All right,] Alvarez ducted to the lot of us. *[Lee, PR, start her up.]*

On this exercise I was part of the infosec team. I'd had plenty of practice slipping past Selection's security—though after a week of hard, twenty-four-hour training on neurotropics and time dilation, I knew just how stupidly naïve I had been to think they hadn't left plenty of holes for me to slip through. Now I had actual training and, more than that, wired reflexes and head-ware. Slicing into the tango's security systems and spoofing their biometric feedback was the work of seconds, which was a good thing: their AIs would have noticed something might have been wrong, but there was a short "delay," so that an alarm didn't go off every time someone adjusted their vest or joggled their cut-rate, second-hand, oldtech biometric contacts.

That was the idea at least.

[We're good.] Lee spoke more often with tightbeam radio than with his mouth. I guess that had to be part of why he'd been picked for S3TA.

[Good.] Alvarez gestured. *[Roll the jeep into the water and switch to Cheetah.]*

Gloria shoved the jeep as I steered, the brakes having been cut with a single quick stab through the hood from Alvarez. The stab hadn't come from a knife ... rather, he'd used his forearm blade, which had popped out with his punch and sliced through metal, tube, and then smoothly pulled out. The jeep slipped into the lake and was gone, as if it had never been.

We ghosted and moved out, loping, springing strides pumping us through the air. Active camo had to work crazy hard to blur us, but moving fast and shifting our stances and speeds made us almost impossible to pin down if anyone did spot the movement. I'd seen footage of a squad fully ghosting. If I hadn't known what I had been looking at, I'm not sure what I would have called it. A blur that moved past at car-speeds?

But that question was just a distraction from another question. Like *why*, exactly, were we training here, in this particular VR sim? This had nothing to do with space or Luna.

Both questions dissolved through my fingers as I fell into *movement*. A focus on dipping and shifting around trees, on wind rushing past my face, on my skin shimmering and shifting, matching the coloration and hue of my skin to the forest behind me. Predator. The term was *perfect*. It wasn't like it was in space, where everything was mathematics ... here, I could shift my weight and change my trajectory. I could bounce and rebound. I could dance. It was like having thrusters on for the first time, but multiplied by a thousand. We didn't go along the road, but instead we cut through a forested area, coming along the bluff that looked out over the base: it was the new pattern of terrorist hide-hole, complete with a brace of hovering camera drones that backed up a few men and women with rifles in picket towers. They covered prefab buildings holding their supplies, people, and at least one computer hub to jack into the government network, all of it camouflaged against aerial observation and satellites.

Not from us.

[I count twenty-five.] Alvarez de-ghosted behind a tree, turning his head to look at us.

[Confirmed.] I nodded.

[All right, two by two. Me and Gloria'll be providing overwatch. Smoke quiet.]

I nodded. Lee blipped up on my AR: he was my "second." Alvarez didn't micromanage us. He could have. In early training runs, when Gloria had been in charge, she'd been a bit RTS: she kept giving us waypoints and patrol routes to go along. It was comforting. Until our first TPK. We got wiped when everyone, all so focused on their little skirmishes rather than the whole fight, got completely blindsided by a godsdamned tank. That was the beauty and the danger of the link we had: with tactical networks, instant communication, head-computers and augmented reality, information became infectious. Finding the right mix of sharing and focus and intercommunication had gotten us all killed a lot.

That was *fun*.

Mostly because each and every simulation was run with full immersion feedback. I knew for a fact that getting shot hurt. Being shot in VR didn't just hurt, though, it was freaking humiliating.

Lee and I went down the bluff, moving slow and carefully, our Cheetahs turning to regular legs. Yeah, uh, turns out all my fancy neologisms weren't needed. Cheetahs were based off old, early twenty-first century augmentations, before the Slump. They fell out of favor after the Singularity Scare made cybernetics the next best thing to becoming a horror movie monster, and were entirely replaced by cloned replacements.

But even *before* you factor in the pneumatics, the synth-muscle, the composite materials and the million other factors that made our Cheetahs better than the old blade-legs, a runner with blade-legs could outpace a standard homo saps. We could outpace some groundcars.

Which is why we used our standard legs as we moved out: keeping our pace slow to prevent the active camo from blurring too much. Though, we also had the standard reasons to be nervous. People noticed things when they made the wrong noise, when plants moved and no one was there to push them. They noticed things like that and then they opened fire. Even if they hadn't heard ghost stories or seen too many spec-fic vids, they were still on guard and twitchy as hell in an era where drone support and stealthed aircraft could put a dozen commandos on your ass. That made anyone bullet-crazy.

Lee came to the bottom of the bluff. In the vids, Special Forces and badass commandos held up their hands to communicate. Hell, before we had gotten augs, we'd done that too. I still sometimes threw up a hand to stop my teammates rather than ducting. Lee never ever forgot: he threw up a stop indicator on my AR, and then tagged three tangos, each one circled by a glowing outline as they moved through the edge of the camp. Pickets.

I moved left and Lee went right. Stealth training—and in the back of my mind, I was still boggling that we were wasting our time with stealth training that could only be used in ground operations—told me to stay light, move slowly and carefully from place to place. Shift your mass on the balls of your feet. Ridiculous, but it worked down here, it worked. But in space ...

[Smoke 'em.]

I fired and Lee fired at the same time. Two bullets bit into the backs of two of the three-man patrol. The third man half-turned before two more bullets bit into him. We made sure to hit them in places that kept them from crying out, but we still had to work quick, as the other team had to be rolling the tangos up too.

We left them where they fell. Lee threw up a branch path, and took left. I went right, crouching and moving slow. I smoked three more tangos who were hanging out at one of the patrol towers and ducted: *[Taking the high ground.]*

[Holding postion,] Lee sent, maintaining security at the bottom of the tower.

As a certified marksman, I wasn't exactly special. Hell, Gloria had certified before I'd even been in the Marines, or done more than play a few vid-games. But I had something she lacked: I knew how to stay still. I could stay still in my sleep, something these Earthers never did seem to figure out, not in the gut instinct level a Spacer did. I clambered up the ladder, moving carefully to keep the active camo moving. Some of the people in the other watch towers had noticed that something was wrong and were chatting in their radios, their voices—speaking some dialect of Mandarin I'd never heard before in my life—squawked over their dead buddy's coms.

I took up overwatch, covering as much of the camp as I could. Before my augs, without a headware, I'd have been deorbiting without a heat shield trying to cover the whole camp: it was too spread out, too cluttered, too thick with foliage and tiny hints of movement. Like, there were at least five (maybe *seven*) vague lumps shrouded by leaves and grass and dirt that *could* be buildings, with dozens of winding paths between each. It covered at least a three-hundred-meter square.

But with my headware?

It *outlined* every possibility, then dimmed out stuff that stopped twigging the computer's pattern recognition. Every time new data came in that made the computer sit up and take notice, outlines would brighten, letting me *focus* on them and identify animals, shifting plants.

Bad guys.

Alvarez smoked the other covering tower as my headware finished laying out the bad guys. By now, alarms had started ringing through the base. Of course, by now they were also down to half their effectives. I worked quick, snapping to wired reflexes to take advantage of my position and my data.

Wiring up had its disadvantages. The first one was that your rapid movements screwed up your active camo, turning you from a ghost to a really obvious blur. The second, and slightly more lethal downside, had to be the fact that it ran your neural augs hot—more processing power meant more waste heat, which was just the only way it could go. But, if you ran too long and got too hot, your brain melted.

Not literally.

The literal actuality was that your brain *boiled*. Earlier training this week had included videos of prototype transhumans with superheated blood shooting out from around their eyesockets. The noises that came after the cameras were splattered with blood were the worst part. I *forced* that memory away as everything slowed to a crawl. Five tangos were coming out of what looked like a bunkhouse, old M1A0s and AK-136s in hand. I sighted and let loose with a few short bursts: two, two, three, two, one. The bullets made little red thumps on their flesh.

Smoke.

They hit the ground and my AR flashed up an ammo indicator. Two, actually: the first was mine (3/31) and the other was a hypothetical counter: one of the tangos had spotted something he thought was worth shooting at and my augs were trying to ID the gun and count out the bullets from the sounds.

It sounded like a PK. I thought the words and the indicator came up: 30/40 bullets fired. A few other indicators popped up and I banished them to the far right-hand side of my view, focusing on another group of tangos going to support the people firing at Gloria's two by two. I smoked them and a muffled *bang* sounded, throwing up a smoke cloud near a building. Silence.

[We're clear.]

I de-cloaked and slipped down the ladder. Lee came out, also de-cloaked. Alvarez joined us, with Gloria and her second: Kinsey. I hadn't mentioned Kinsey because I really badly wanted to kill him. Not actually kill, kill him, but rather to set my augs to edit him out of my vision and audio input.

"You call that overwatch, PR?"

I didn't know how Kinsey could turn ducting into whining. But he managed it.

[Well, gee, I've got a CKC up in the double digits.] I scowled at him.

[PR, shut it,] Alvarez snapped. And wasn't that just the way of things? Kinsey threw shit and I got the splatter.

The camp around us faded and shimmered and we disembodied. It was like becoming fog and drifting through your memories, if your memories weren't a gooey mixture of chemicals and neurons but instead the clear, cold facts that computers could do. Computers didn't hide your mistakes behind rationalizations.

[All right.] Singh, who had been overseeing our training exercise, ducted into our conversation, like the voice of the gods coming down from on high. *[Let's see what you did right, what you did wrong, and how to apply this to an actual mission.]*

[Permission to speak, ma'am,] I broke in.

[Granted.]

It was really weird, ducting from the VR to out of the VR. Sort of like reaching beyond the universe into something else. I knew that VR wasn't real. It just felt that way a lot of the time.

I had a weird spine-tightening flash of terror. It was here and gone so fast I nearly didn't know what had happened. I sat there, blinking a few times.

[PR?]

I shook my head.

[Uh, why are we training like we're going to be doing this kind of thing in rural China? We're going to be past Angels-6 and in one-third Earth gravity when we hit the Loonies.]

Singh actually took a little bit to think before responding. That could have been because she was considering what I had said, or because she was checking to see if we actually needed to know such things.

[There are two answers to that, Dru.] So, so damn weird to be called Dru by a superior officer, I don't care how weird the S3TA is supposed to be. *[The first is simple: this kind of organization and combat will still happen on the Moon, even if the environment is different. The second is obvious, if your cynicism detectors were on: the S3TA doesn't just operate in space.]*

Right. Of course. I had signed up to shoot Loonies and help close this whole war up. That didn't mean my eminent Loonie shooting skill couldn't be transplanted into ... well, wherever the CAA needed me.

Fantastic. And the creepy thing was I wasn't sure if that was even *sarcastic.*

It felt good. Being so *fast.* So strong.

I didn't have much more time to think about that. Singh started going through the training run. She examined our movement, our sighting and ammo usages. By the time the whole thing had been ground through our processors, it felt like my brains had been kneaded by a giant with calloused fingers. When we slipped out of VR, I took a few moments to shiver inside the pod, rubbing my shoulders. I sniffed and tasted iron.

I reached up in the darkness, keying on my night vision with a thought. Blood. I rubbed at my nose, then at my face with both hands, sniffing again and again. That just ended up smearing more blood on my face. I pinched the bridge of my nose and ducted.

[Got a bit of a nosebleed here.]

[Hit the Doc.]

The pod snapped open. Alvarez still looked funny. I had gotten so used to him with a single cybernetic leg, with silvery skin and clear machining. Now, when I looked at his legs, I saw the same thing anyone else would see; a middle-aged man's legs, complete with hair and a complete lack of appealing *anything.* He—along with Lee and Gloria—were getting suited up in their jumpsuits. Gloria paused, half into her suit. She reached out, catching my chin. She whistled a low note as she tilted my head back. I sniffled at her and mumbled. "Bluuguh, this is the worst."

Gloria snorted. "Weren't you *shot* once?"

"Hey, you gonna just sit there and hemorrhage to death?" a snide voice cut in.

I jerked my head to the door and saw Kinsey. He was pinching his nose, his fingers smeared with red, and stood at the door. I'd be damned if he got to wait in line before me. Gloria kissed my cheek before I slipped away, and I ducted a quick *[hug]* at her.

Kinsey and I walked shoulder and shoulder down the corridor. I held my nose and glared at him.

"So, think it's CPRS?" he asked.

Cybernetic Psychosomatic Rejection Syndrome. Our boogeyman. It made crawls run down my spine.

"Shut up, Kinsey."

"What, you think saying it out loud makes it more likely?" He grinned at me. "I thought Spacers were sluts, not superstitious. Isn't that why you're racking with a girl old enough to—"

I scoped out the corridor. Since no one else was there, I grabbed Kinsey by the front of his jumpsuit and slammed him against the wall. Hard enough to *dent* the wall. "You got a problem, Kinsey?"

His hands grabbed my wrists and for just a moment, I could see a real fierce hate in his eyes. But he shook his head. "Nah, PR."

Hot blood dripped onto my lips. I stepped back and Kinsey walked away—leaving an unmarked wall behind him. I glared after him, then rubbed my arm. I'd need to ask the Doc to check their strength inputs too. I shook my head, then hurried to catch up before he got to the doctor's office. I shoulder checked Kinsey, but he ducked out of the way before I could get the pleasure of slamming him to the wall again. Still, I took advantage of his movement and slid inside the office first. The Doc opened itself to me: a robotic pod with its cover slid back to reveal what looked like a bed surrounded by knives and spider fingers. I kicked the door shut behind me and stepped over to the Doc.

"Nosebleed. Diagnose. And check my strength inputs too, p—" I stopped myself. It was a robot. I didn't need to be polite to it. Then, feeling doubly stupid, I added: "Please."

Kinsey, out of the corner of my eyes, made a jerking off motion. I flipped him off.

The Doc shifted and resettled, a face mask sliding out of one of its many equipment banks. I pressed my face against it and waited. I could have looked up what it was scanning me with. X-rays. T-rays. The Hell-Rays. I'd rather not know, to be totally honest. In a few moments, a cool female voice (pre-recorded) spoke in the air.

"Implant shift. Please enter automatic doctor chambers for adjustment."

The Doc changed its look. Away went the knives, away went the prodding pokers and the face mask and the scanners. Instead, it looked like a white bed, and soon, it was even horizontal rather than mostly vertical. I slid in and closed my eyes. The Doc whirred to life. Some people prided themselves in being able to watch the doctor move around and change their augs ... even watch him rip into your guts or your head.

I just kept my eyes closed and felt the hiss of painkillers. My head went numb. Something shifted in my nose. And then it was done. A tiny adjustment of a tiny machine, with tiny tools. The flushers hissed in and the numbness faded as quickly as it had come. The Doc opened and ...

Kinsey was watching me. He leaned on the doorway, his eyes narrowed, his pale face spotless.

"You done?"

"Yeah." I stood and scowled at him. "Enjoy your time with the Doc."

I stepped past him and into the corridor. Alvarez, Gloria, and Lee were walking toward the caff. I moved in after them and Gloria handed me my jumpsuit. I wriggled into it, hopping on one foot at one point. Gloria grabbed my arm to keep me from falling over.

"This is the third resetting you've done this week," Alvarez said, glancing sidelong at me.

"So?" I asked, moving into lockstep with the group once my suit was on, my hand squeezing Gloria's for a few seconds.

"So, I'm saying you should see an *actual* doctor."

I wanted to tell him it wasn't anything. That it was just the implants settling into place. But someone—I forgot who and I forgot when—said that I had a risk the other guys didn't. I was still developing. Young people's brains were still molding into their old people shapes, and while most of the implants were nonintrusive, hair-thin monofilimants threaded from neuron to neuron ... there was still a chance that I'd flunk out. Not because of somatic rejection, and *definitely* not from CPRS, but just because my brain was bleeding itself to death trying to handle the pressure. I remembered the last time I'd avoided seeing a specialist. How had *that* turned out?

I opened my mouth to respond—but out of the corner of my eyes, I could see Gloria looking at me with concern.

I gritted my teeth. "Sure. I'll see an actual doctor."

"Good." Alvarez slapped my shoulder.

What a jerk. Caring about my future, wanting me not to die. I rubbed my shoulder and followed him through the door into the cafeteria. The caff was built in the same style as the rest of Fort Kong. Old fashioned and clunky. Still, the gruel served here beat the hell out of the gruel served in earlier parts of Selection.

While I ate, thinking about seeing a doctor, thinking about how much I'd despise flunking out now, thinking about how I'd despise dying of a brain hemorrhage even more ... I realized something.

I had gotten through the whole day without thinking about Sarah. No little worry-worms gnawing at my gut whenever I leaned against Gloria. No flashes of memory. Just ...

I just felt like I was part of something bigger than myself. And it was a weird, eerie feeling—spooky in how *nice* it was to be in a team. A group. A *unit*. S3TA felt home in a way the Marines never had.

No ...

No wait ...

There was *something*. A jingle ran through my head, like a song I couldn't get out of my head: *Drusilla Zhao. Lance Corporal. Service Number: 400122B. Born October 9th, 2050.*

For a second, I felt like I was drowning. Water, rushing down my throat. I choked.

Then Kinsey sat down across from me and started eating. The way he slurped rice noodles made my skin crawl. I dug in and forgot about whatever it was I had been thinking about before. I had things to focus on: the mission, tactics, movement, the feeling of being a ghost. Not Sarah. Not the increasingly distant thought of peacetime or being out of the military. My skin shimmered faintly and I blinked. Had I ... imagined that?

I glanced around the mess hall. Kinsey was smirking at me, like a gormless son of a bitch. His eyes glinted and he leaned forward.

"Feeling okay, *Corp*?"

"Shut up," I muttered.

"Hmm?" Gloria looked at me.

[*Brb.*] I sent to Gloria, before I stood up and went to find Singh, ducting through our private net: [*I need to talk to you, Mary.*]

[*Sure thing,*] she said, throwing up an AR glyph that showed where she was in Fort Kong. It wound me through a series of corridors and down an old, tight flight of stairs. I skipped over the railing and dropped the whole way, letting my legs flex and take the impact with a faint *clunk*, the shock absorbers built throughout the leg-systems compressing down to almost half their length. My hips jarred only slightly. I stood and then came to Singh's office.

Mary Singh sat behind a desk, her hands clasped before her. To anyone else, that might have looked like she was waiting for me. But she keyed me into her AR view and I saw the desk was covered with virtual files, not paper copy like what we got to suffer through. I took the courtesy of not trying to read them, though I noticed they were all hard-crypto, way beyond my pay grade. One of them, though, I noticed its encryption ...

Mary had a little lamb, little lamb.

Mary had a little lamb

Her fleece was white as snow.

The hell?

Singh sighed. [*What do you need, Drusilla?*]

I sat down across from her and mentally banished her AR view. I brushed my hands through my hair and sighed. [*I think I have a bit of implant drift.*]

[*You have seen the doctor at least four times.*] Singh frowned. [*We'll bring you to an actual neurospecialist.*]

[*Thanks.*] I paused. [*I'm going to flunk out, aren't I?*]

She shook her head. [*There are possibilities. Drusilla, we monitor all of you constantly. To be honest, Selection Overwatch thinks you're still within acceptable parameters. But I never let SO override a man or woman under my supervision. You're all too valuable. We at the S3TA pride ourselves on individual focus. Other branches of the military have chains of command. We have distributed operations. Other branches of the military have masses. We have handfuls.]* She smirked. *[And we shake the pillars of heaven.]*

I grinned at her, another rush of pride hitting me. *[Fuckin' A, Mary.]*

[While we wait for the neurospec, why don't you read through these files.] She made a short gesture and her implants pinged mine with a short burst of information. I accepted it past my firewalls and felt the new file slot into place in my headware. *[They're on my first operation with the S3TA against Singularity City.]*

I cocked an eyebrow. I hadn't even heard of Singularity City. She must have seen the look on my face—or read my kinesic feedback by watching blood flow on my face with enhanced visual input. Or read my mind using our head-link. No one quite knew what admins were capable of doing ...

[Read. You might notice someone familiar in there. Now, get back to work.]

I stood. Saluted. She nodded.

I turned back, walked to the door, and then paused. My hand slid along the doorframe and my fingers told me the metal composition. I turned back to Singh.

"Mary," I said, out loud. "I also have to ask ... is there some way you could get Kinsey off my godsdamn back?"

Mary looked at me. Cocked her head. *[Who?]*

My eyes widened slightly. Something echoed in my brain. *Fallen Angels.*

I shook my head. "N-Nothing."

I turned around and walked out of the office. I already knew that Mary had to be ducting or calling more than just a neurospec. Psychiatrist. Men with straitjackets. Or maybe just a squadron of men with armor piercing bullets. I started to run down the checklist, throwing up an AR bullet list as I walked up the stairs, my cyberlegs making a psychosomatic whir.

Initial Symptoms of CPRS

- Emotional Isolation (*How* fast had I gotten over Sarah? Love of my life, just gotten over, just like that? Just like *that*?)
- Trouble concentrating (I kept letting my ducting slide … didn't I? I couldn't keep a coherent …)

I came to the top of the stairs and paused, leaning against the corner of the corridor. A conduit line jabbed my back, but I didn't care. I rested one hand on an old, locked wheel that had once regulated water pressure for some system that had been gutted decades ago.

- Trouble sleeping (Catnaps don't count as sleeping … do they?)
- Loose thought associations (Thank the gods for bullet-points. They kept me focused …)

I heard some of the other members of Selection talking, walking through corridors to their rooms for more training and reading. I rubbed my temple and tried to focus again. You know, you know, I was reminded right then of just how great it would be to be scared of something. Being terrified of opening doors had really focused me.

The bulletpoints scattered as Kinsey bit into an apple. He was leaning against the corner next to me. He smirked.

"I'm a bug," he said.

"I noticed."

I glanced down the corridor, but no one seemed to be coming. The walking and talking had faded: everyone was in their rooms, reading files.

"I'm a ghost."

"I never knew anyone even half as annoying as you are," I said, gritting my teeth. "Most of my ghosts should be trying to get into my pants to see if sleeping with someone with cyber-legs feels better."

"You're nothing like what Shiva said you were like."

That stopped me cold. I blinked—and for a moment, it crossed my mind that I might not be crazy. Were these symptoms of CPRS-induced schizophrenia ... or symptoms of a constant work cycle, of a brain supported by enhanced augmentations and pushed beyond normal endurance? And you find comfort where you find it, don't you? Didn't I see Marines who hated each other's guts shack up in space because of warmth and closeness and intoxicating hormones? I was in a gods-damned aircraft carrier built to usher in the end of the world with nuclear fire, and I was wondering why I clung on to anything that made it feel less alone?

Sarah was *dead*. That was enough reason to need, right? Or was I just rationalizing? I kicked myself out of this mental circle jerk and turned to face Kinsey. Who might not even *be* there at all. But there was a chance, just a *chance*, that he might be there. Just not standing there, eating an apple. He might be in my *computer,* painting himself in my vision and filling my ears by adjusting my nerve endings.

"You know Shiva?" I asked. Salty sea breeze wafted up my nose for just a moment.

"I know them all," Kinsey said. "Shiva. Rama. Buddha. You."

I narrowed my eyes.

He grinned. "What? You didn't think Shiva was the *only* AI out there. Things are more complicated than you might imagine ..." he murmured. "This little spat between the Earth and her satellite will only last for a short time. Once it's over, humanity will have to *grow* up. Mature. Reach for the stars as one unified people."

"Oh? Is *that* all we have to do?" I asked, my voice hissing slightly as I stepped closer to Kinsey. I glanced back to make sure no one could see me talking to literally no one. Assuming Kinsey couldn't edit *their* perceptions too. "Gee, I'm glad we have someone like you to finally tell us what to do. Why didn't *we* think of that!"

"Hey, don't shoot the messenger," he said, lifting up both hands. I turned away from him and started to rub my temples.

"Okay. So. My options are that I'm insane, or that a cabal of secret AIs has infiltrated my brain with ... what?" I turned back to him.

"A muse." He gestured to himself with a swirling gesture.

"And you've been acting like a dick to me because ...?"

"I don't like you. I haven't liked you ever since we met." He shrugged, slightly. "You're a moody, whiny, flip-flopping bitch."

I didn't respond, I just scowled at him. By this point, I was pretty much sure that he had to be a hallucination ... but then again, if he was a hallucination, wouldn't I think he wasn't? But if he was a program sent by Shiva, why would he be parroting the party line in Drusilla central? And why wouldn't he show up on a diagnostic? Wouldn't the Doc or the techies or any of the other people who had admin access to my brain have noticed him?

Unless they'd put him there.

Kinsey smirked at me. "I can see the wheels in your head, Dru. They don't go anywhere good, do they?"

I tried walking through him, but he stepped aside before I could shoulder check him into a wall—damn, that would have been satisfying. Course, if he was a figment of my imagination, I'd just imagine him. And if he was a bug, like he claimed, he could use direct nerve-induction to *simulate* a shoulder bump. Ugh. Great. I glared over my shoulder as I walked up the stairs. Kinisey didn't follow me as I walked up to my quarters. As I came in, Gloria glanced up from our bed. She had her hands clasped behind her head and seemed to be studying the ceiling. I sat down by her feet and faceplanted myself into her belly.

"Gloria, I think I'm going crazy, I mumbled into her skin. Her hand dropped and she started playing with my hair.

"Me too," she said, sighing. "If I have to read another damn alphabet soup article about this, that, or some other thing, I might go AWOL."

"No, I mean ..."

Her finger started twining harder. She shifted and I could feel her eyes on me.

"What?" She stopped twining—only cause my hair had hit that sweet spot between comfort and pain that Gloria could ride like a pro. "You seeing things?"

[Maybe.] It was too much of a word to be said *aloud*. Her palm shifted and then cupped the base of my neck. I rolled my head up, looking along her sleekness, and saw that she was looking at the door, then the corners of our little room. Tugging me up, her lips and mine almost met. I felt a fluttering excitement—*not now, Dru*.

"Dru, I think you might be onto something." Her breath was a drug on my lips.

[???] I ducted the *feeling* of confused questioning for her.

[Okay.] She kissed me. The mewl she made was such good camouflage because it was part real. I did the little trick with my teeth for that. Her fingers gripped my hair tighter. *[Do the words "fallen angels" mean anything to you?]*

Something squirmed down my back, like a felt spider had been shot down my spine by a railgun. I used some tongue, feathering along hers. *[Yeah.]*

[I've asked half the other members of the unit. Half don't have any idea what I'm talking about, or at least, they say they don't, but their kinesics show a clear emotional connection.] All this flashed into my mind faster than the tiny shivers that

made kisses so delicious. *[Increased heart-rate, blood pressure, microexpressions indicating fear, all that jazz.]*

I drew back. Not cause I needed to breathe. No. But there's a limit to *intense*. It goes from good to painful. *[So, you think we're … what? A control group? An experiment?]* I ducted, wondering if my thoughts were as panicky as they sounded in my head.

[Maybe.] She sighed aloud. *[After the Singularity Scare and all this research into augmentation, why wouldn't the CAA be interested in the effects of augmentations on our brains? What if they want to see what happens if they stimulate us with these things?]*

A frown deepened my worry lines. *[They need us. We cost money. You don't spend seven million credits per soldier unless you get a really damn good soldier back.]*

[It's the Alliance, Dru. They tax two-thirds of the human race. They have enough money that even fifty million credits can vanish without anyone noticing.]

I knew that. I had thought about it. But it still smelled wrong to me, as if that couldn't possibly be the right answer. I glanced at Gloria and saw that she wasn't quite buying it either.

"There's an easier solution. Less massive." I grinned at her, weakly. My voice sounded weird as hell to my ears. "We're all hopped up on neurostims, battered psychologically from being sim-tortured, and we get killed every other day in VR. We've all got our arms and legs hacked off, our skin replaced, our lungs—"

"Okay, okay." Gloria cupped my head again. Stroked my hair again. I leaned into her again, my eyes closing again. Echoing, repeating *déjà vu*. It felt like it *should* be my memories of Sarah. But those memories felt so distant and dimmed. It should have hurt. But it only ached. "And they monitor us closely enough, you'd think if there was something to what we were talking about, the men in black coats would take us away or something."

She lay back, drawing me down next to her. My hand slid under her shoulder.

"Yeah."

Gloria snuggled against me. I mulled it all through in my mind, ticking off the reasons for and against. But the possibilities were all so nebulous ... and each one ended badly. We were being yanked around by a sinister government conspiracy. Some AIs were smart enough and connected enough to slip whole programs into my head without anyone noticing—and worse, the program hated my guts. I was going insane from CPRS.

Or, heck. Here was a real spooky idea. What if I had snapped a long time ago and this was just a fantastic delusion? That one kept me up way later than it should have. I ran through the evidence in my head.

One, I was just some puke teenager. I barely had an inkling of what I wanted to do with my life, and yet here I was: Space Marine. Decorated veteran. Member of top secret military unit?

Two, augmentations like what graced my body were way ahead of anything on the commercial market. I hadn't even imagined it was possible for adaptive camouflage to be *this* good, let alone to be mixed in with armored skin, and it all looked and felt just like normal skin?

I stopped ticking through issues, realizing that I had cast up the thought bubbles as AR, hovering over my face as I lay in the darkness of the room. I waved my hand and then looked down at Gloria. Her breathing was uneven enough to indicate she was still awake or having a crappy dream. Either way ...

"Gloria."

"Yeah, Dru?"

I chewed on my lip. I remembered the bulletpoints describing psychosis. But. Gods. How do you bring up a thought like that to your new girlfriend? But ... Gloria wasn't like Sarah. She was older. She'd been around before, right? But thinking that—putting it in those words—made me feel like I was shrinking. My throat caught.

Gloria shifted. The blankets crinkled and popped as she sat up, moving to be face to face with me. The blankets pooled around her belly and her eyes glowed as she kicked on the most blatant sensors. Even with only my passives, I could see all the EM scanlines popping out of her augmented eyes, bathing the room and giving her as much visual feedback as most high end optics.

She looked down at me with those glowing, gentle eyes. "Sarah, isn't it?"

I flushed, hard, and tried to jam up any leaks.

Gloria chuckled—but it was easily the saddest chuckle I'd ever heard in my life. "You're not leaking, Drusilla." Hearing my full name in her warm, chocolate voice felt decadent. Like silk spacesuits.

"So, I'm just fucking obvious?" I asked, looking up at her, wishing I could stick my head underneath the hardass board that the S3TA gave out in lieu of actual pillows.

Gloria shrugged one shoulder. "I might just be really smart, you know. I've never dated a ... well, a widow before." She caressed my cheek with one hand. "But I've lost people before. And you feel that hole, and you want to fill it, but filling it feels like you're betraying her ... doesn't it?"

Even nodding felt hard.

Gloria shrugged a bit. "I can't fix that. I can't ... fix anything. It's not my job. And I've seen people trying to *fix* other people too many times."

Her hand cupped my cheek. Her thumb rubbed my lips and I felt the twin warring impulses of wanting to wallow in the physical comfort and squirm at remembering that she was ... uh ... older.

"So, I just love what I got," she said. Casually. Like … like … it was just a word. Was I stoked she'd said it? Was I squirming uncomfortable, not sure if I felt it? Was I *offended* she'd said it so easily? Was I blind stinking jealous she had the godsdamn *cast-iron* will to just drop it? Circle E for all of the above.

[Really?] I ducted, before I could stop myself. One downside of direct thought-to-radio transmission, huh?

"Yeah. I guess so. For one thing, we keep having sex. For another thing, you're tough, cute, and pretty cynical for such a dork. If I hadn't had my mothering instincts surgically removed when I was eighteen and saw my Mom give birth to my little sister in an Alabaman refugee camp, I'd even say you make me feel … momly."

I snorted. "Momly? Gross, dude!"

She switched to ducting, her cheeks flaring with blood. She was embarrassed. [Hey, I said if I did. As is, I don't have time to get sassed by a girl young enough to like C-Pop.]

I made a face and laughed, rolling onto my back—feeling tension unwinding like a spring. Gloria shifted, moving so that she was over me. The look in her eyes wasn't even close to "momly," and I was kind of relieved.

[So, if there's a conspiracy to screw with our heads, you're with me when we go rogue and try to uncover it.]

[Hell no,] she ducted back. Smiling. She kissed me, still ducting. [I'm keeping my head down. I want to walk out of this with commendations, a cushy retirement, and maybe some augments to tide me through civilian life. And … you.]

On the one hand, that seemed kinda craven. But on the other hand … it also sounded like the best damn advice I'd ever heard in my life. Then the last thing she said sank in. My whole face heated.

Then Gloria showed me the best way to stop worrying about the future. The *very* best.

Chapter 6: AWOL

7/12/2068

Hong Kong, China

T-Minus L-Day: 2

I lay on my back and watched as a skinny girl with pitch black skin and pink hair worked on my brain. Well, it wasn't my brain: it was an almost perfect emulation of my brain, scanned down to the very core and then scanned right back out again, projected above my head by the spider-limbed autodoc that I was reclining in. Hormones were indicated by different colors, neurotransmitters and other chemicals and cells flaring their own hues, symbols, and indicators. In the end, it looked like a Jello mold that had been set on by the kind of fungus you never ever want to see anywhere but in a locked down agrilab.

"You are suffering from mild CPRS," the skinny girl said, without preamble.

Well. I glanced at the corner of the room, where Kinsey shrugged at me.

"The technical explanation would only make sense if you have a degree in applied psychosurgery, so I'll put it in the simple babytalk you Grunts use," Skinny Pink said, smirking slightly. I guess they'd picked her for being good, not for being nice. Or professional. "Your augmented reality wires have connected two parts of your brain that are not normally connected, causing you to create a hallucinatory personality that's just your brain talking to itself. This Kinsey. Is he a dick?"

"Yeah. Kinda."

"That follows." She sighed. "There are two solutions, well three, but the third is unacceptable. One, we can hack out your AR circuits and you can use smart contacts. The second is that you can take a regulation pill that should blunt the worst of the issues. And the third, which we are not going to do, is the old suck it up and ignore him option."

"Yeah, let's try the pills."

"You don't actually get to make that decision," she said, rubbing her chin as she looked at the hologram. Her face was all consideration and thought. On the problem, that is. She didn't look like she gave a flip about me personally.

"Then why did you give them to me?" I asked, scowling as she swiped her hands through the air. The hologram projectors sensed her movement and the image of my brain snapped off as the lights in the office brightened. It was a pretty spartan place, with just the white walls, the cot to sit on, and the imaging system. It looked a bit like the MRI I was used to, but included some very thin, possibly metallic tongues that had pressed against my forehead and done gods knew what.

"I like people knowing their various options, even if they're stuck with what they're ordered." She grabbed a small chip off the counter—containing the hard copy of the scan, without a doubt—and headed to the door. "Wait here and talk to your hallucination."

"I resemble that remark!" Kinsey glared at the doctor as she walked out.

"I wonder if she's racist or just mean ..."

Kinsey looked at me.

I frowned. "She might as well have called me a transie monster."

I felt really silly sometimes, thinking back on how I had been so scared of the transhuman boogeyman. They made great bad guys in movies: like Nazis from the old twenty-first century games; no one, and I mean no one, could complain about sticking a transhuman into a game to make them worthy of killing. And I could even understand it on an intellectual level. Reading the documents about Singularity City—which had included a few mentions of one Staff Sergeant Noah Antwiler, which had made me disgustingly nostalgic—I knew that most of the really, really bad things from the Singularity Scare hadn't been documented. The brain-farms. The forking. The neural pruning and morphological experiments.

That whole city—really more of a geodesic dome that had grown up almost overnight in Sweden—had been leveled in the fighting, then burned. Literally burned: there were documents that I had leafed through detailing the amount of thermite, napalm, and CS30 that *we* had gleefully thrown around. The footage of the scar that had been hurriedly bulldozed and turned into a memorial park stuck in my brain like a mining pick.

In that place, I'd have been a regressive square, not a cutting edge freak.

We. That was a funny word I'd used. I paused for just a moment, putting my hand over my face, touching my Kevlar-tough skin. Who was we? The Alliance? The people who, for all I knew, were using me as a tool? Was *we* unaugmented humans? The *natural* people I'd been taught to see as my side. Even now. When I was freaking comic book awesome. I could turn *invisible* for crying out loud!

Who was we?

That question got chased away when the door opened and the neurospec came back in. She held a small bottle of pills in her hand and tossed it to me in a parabola. I caught it without even trying, and my AR popped up a description of the bottle, caught from the tracking built into the bottle itself. I could actually send it a mental ping to dispense a pill into my palm. Instead, I looked at the doctor.

"All right," she said. "This should suppress some of the feedback loops caused by your augmentations. That, plus the latest tuning trick I've programmed into the autodoc, should cut down on your hallucinations."

"And how many do I take?"

"One a day, right before bed." She smirked. "That should be easy enough for you to figure out. Ciao." She turned and headed out through the door, leaving me to my own devices.

I shrugged, slipping off the table. "Yeah, thanks, later ..." I muttered to the empty ward.

I walked out of the room. The neurospec wasn't waiting for me outside. Rather, I found myself in the antechamber with no one to keep me company but a bored looking secretary. I looked at him sidelong as he tapped at his desk. It looked like he was playing a MUD in text-only form. I shook my head and walked fully out of the clinic proper ... and I vanished. Oh, I didn't activate my camouflage, but I walked through Hong Kong in the press of people with my hands in my pockets and my shoulders slumped. There was nothing to really cut me out from the rest of the crowd: no armored car, no special guard, nothing to signal me as important to any snooper-sats.

My hand closed around the pill bottle in my pocket. I let it go before I crushed it into a tiny plastic sphere. I pulled my hand out of my pocket, only half paying attention to where I was walking: my augmented senses and body made it easy to follow the path laid out in AR, which would guide me back to a few double-blind entrances to Fort Kong. Of course, going there would take a while ... we—the whole S3TA—were trying to be as careful as possible.

Still, I had a lot to think about. And there weren't any other Selection members to listen in. So, I thought away: I thought how much I both wanted and didn't want to wash out. About Kinsey and about the pills in my pocket. About—

I walked into a wall.

It was the kind of embarrassing thing that was put on vid-sharing websites, and I didn't even have a pair of HUD-goggles on to make it look halfway reasonable. I rubbed my face and stepped backward, muttering cusses under my breath. My AR fizzed out and I was left feeling half-blind: I had no contextual information, no mini-map, no guideline. I turned around and around and took in the scene with my actives and passives: I was standing in an alleyway in Central Kong, which had been built over and up into a Steel Sky situation like Shanghai. There weren't stars overhead, there was just more city ... a walkway, actually. The sides of the place were made up of doorways and flat walls, with wallpaper applied patchily at best: I could only see a few fuzzy holograms and symbols advertising cigarettes. A light flickered over one of the doors. I frowned and expected a gang of bad guys to come out of the doors.

That didn't happen. What did happen was one of the doors unlocked with a cuh-CLUNK. I walked toward it. The door was painted green. I almost reached out for the handle before I jerked my hand back, frowning. Someone was screwing with me. Someone was leading me into blind-corridors with AR guidance and unlocking doors for me. Someone ...

Shiva.

The thought popped into my mind and I tried to squash it. But it was seductive, wasn't it? If Shiva could hack into my augments and guide me here, then hack into the doors to open them ... then he could slip a program into my mind. Even if he hated me, a program was better than being nuts. Right?

I opened the door. I had to have hope.

The door opened into a grungy hallway, with more doorways to either side. Each one was numbered, and they were so close together that the rooms they led to had to be closet-sized. Even in space, that was cutting it pretty close. Of course, space didn't have two billion people living under a steel sky. I frowned and walked down the corridor. One of the doors opened and a guy glanced out: skinny and tired looking.

He spoke a strange mishmash of Cantonese and a slangy dialect that I didn't understand. The words I understood were *get* and *hell out*. He drew a knife. I held my hands up and hurried down the corridor. As I got to the end, I tried the door that would lead out to the main street—I could tell, thanks to the sound leaking through the doorway. I frowned as I found that the door knob was locked. There was a door to the left and to the right, and both of them had faint signatures from beyond them, but neither sig had a conclusive shape or density to tell me if they were sitting humans, cats, or small refrigerators. This time, I didn't even try the knobs, I just pinged them mentally, trying to see if their computer components were open source. They weren't.

They were cheap, though. I could easily ping them both to see which one was unlocked ... and there it was. I opened the one to the left and found myself looking at stairs going straight down. I frowned and started walking down them. Logical counterarguments were plentiful: I could just break down the front door and keep heading back to Fort Kong. Hell, even an un-augmented human could break that door down.

I could. But then I'd be heading back with pills in my pocket. And the only rationale would be: *You're crazy.*

I looked at the door. Everything Selection had drilled into my head said to kick the door in and go. But there was a deeper, more primordial part of my brain, that turned me back at the stairs. I glared down them, thinking about the pills, about this obvious frigging trap.

Stupid. Reckless.

Crazy.

I went down the stairs.

I had the excuse, didn't I? My shoes thumped and thumped, and my hands remained in my pockets, and even as the lights went from grainy to almost completely non-functional, my eyes saw everything. I stepped onto a landing and past a bum who snored, clinging to a smartphone, his head tilted to the side. His thermal indicator continued to shine out of my peripheral vision, a glyph popping up to tell me that a heat signature was behind me. The glyph faded as I went around the bend of the dark stairs. I came to the bottom and looked down the corridor that I was spat into. Grungy.

After a lifetime of clean corridors in space—or at the very least, clean parts of the Earth—it felt like a surreal dream to walk down a corridor that dripped with water damage, that smelled like a sewer. Each of the doors' RFID tags pinged them as locked, save for the last one at the end. I frowned and opened it while standing to the side: there wasn't any gun waiting to blow me away.

It was here that I thought for maybe the fifth time that this was a really stupid idea.

But I was down here already.

I stepped into the room. There were four people in the room, two in the dark corners, showing up bright and warm on my thermographics. My AR identified potential weapons strapped at about kidney height and tagged them for future evaluation. The two people who were in the open were both nondescript, pure Han. One of them had a handheld computer, and the other one was cradling a shotgun—the make and number of shells loaded popped into my vision. I banished it with a thought.

The man with the hand computer smiled at me, leaning back underneath the light. It was a practiced smile. I bet that his mirror had seen it at least fifty thousand times. To regular humans, this room was lit about as well as one of those interrogation cells you see all the time on vids, with a single lamp hanging overhead. Maybe they had light amplification contacts on.

"Drusilla Zhao," the man with the hand computer spoke.

"Why am I here?" I asked.

"You are here because we wished you to be here. You are here because we believe that you might be amenable to our purposes."

I looked at him, then at the man with the shotgun. "And you are?"

"We represent several interests that have a stake in the current situation—" translation, the war "—ending the way *we* want it to. You are in a position to divulge secrets that can drastically alter the course of future operations. In exchange, we can make you vanish."

"Vanish?" My brow furrowed. I was pretty sure I knew what he was talking about, but I was playing for rope.

"Don't play coy. You know how the world works by now, no? The right money, the right favors, the right technology can manage anything." He gave me a little smile that was not a smile in any way, shape, or form.

I frowned. "So, I tell you ... what, exactly? I'm just a grunt."

He shook his head. "In anywhere from two to four days, the S3TA is going to begin operations in the orbital theater. I've been briefed on their capacity and my employer believes it's enough to drastically tilt the current situation one way or another. You can return to Selection, and when you are briefed, all you have to do is witness it. An uploaded program to your neural hardware will shunt it to us."

I kept my eyes on him, not wanting them to know I had noticed the men in the corners—if they hadn't twigged it already. But still, no sense in giving them any extra cues.

"And you'll just make me disappear before the mission goes off? With, I'm guessing, a few million extra credits in my pocket?"

"Exactly."

[Take them down.]

Colonel Mary Singh's voice ducted into my head. I had a split second of indecision. But then something flared on the man's face—his eyes widened, blood pressure rose, heat flared, all indicators of microexpressions that all came out to one thing: he knew. He started to make a gesture when I kicked on my wired reflexes. The man with the shotgun hauled it up. I darted to the side, kicking on Predator. My clothes were not adapted for it, so I flexed my arms and ripped most of my shirt off. The tatters and the dimness of the room added to the adaptive camo.

The shotgun roared. The AR counter ticked down.

Snap hand up, grab the wrist, bend. He screamed. I slashed down with my other hand and his throat got a lot narrower. As he fell, the man who had been talking grabbed for a pistol. I kicked him in the temple, then turned the choking man whose wrist I still held to face the man in the right corner. Bullets thudded into the choking man's chest—his smashed throat burbled with blood.

My head felt hot.

The dead man's shotgun hit the ground. The man in the right corner was tracking, trying to decide if he should shoot or not. My toe caught the shotgun and I popped it up. One arm kept hoisted around the dead guy's armpit, keeping him up.

My squishy shield's friend realized he was past worrying about friendly fire. He opened up. Bullets thudded into meat.

I snapped the dead guy around, the shotgun sticking out from under his armpit. I fired and caught the right corner man in the chest. He flew backward and hit the wall with a crash, but the body armor he wore absorbed the impact. The left man had started to fire more controlled bursts. Two bullets struck my shoulder, but hit at an angle and skimmed off. I swiveled the corpse-shield around and three more bullets hit his pulped chest.

This time, I grouped the shot-blast higher. The left corner man hit the ground without most of his head.

I let the corpse drop, hopped over him, landed, and plunged my forearm blade through the right corner man's eye socket as he reached for his gun. He twitched. I flicked the blade out, spun, then brought my elbow down on the talking man's chest. He curved in on the impact, dropping the gun he had been going for—my kick hadn't been quite strong enough to take him down. When I jerked my elbow up, my forearm blade glinted at the base of my arm.

I kept my arm cocked, the blade dripping. It slid into my elbow, the blood slurping off.

I looked around the room and my wired reflexes kicked off. Ten seconds.

My head felt achingly hot and my nose throbbed in time with my heart beat. I rubbed at it and my fingers came away red.

With a thought, I deactivated Predator and thought, mournfully, that I had really liked that shirt. Then it hit me: I had just killed four men and I was worrying about a *shirt*.

[*Very good job, Dru,*] Singh ducted. [*Get out of there before the police arrive. There should be a replacement shirt in the room across from you, as well as a stealthed sidearm, just in case.*]

[*All right, sir ... um ... can you tell me what the FLYING HELL IS GOING ON?!*]

I walked across the hallway, moving quickly. The door had unlocked and I found a change of clothes—I just took the shirt—and a sleek, carbon composite side arm. I holstered it.

[*No need to All Caps, Dru.*] Singh sounded amused, the bitch. [*We suspected a mole. When someone replaced our neurospecialist at the last minute with some unvetted brain-butcher we knew we had one. So, we let them slice into your AR. When we saw where you were being led, we dropped off the kit and let you walk in. I knew you'd do the right thing.*]

I had been this close. This. Close. To spilling the beans. I wondered if Singh knew that. Oh, who was I kidding, of course she knew that. I came to the stairwell and rubbed at my nose, which still bled sluggishly, though my head didn't feel as hot as before.

[*And you didn't warn me ...*]

[*You're still not the best liar, Dru, and we figured they'd have a kinesic in there.*]

[*A gym teacher?*]

I came to the stairwell and the front door was unlocked and there was a comforting, glimmering path that I knew would lead me back to Fort Kong.

[*An expert at reading microexpressions, I thought that was in your briefings.*]

[*It is. I'm making a bad joke. Can't you tell that me being diagnosed with CPRS and then getting corralled into killing some criminal traitors that I didn't even know existed until after I was finished stabbing them to death really puts me in a comedic frame of mind?*]

I almost walked through someone, that's how fast I was going.

[Dru, our actual neurologist is examining the scans that the fake one took. You don't have CPRS.]

I stood next to a traffic light. Other pedestrians crowded around me. They talked on their phones, they read newspapers off of handhelds. They listened to music. Some even watched vids or played AR games with their HUD glasses. Others talked to each other, or watched the endless, glittering wave of traffic drive by. All of them seemed a million kilometers away as I listened—well, mentally listened—to Singh's ducting.

[In fact, your implants should be coming in fine. The nose-bleeds are a minor symptom of settling and should clear up within a week.]

I stopped myself before I sent back "and Kinsey?" I didn't even think his name, clamping down on the thoughts so hard that my breathing stopped and my heart skipped a beat.

Because Singh hadn't mentioned Kinsey. And if she hadn't mentioned Kinsey, then it meant she didn't *remember* me mentioning Kinsey. It was a tenuous grasp, an idea, an idea that I wanted to cling to, even with the muddled narratives I was able to tease out of these last few days.

Shiva. If Shiva could implant a program, why not change a memory? Why not blank out me mentioning Kinsey to Singh? Why not?

If it was to keep a secret, a secret this important ... then why not?

That was hope. That was hope that there was something bigger than me looking out for the future of the human race. And maybe clinging on to that slenderest of hairs was better than realizing that I'd just shot the only people who could get me out of this mess and into some quiet part of the Congo. For just a moment, the *thought* of that made me ache with the same kind of desperate longing I had felt for Sarah when we had been separated by an impossible gulf of space.

The world would be someone *else's* problem.

And after *this* day? After being jerked around *this* much?

I really wanted someone else to take that problem. Let someone else worry about what was real and what was a lie.

The light changed colors and I started to walk across. I ducted to Singh.

[*Who were those guys anyway?*]

She chuckled over the ducting. That was something that I had yet to figure out how to do.

[*Why, Dru … that's need to know.*]

Of course it was.

Chapter 7: Launch

7/14/2068

Cape Canaveral, Florida, NAU

T-Minus L-Day: 0

The thing that I remember most about the Cape Canaveral launch facilities was the big old sign with weeds growing around it. First thing on the sign we'd passed by in the night, visible only thanks to my augmentations, had been Cape Canaveral. Then, over that in sloppy whitewash, there had been Cape Windrip. Then, over that had been even newer paint: Cape Canaveral. Again. Of course, new was a relative term for stuff that had been slopped on almost forty years ago. The buildings were desolate and abandoned and not really worth remembering—unless you were, for example, a teenage Spacer, walking through them with jaw hanging wide, looking around at the place where the American colonization of space was launched from for so many years.

The launch facilities were not where we were being briefed.

The launch facilities were the cover, the place we were shoved into camouflaged trucks under the cover of night. The cover wasn't just for us, though. It wasn't *just* a way to hide us from Loonie orbital surveillance and intelligence tracking.

The cover was also for Alpha Base. This sucker had been pre-built for us by President Windrip, and it happened to be the biggest computing base in the world. And, best of all ... it had been designed by a paranoid nutcase at the behest of paranoid nutcases. Meaning that it was designed to be off the grid: it had its own nuclear atomic batteries (no, really, they were called atomic batteries and they were hot as *hell*.) Those were supplemented with some old-fashioned fossil fuel burners that could have been switched on if the base ever needed more juice than the atomic batteries could put out at once. Those had been swapped out sometime in the 2050s for fission reactors. At the time, they'd been cheaper than fusion reactors. Considering the Earth's current lack of Helium-3 thanks to Luna's secession, those fission reactors were paying off. But the last, most important feature of Alpha Base was that it had absolutely no communication going in and out, beyond a single cable that ran straight into one of the most secure intelligence installations in the world: the Atlanta Castle.

The end result was that, while I read and reread and re-re-read the mission briefs, I was secure in knowing that the closet I was living in would never be noticed by the Loonies. Or our own side. Or anyone else, for that matter. I frowned and flipped to the last page of the mission dossier, rubbing my neck, which had started to crick up.

Hey, Dru, I'm sure you were wondering. *What about the goons you iced a few days ago?*

Yeah. I sometimes, in the seconds I spent not eating, training, and sleeping, thought about that. And the more I thought, the more I didn't like the facts I had to face. I couldn't trust my eyes. I couldn't trust my *side*. I couldn't even trust my own thoughts. And you know what?

I was *glad*. Glad that I had no time to think, no time to brood, other than a few snatched seconds between training. Because there wasn't a *godsdamn* thing I could do about it at this point. It was like riding at a sandcaster on a thrust-pack in open space. All I could do was pray.

I shook my head, then brushed my hands through my hair, tugging it back. Ugh. I threw up a mental clock in my AR and groaned, softly.

Practice was coming up soon. My fingers were still twitching from the last time we had run VR—it felt like an hour ago, but it was closer to ten, fifteen minutes. Our schedule here had gone from insane to sadistic within an hour of arriving— stepping off a VTOL with a slight nosebleed and Kinsey in my peripheral vision.

"Hey, it's like going on a historical tour. Appropriate, considering I get to walk around with a Neanderthal."

After stepping off (and in my case, being insulted) we'd slipped into the place—moving in dispersed units, with active camo at night with our VTOL (which had been stealthed) being shoved under a camo tarp as fast as possible—and then, with orientation finished (we'd done virtual orientation in our AR on the way there), we were thrown into VR simulations. Just like the beginning of Selection, we were pumped with neurostims and we went through the mission permutations again and again and again. We had the plan in our head. And more than that, we knew how to break the plan.

I had practiced what to do if every single other member of the strike force was incapacitated except for me. I knew what to do if I was captured and taken to any number of specific locations. I knew how to handle everything up to and including an immediate, unconditional Loonie surrender, an alien invasion, or a portal to Hell ripping open. All the impossibilities, possibilities, and permutations.

And now, it looked like we were going to practice again. At least, that's what I thought, until I noticed that the indicator glyph for *this line will lead you to practice* had changed shape and color in my AR, and the silvery arrow that pointed me through the corridors of the Alpha Base didn't aim for the normal route.

Launch. We hadn't been told quite when we'd be launching, but we knew it was going to be soon.

Kinsey leaned against the wall. In the narrow corridors that predominated down here, it was irritating to have to try and slip around him, but I did it anyway before I even realized I could walk through him.

"This place is a tomb, did you know that?"

I stopped, my eye half on the AR clock. It hadn't started flashing red yet. I turned to face Kinsey.

"The militias didn't even know this base was here." I frowned. "Hell, it wasn't even declassified until—"

"Not for humans," Kinsey said. "This is where the first AGIs were born and where they died." He looked at me. "You know, Shiva says your species is worth saving. But here, in this place, I'm starting to rethink that idea."

"Maybe you shouldn't discuss this with the person you're using as a walking server," I said, my voice tight. "Oh, wait, I know, if you hate me and humanity so much, why don't you just ... leave?"

He looked at me and I cut in before he could say anything.

"Use your super awesome computer manipulation abilities to get some factory somewhere to build you a robot. Then upload into the robot and do whatever the hell you feel like." I shrugged.

He scowled. "And loyalty doesn't mean anything to you, does it?"

I smirked at him, then started laughing as I walked down the corridor. He looked royally ticked off. Loyalty. *Loyalty.* What had loyalty gotten me in my life? No. Scratch that. What had *anything* gotten me? I was alive because of luck, here because of a genetic fluke, and in this world because of the aggregate mistakes of umpteen generations of barely evolved chimps trying to kill each other and get laid. And now a *computer* was lecturing me about stuff like duty? What was next, a speech about the necessity of valor and filial piety?

I followed the silvery arrow in my AR and soon, Lee was walking to my left. He nodded, ducting, *[How are you doing, PR?]*

I measured everything in my head. There was only one word that fit.

[Surviving.]

We got to our destination: a hangar bay, where all the members of the Strike Force were getting in and setting themselves up. So, that was that. The Launch was going off. I felt a distinct lack of excitement, the same kind of detachment I had felt oh-so-long ago, when I'd been falling toward *Hope*, the Loonie's borrowed space truck. I thought about that last time, even as I moved to my locker and started checking my equipment. Any unaugmented humans in the room would have to be freaked right the hell out: here were about thirty-six people, all of them working in complete silence, save for the clunk, click, and rattle of equipment organization.

To me ... it was as loud and raucous as it should have looked. AR glyphs and movement indicators floated through the local virtual space, mixing with hazy arrays of timetables and competing loadout indicators and requests, while tightbeam and broadbeam ducting shot back and forth, a babble of voices requesting, asking, and commanding. I threw up my own timetable, just in case anyone needed to know my ETA for readiness, and then set to work. I checked over my PPR—no more slug throwers for my main weapon, back to the old trusty laser rifle—my P3 sidearm, my EMP charges, scrappers gel, slick-grenades, snooper swarmbots, fiber-cables, COT bands, seeker bracelet, and of course, my adaptive camo-treated armor vest. Then I got my virtual equipment: spoof programs, exploits, sniffers, screamers, hacks, jacks, macs (just kidding), worms, and the all-important ICE and firewall updates that they had slapped on us, just in case.

I did a quick rundown on what to use where. EMP for scrambling drones. Gel for doors. Slick-grenades in case we get an abundance of soft targets with permeable clothes. Snoopers for forward observation, COT for generalized breaking and entering where ripping the door open with my cyberarms would be too obvious.

Oh. And of course, the seeker bracelet. Cause who didn't need micro-rockets with mass reactive explosive tips, huh?

Finished with the check, I made sure that I'd installed the virtual gear. Then I paused and ... tried something I had never tried before.

I ducted to Kinsey.

[Can you hear this?]

"Of course." Kinsey leaned against the locker.

[So, you're either a delusion or you're a program implanted in my brain by a godlike AGI and I'm sick of trying to figure out which is which.] I glanced at him as I adjusted my timetable slightly, the AR graphic claiming I was double-checking my firewall. And, considering what had been going on ... that sounded prudent as hell. *[Prove it. One way or the other.]*

Kinsey pursed his lips. He glanced aside. "How?"

[Use your fucking imagination, Kinsey.] I frowned.

He nodded. "How about this ..." He grinned, then leaned in. "I wasn't supposed to tell you. Shiva says you're not ready, that I haven't finished my job, and that now's not the right time. But you know what? I think the old goat is too nervous about breaking your fragile, bitchy psyche into a thousand little pieces."

He licked his lips and I felt time seem to slow down, as if my wired reflexes had kicked in.

"Sarah."

He paused, his eyes glinting.

"Is."

I looked away from him. I could feel his breath—simulated and tingling—brushing along my earlobe.

"Alive."

The words floated before me. My mind had thrown them up in AR, as if they were a subtitle for a language I didn't speak anymore. I jammed on the privacy filter, my eyes blurring as I felt blood well and drip down my nose, spattering my gloved hands. My fingers clenched and I looked at the words.

Sarah. Is. Alive.

My eyes swam slightly and for a moment, the words were backward.

slegnA nellaF fO hselF ehT

I shook my head and the words were still there. But they weren't backward, and they weren't what they had been.

The Flesh of Fallen Angels.

My timetable started to flash red, as it was slewing more and more out of the way. I made a motion of picking up my PPR and slinging it over my ...

It crashed to the floor. I swayed.

[Dru, you okay?] It was Singh.

I closed my eyes.

My head buzzed.

slengA nllaF Fo hselF ehT

I opened my eyes. When the flying hell had I dropped my PPR?! I saw Gloria looking at me from her place in the kitting up chamber and I flashed her a smile.

[Nerves,] I ducted to Singh, grabbing the PPR and slinging it over my shoulder, the strap wrapping around my armpit as it had been designed to do.

"He was right," Kinsey said. I looked at him, scowling. His face, though, made me reconsider. He looked shocked. His eyes were wide. I swore, he almost looked guilty.

"Who?" I frowned. "And what were you going to say?"

But he didn't say anything. I shook my head, trying to ignore the annoying delusion or possible godbeing computer virus. I had no idea which one it was. With my PPR loaded and my timetable flashing at me, I only had time to blow a kiss to Gloria before hurrying toward the liftoff vehicle.

Once on board, the door closed behind me as I spun around to face Kinsey, but he was gone. Of course, he was in my head, but as I thought about ducting to him Alvarez slapped my shoulder, his gloved hand thumping loudly on my armor.

"Ready to kick ass, PR?"

His voice held none of the old growl it had back in Selection. Chronic pain, it turned out, had a way of making everyone nasty. I nodded, gaining strength. Kinsey was such a dick.

The inside of the LV didn't look like a ROVer. Rather than a mostly empty cargo space that could be configured to suit various transportation needs, the LV was a very narrow, very thin corridor with twelve doorways. I got to mine, stepped inside what felt like a coffin, and then smirked at Alvarez.

[Service guarantees citizenship, huh?]

He looked at me funny as he started to check and double-check the systems on my room. I was doing the same. I explained. *[It's from an old spec-fic film my g ... someone I used to know forced me to watch. Starship Troopers.]*

[I think I saw that once ...] He turned around, checking the room across from him.

The door closed and I felt a murmur of ducting conversation flittering around, a rattling off of checks and clears. I slotted my equipment, stood up, and waited as the crash-resistant foam slurped around my body. I had been through this in simulation, and frankly, after spending a month or so encased in foam and drugged to the gills, this was no big deal. I could even play games on my AR.

Didn't I have an email to write? I opened up the program, but I didn't know who I would send it to. Sarah was dead. Maybe I wanted to send something to Gloria? But that was …

The LV started to shift and move. Out of either a hope to allay any fears or worries we might have—or maybe just to sate our curiosity—the forward cameras to the LV piped into our eyes. To the left and to the right, the other two LVs taxied toward the edge of the hangar bay. Then, the ceiling opened. Dirt and bits of rust scattered from the ceiling as machines long abandoned lurched to life. The Loonie optics might spot that almost immediately, if they were looking at Cape Canaveral.

But, then again, the chances of that were fairly low. Hence why this was one of the major launch sites. The LVs shifted onto their backs, smart-material struts extruding out of their bellies and tucking up against their sides. And then the engines kicked us all like a god kicking us in the butt. The view became incredibly blurry until the computer edited and stabilized the feed for all of us.

We were going up.

And across the world, dozens upon dozens of other ships were going up as well, each of them moving along an intricate dance, a network of flight zones and orbital pathways that were known to be cleared or would be clear very soon. Across the world, camouflaged laser arrays were targeting every hunk of debris in the secondary areas, trying to blast them out of orbit, or at the very least, push them away from the flight paths.

The three LVs from the Cape, though, they were joined by a half a dozen LVs from other positions. Those LVs looked subtly different in the cameras: they weren't quite as sleek. They weren't quite as black.

They weren't *quite* impossible.

The technical specifications on the LV still made my head hurt. I hadn't quite been told all the technical details and the scientific explanations, but I had been told what would happen. Once we were out of the atmosphere, the LV's special materials and heat-shunts and magical technology (which was the only explanation I could think of) would kick into full life and the craft would look dark. Quiet.

Cold.

Very.

Very.

Cold.

This had been beaten into my head ever since I had been given my first space strategy game: stealth is impossible in space. Even a basic optical set, the kind that could be slapped onto a wrist watch, could detect a spaceship easily if it is angled in the right direction. The background of space is so cold, and the heat required for human beings not to freeze to death was so (comparatively speaking) hot that it made detection pathetically easy. Add chemical rockets into the mix and it went from being a single bright white light in a black room to being a single bright white light in a black room ... that was also waving a huge flare in the air and shouting at the top of its lungs, "SHOOT ME! SHOOT ME! SHOOT ME NOW!"

The CAA had to beli ...

No, scratch that.

The S3TA had to believe that this would work, or they'd never have stuck thirty-six of their operatives on them and launched them through hundreds of kilometers of debris-studded space, past Loonie-held space stations, missile defense grids, and whatever else the bastards had thought of while they had been sitting in orbit and throwing rocks at us. I had to admit, my jaw was clenched tighter than my suit as the ship rocketed out of the atmosphere. The pressure and the rumbling faded. Then there was another series of sharp, hard kicks. Material foamed and hazed around the cameras, which then went dead.

According to my AR specs, we had just deployed the active part of our camouflage.

And now ...

I waited.

As I waited, I imagined. The other ships, the more obvious ones, had had a lot of money put into making them look and act real. I heard rumors of vat-grown muscle and bits of organs, bone fragments, and stuff that would look like armor, weapons, and so on. It was the kind of insane tactic that you could pull off when you were desperate, rich, crazy, or all of the above.

Battlefleet Potemkin. That had been the name I had heard, and I suddenly remembered what it was from. Back before the Slump, the Chinese Government had been relocating people from the Three Gorges area so they could build the dam that would later have the same name. Or ... had the region been called something else and the dam changed that? I shook my head slightly. The villages had been called Potemkin Villages, because they were fake.

Which was weird, because Potemkin wasn't any Mandarin word I knew.

"That's because it's Russian."

Kinsey's face pressed against the doorway window that looked out into the hallway of the ship. He smirked at me through the glass.

"The first ones were made to fool the Empress Catherine into believing that her latest conquests were worth the blood and gold she had spent. The general, Potemkin, built the fronts of houses along the river. As the Empress rode past, she saw the fronts and saw a bountiful land. Well worth the price."

I scowled at him.

"Oh, it's a very Chinese tradition to believe they invented everything. To be fair, your culture did invent almost all the worst parts of your species. Gunpowder used in warfare. Centralized bureaucracy. Empire. Possibly even ethnic cleansing, though the Hmong never did have the decency to die out properly, did they?"

[Shut up.]

"Why so defensive, Dru? You're a Spacer. You were born hundreds, even *thousands* of years after the worst barbarities of your species popped up. Oh, right, because you decided to strap swords to your arms and join in on the mass slaughter. What a wonderful, well-thought-out idea *that* was."

I closed my eyes. By my calculations, it would take too long for the LV to get to the Moon. Anything longer than five more seconds with Kinsey talking to me was going to kill me. Or him. Could you strangle a program with your bare hands?

"You could try, if you weren't locked into your launch capsule. By the way, the Loonies have started firing. And here's something for us all to think about, reflect on ..."

I realized something. The way Kinsey's stupid face was twisting, the way he looked to the left and the right, the way his voice stressed words just *so*. I was no kinesic, I didn't know how to read microexpressions like Colonel Singh could without AI help, but I knew when someone was scared. And Kinsey wasn't just scared. He was freaking terrified.

"See, this ship is stealthed. Metamaterials, quantum thermocouples, and the simplest one of all, a Faraday cage. We can't get any signals in and out of this ship." He rested his head against the glass of the window. His illusory status felt very confirmed now, as the engines had died and the familiar and oh-so-beautiful grasp of microgravity embraced me ... but he remained rooted to the ground.

[You're trapped here, aren't you?]

"Yeah." His voice was raspy. "I don't want to die. And we can't dodge. The fake ships, they have fuel for dodging. They can at least pretend to get out of the way. We're fu—"

[Kinsey. Shut up.]

And for a wonder, he did.

Chapter 8: Potemkin Landing

I stuck my head out of the front of my pod and got shot in the face.

It was a stupid, rookie move, and I never would have made it if I wasn't so damn grateful to be alive. The past three days had been like sleeping below an anvil hung by a monomolecular thread with a psychotic and malicious monkey sawing very slowly at the string, and it was even money whether or not the string would snap and the anvil would pulp you before you even knew what was wrong.

Then we got over the Moon.

And that's when the LV had exploded.

The fact that it was a planned, thought out, and actually quite ingeniously designed explosion didn't change the fact that our thin skin against the void had peeled apart like a bursting fruit and seemingly randomized blasts of superheated gas had sent each one of our little pods tumbling to (hopefully) predetermined parts of Luna herself.

In the VRs, the ride down had been like being inside one of those ludicrously wasteful and horribly loud washing machines that appeared in the fiction Sarah had made me watch from the turn of the twenty-first century. I could still remember what she had said: "It's like a spa for your clothes!"

The actual ride down was ten times worse because, well ... it was real.

I got pinned to the side of the capsule, then mashed forward by a "secondary explosion," which was supposed to be a clever way to disguise a deceleration burn. Then, through the view port, I saw the gray surface of the Moon zooming right at me.

Luna bitchslapped me worse than any crash I had been in before.

And, so, head ringing, PPR in my hands, the door exploding open and flying gracefully out thanks to some automatic explosive bolts, I stepped out onto Lunar gravity.

And someone shot me in the face with an armor penetrating bullet.

Funny. The fact it was a Teflon-coated slug with a narrow tip and dense core actually saved my life. The bullet zipped through my faceplate, zipped through my cheek, then zipped through the back of my helmet and started its long, stately, hyperbolic trajectory away from Luna. The actual kinetic energy transferred into my head was minimal.

Someone please tell my nerve endings that. Pain exploded through my body, then was damped by augmentics as I executed a movie-perfect drop. My suit's back slapped the ground and moon dust billowed outward. I lay there, holding my breath, trying to ignore the sluggish bleeding and the prickling feeling on my hardened skin. I still had capillaries, but I didn't know if they'd burst the same way as normal skin would. After all, normal skin wasn't bulletproof.

Mostly bulletproof.

Semi-bulletproof.

If I was hit at an angle.

At long range.

With a low caliber.

How many godsdamned times can I get shot in the head before it sticks *and I* die *for once?*

A yellow and black suited figure bounded closer. Their suit looked roughly the same as the kind worn by the Loonies I had fought and killed almost half a year ago, and seeing it was so ludicrously comforting that I almost laughed into the vacuum, but I was busy doing everything I was taught not to do when I had been a Crèche kid: holding my breath. Of course, nowadays, I had lungs that could recycle the oxygen and CO2 and had internal caps that would prevent a vacuum to rip air out, so holding my breath actually made sense. It didn't make it feel any less weird. And I still had to work fast; it'd only keep cycling for about ten minutes.

The Loonie kept his rifle aimed at me as his patrol partner turned to face some com-relay. They had a laser link.

I kicked on my wired reflexes. And then, remembering my lower gravity VR training, I pushed myself up with one hand. I bounded into the air, and my right arm's blade snapped out. I plunged it down, through the faceplate of the man who had shot me—unlike him, I managed to get a good hit through his neck. I used my momentum and his added weight—leverage, perfect leverage—to haul myself down toward the man's partner. My boots kicked up the basaltic moon dust—white, grainy, familiar looking—and I slammed my blade through her throat, my augmentations reaching out into her suit's computer system. She had some shortwave, point to point radio. I sliced into the system then started spoofing her, bringing up an audio recording of one of her previous logs contained in the suit.

Using that, I synthed up a voice and ducted it into her radio, "Uh … just a second, I … OH SHIT!"

I jerked the blade from her back, letting her slowly—oh so slowly—fall. I moved quickly (though not as quickly as before, my wired reflexes dimmed down to avoid melting my brains), grabbing my equipment, my breath still held tightly. I touched off the emergency self-destruct in the pod and bounded away, a timer ticking through my AR.

Timer. It had to be a timer. It couldn't have been a radio signal that could set it off.

The timer blinked from red to green to indicate I had reached a safe distance. I ensured that by dropping into a crater. I felt the thump rush through the ground and when I looked, my eyes focusing and zooming in to make sure, I saw that the two bodies had been pretty much obliterated.

A focused forensic investigation would find all sorts of holes in the narrative I planned for them to find—one involving the pod blowing up and taking the two of them out as they investigated—but I hoped the Loonies would have other things to worry about by the time the techs showed up to sniff around.

With that finished, I rolled onto my back and calmly removed my helmet. I thanked the gods that my painkiller apps were still running, but I couldn't deaden the sensation forever, not if I wanted to keep an accurate tab on my medical condition later on. Nothing was more embarrassing than suddenly passing out because you didn't notice a sucking chest wound. I applied a medipatch to my cheek but didn't have time for anything more fancy than that. Now, for the helmet. I closed the front visor down—it was just like the GISS helmet—and glued it shut with my repair spray. Once it was solidified, I slipped the helmet on, cycled it, and then disabled the internal lock that had kept the rest of my suit's air from hissing out. Air flowed into my helmet and I breathed in, testing the helmet cameras. They worked, and were about as good as my eyes. Good enough.

I stood, then activated my pain receptors.

"Son of a bitch!" I shouted into my helmet, comforted in the knowledge that no one in the universe could hear me through a vacuum. "Godsdamn ... I ... ARRGH!"

I put a gloved hand on my helmet's cheek. It provided exactly no comfort.

I screamed and shouted and swore.

Before I'd even gotten half of it out of my system, an AR timetable popped up in the corner of my vision, reminding me of what I needed to do: find my location, find my nearest target of opportunity, and then move from that to Target Omaha. Heading straight for Omaha would be what they expected. If they didn't think we were going to risk a run for that ... well, that was the theory at least.

"Well, you can add two to your kill numbers," Kinsey said.

He stood, suit-less, on the edge of the crater I had jumped into.

"Kinsey," I spoke out loud, pointing at him. "Shut the hell up and go away or you will get me killed. Got it?"

He vanished like a soap bubble. Thank the gods.

I kicked on adaptive camo and moved up to higher ground. My camo was no good against thermographic scanners, but I had to hope that it was still better than nothing. I swept my cameras around in a three hundred and sixty degree sweep.

I stopped ...

And I saw it: thrusting up, a long, low, L-shaped curve in the distance.

Target Omaha.

The Shi-Armstrong Railgun.

I skidded down the crater, deactivating my Predator and switching to Loonie colors. I went to the buggie—a small, two-person unit with smart-wheels that could turn three hundred and sixty degrees and were each an electrical engine unto themselves—and sat in the driver seat, mentally hacking the computer system. It was a matter of moments to penetrate the initial security and spoof the IFF signal. That, though, would only work so long ... I could already feel network security sniffers poking around in the code. I focused on the non-virtual world, gunning the engines. The wheels buzzed to life and I pulled out of the crater, leaving behind the ugly scar that the landing and explosion had made.

I brought up the timetable. Targets of opportunity, we had about twenty-five minutes to hit any we had, and then thirty minutes to arrive at our designated positions around the railgun. Changes in the timetable, though, were permissible under operational parameters. There weren't any other S3TA members in the range of my radio, so I had to take my chances with what I thought I could manage.

And a plan was forming in my brain. Still, I started to work the pre-designed program into the car's radio. It started transmitting a secret code underneath its tracking feed, and sprayed it around rather than just linking directly to the control tower that was supposed to monitor the computer systems.

I was in luck.

[PR?]

[Lightfoot, pleased to meet you. I have a buggy I've spoofed. You?]

[Still legging it. Head here.]

He threw a glyph onto my AR. I spotted it a kilometer down the path I was trundling along. The scenery I passed reminded me of the time in simulations: Cold. Desolate. Eerily historic. I felt disconnected from the war, even as I rode past a small wall built to indicate where buggy drivers should avoid hitting what looked like an unstable patch of dust. I could have been one of the original Apollo astronauts.

Save for the cybernetic augmentation.

And the laser rifle.

And the buggy.

And my skinsuit with nanotube armor and reactive camouflage.

Still, it was hard to ignore the parallels.

"You're an idiot."

And that was another thing to keep me rooted in the present. I didn't spare Kinsey a glance, but he made himself known, sitting without a spacesuit inside of the buggy. He tapped the dashboard.

"Oh, gee, Kinsey, there's a perfectly good reason for why I'm not jacked into the Loonies' radio traffic." His voice dripped with mocking sarcasm.

I frowned. *[I don't want to draw any extra attention.]*

Kinsey made a face.

We reached the glyph. I didn't see Alvarez—at least, not at first—but then his active camo shifted and changed, his armor setting itself to Loonie yellow and black. He climbed into the side of the buggy, strapping himself in and hiding his PPR.

[All right, Gloria and Lee made contact, along with Jackson, Tipelly, and Kinner. Applejack is dead.]

I closed my eyes, relief exploding inside of me. Gloria was okay. Okay. Okay. Okay. Gloria was alive. That thought buzzed through my brain—feeling weighter than it should have. Which was saying something. She was my *girlfriend*.

Gods. It took being shot in the face to get me to say the simplest things, didn't it?

Alvarez kept ducting. Kinsey looked at me with deep, sad eyes.

[Gloria, Lee, and Jackson are hitting a depot. Tipelly and Kinner are going to meet with us to take on the railgun. The other squads, as far as I know, landed fine and will be hitting their targets in a few minutes.]

I nodded again, taking a gentle turn. The medipatch on the hole in my face was doing its best with the localized painkillers. But nodding and jouncing around on a buggy wasn't making things easier on it.

[*So, where do we go?*] I ducted at Alvarez.

[*Along this road.*] He grinned. [*You speak Hindu, right?*]

I looked at him as if he were crazy.

[*Hey, you slept through at least some of the classes.*]

[*I was on neurostims, you dickhead.*] I sent a smiley face to his AR, looking back to the road. Moving my lips would hurt too much. Hell, the only thing keeping me from screaming was the fact clenching my jaw was what kept it from hurting worse. Forcing myself to focus on the road again, I saw how it branched into three directions, but the local information coming out of the signpost flashed onto the windshield, indicating that two of the roads were classified Military Business Only. I rolled my eyes. The Loonies hadn't even gotten around to rejiggering their signposts. Even in pre-infotech Britain, they'd taken signposts off to confuse invaders.

I turned down the rightmost classified road, Alvarez indicating that it was the correct one.

As we headed down the road, I caught a subliminal flash at the horizon. I looked up and saw that a dome of smoke was expanding over something a few kilometers away. Bits of fragments were sailing out like tendrils of some weird flower. Some were even heading straight up, thrown completely free of Luna's meager gravity well.

[*And that's one depot down ...*]

I shook my head as Alvarez grinned like a wolf. The pain was getting worse as my little medipatch continued to fail gloriously.

We got to the front gate of the railgun. Our armor was the wrong make, but the details were fine and small. We just needed to get our foot in the door, so to speak. As we advanced, Alvarez spoke over the radio, sending along spoofed ID codes. He, of course, spoke in the Loonie dialect of English, Spanish, Hindu, Arabic and other languages kicked up here over the years.

"This is Patrol Sergeant Hakim, reporting in for refueling. Over."

"Roj, Hakim. Welcome back to the barn. Any falling Plodders hit you in the head?"

"Nope." Alvarez sounded completely at ease, chuckling. "Stupid assbackward Plodders wouldn't know how to land on Luna if you faxed them."

The person on the other end laughed. As for me, I just closed my eyes and clenched my jaw harder. Plodders were what Loonies called Earthers when they thought they weren't listening. Idiots. *Argh.*

"Oh, yeah, it's only offensive when *they* do it. When you call them Loonies, it's absolutely freaking fine," Kinsey said, sitting on the dashboard. The pain did make it easier to ignore him.

We went over a few more minor bumps in the road, the buggy juddering oddly under my control. Virtual Reality was almost perfect, and the black-tech stuff that Selection had used was creepily good. But there was one thing that was persistently hard to fake, and that was gravity. It was something about how it affected so many autonomic functions that were subtle but easily noticeable. That meant that the buggy moved just slightly wrong and I kept finding myself having to correct and change my positioning and stance to keep from tumbling against the straps. Each bounce had the added fun side of sending a new jolt of pain through my face.

[You okay, PR?] Alvarez ducted. *[You're leaking a little.]*
[I was shot.]
[Oh, and you mention this now?] He sighed. *[Where?]*
[The face, hence the whole faceplate ...]

He bobbed his head in his helmet.

[Keep it down and play things by ear. Once we're in a shirt-sleeve, I'll try and fix you up. Okay?]

We hit the perimeter. There were automated turrets, glinting faintly against the dark silvery-gray of the lunar surface. My AR tried to identify them, but rather than risk being noticed sweeping any advanced sensors over what should be familiar stuff to me, I looked forward. The road ran into a gate. The gate looked almost absurdly out of place here, a mundane normal modern gate. It was like it had been dragged from Earth and slapped down on Luna.

Two Loonies in yellow and black armor stepped out from the gate. They had nasty looking guns whose silhouettes made my AR go into fits before classifying them as "homemade." They looked lethal enough. They were the first hint that military intelligence wasn't an oxymoron this time: Loonies really *were* dead set against any kind of uniformity or standardization. As I hit the brakes and came to a juddering, crumbly low-gravity stop, I got a really great diagnostic of their armor.

It was completely different from the two people who had shot at me when I landed. Homemade too, if my AR didn't miss its guess.

"Yo," the one on the left spoke through the radio, his suit helmet lighting up. How quaint. "Spot any ghosts out there?"

I had to talk.

I had to talk with *this* face. Panic. Uh. I opened my mouth.

Painpainpainpainpainpain-

Click.

Shift.

Speak. **Speak.**

"Not a one," Dru said, hoping she got the accent right with a big-freaking hole in her cheek. Moving her jaw and speaking made her want to scream, but she bit down the impulse, as Alvarez took up the mantle of talking, hopping off the buggy

and landing beside it as if he had done that kind of thing a thousand times in his life. The guard on the right gestured ...

me

... toward a parking lot cut out of the ground near one of
the support struts for the railgun: this close, the whole thing
looked incredibly spindly. It was almost a kilometer long, a huge
tube of concentric rings, built along a rail. The loading building
was at the end, but this was the administration building, which
looked like it had been bulked up into an actual bunker over the
past half a year. I looked around carefully as *I* drove to the parking lot, and Alvarez kept his POV feeding into my AR in a small
inset box in the upper right-hand corner of *my* vision.

"I swear command is yanking our chains. The Plodders
didn't even get past L1 with their attack."

"It was pretty freaking stupid." Alvarez was walking with
the guards, and they were buying him hook, line and sinker. He
ducted me, [*Keep an eye on me, make sure that my spoofing is
still on task.*]

I parked the buggy and mentally opened up a second window, starting to read through the programs that were running
through the net around here. There were checks that Alvarez
had fooled, but those checks had checks, and the checks had
checks. I tracked it back to dispersed security terminals laid
throughout the bunker. So, there was no one guy I could go and
quietly kill.

It was time for my virtual cargo. I ducted Alvarez, [*Putting
in Worm 2.*]

[*Do it.*]

I reached the entrance, waving to one of the Loonies who
waved back to me.

Siccing the worm on the base was as easy as opening the file
in my augmentations, then releasing it into my suit-computer,
then weaving it into one of the many routine checks pinged off
me by the base's computer system. I had just gotten inside of

the airlock proper and was trying to figure out how to explain why I wouldn't be taking my helmet off immediately … when the worm did its thing.

The lights shuttered off and the airlock door half-opened. Radio signals started bursting from everyone and everything, and rather than being coordinated and streamlined by the invisible layers of programming that surrounded everything in a technical civilization, they bounced. They tangled. Thirty panicking voices, alone in the dark, mixed among a howling static, prerecorded lines of pure nonsense, screamer attacks, AR fog filling any HUD goggles or cameras.

I shoved the airlock door open, jacking on my active camo. Air was venting from the primary chamber, and the worm had jammed up the door closing mechanisms as best as it could. Unfortunately, for me at least, the doors were all partially self-automated. Some had detected the subversion of the local system and shut themselves off from the wireless signal before any nasty program got in. That meant that parts of the base remained sealed off. My AR started to map what I could see. My PPR at the ready, I came around the corner, Alvarez ducting to me: *[Good work. Wrapping up out here. Report.]*

I fired two short pulses. Two shocked and terrified looking technicians wearing face masks and pressurized coveralls were trying to get through one of the interior seal locks. They both fell, holes burned through their backs.

[Scratch two tangos. The base is checkerboarded.]
[Hitting their power plant in five. Brace.]

I nodded and kept walking for five paces, checking corners and doorways I headed past. Adrenaline and focus was doing a hell of a job as a painkiller—letting me focus on the sounds filtering through doors. I placed my palm against each door, listening. Nothing. Nothing. Nothing. My AR flashed up the warning about Alvarez's bombs and I ducked against a wall, crouching down to make myself as small a target as possible. It wasn't as large a thump as I expected, more subliminal than anything else over the semi-audible hissing of air leaking through the spamming base.

The secondary effects were a *lot* more noticeable.

The lights went out. A moment later, emergency biolumes kicked into gear. And I started checking doors again. I found three tangos at door six, all wearing pressure coveralls with weapons. They were communicating awkwardly, using a strung together fiber cable that they thought was hardened against the worm trashing their IT.

They'd be right.

One of them half noticed my ghostly, rippling form, or maybe the two camera lenses that had to be visible for me to see a damn thing. She raised her hand to stop her fellows, her mouth moving underneath her face mask. My AR subtitled it: Uh, do you—

By the numbers, one, two, three tangos down. I stepped over them. Alvarez pinged me.

[Light opfor out here, how's the opfor in there?]

[Random and light.]

[We're heading in. Fan like this.] He threw a series of glyphs into my AR. He'd gotten his hands on the map of the base, and showed me where I was going to handle things. The place was mostly barracks and life support, with a few computer labs for trajectory analysis. I got to go after one of the life support facilities.

Wonderful.

"Pretty dirty way to fight," Kinsey said.

[Can you do anything useful?] I asked, taking a corner carefully. There wasn't anyone around it, save for a single tango who hadn't gotten a face mask before the blowout had hit them.

"I'm a pacifist. So ... no. If anything, I'm obliged to distract you."

[And if I get shot?]

"The electrical power in your headware will last long enough for me to download onto the local net. From there, I just beam myself to Earth." He let out a sigh. "Weight off my mind."

I got to a sealed door. I frowned, tapping around it until I found the access port. I punched the port, crumpling the metal, then ripped it off the wall. It bounced once, twice, then hit the far wall. From there, it was just a matter of extending my forearm blade and stabbing it through the pressure tube that was holding the door down. There were a few other tubes to puncture, as the door was built with several redundancies. It was still the work of just a few moments. I knelt, worked my fingers along the seam, and pulled up, moving carefully to not overstress my arm joints.

The door slid smoothly upward and air blew past my hand. My other hand grabbed a slick-grenade from my belt and I chucked it in, sending a mental signal to the grenade.

I think ...

[Twitch.]

"This is sick," Kinsey muttered. The door shut as the grenade went off.

I pushed the door open after a few seconds. The air blew past me, but by then, the Twitch had fully gelled. Five tangos were in the place: two techs and three soldiers. They had face masks around their necks, but hadn't put any on. They had weapons beside them, but they weren't holding them. The Twitch had hit each of them enough to spread the contact-toxin. They twitched and flopped on the ground, the air evacuating around them. I stepped over their bodies and checked over the life support gear.

It wasn't anything special—the same kind of life support tanks and filter systems I'd worked on for years on the Hub. I quickly spread scrapper's gel over the important parts: the nozzles connecting the algae vats to the processors. The filters.

The computer that used to run the place. The power connections. The backup nuclear battery for the heating systems. Once I had put the minimum amount of scrapper's gel onto the places, I reconfigured the gel spreader with a thought. The tip turned from a nozzle to a long, thin copper cable. Using that, I electrically touched off each line and drop, which caused them to flash and sizzle soundlessly in the near vacuum.

The room was wrecked in five seconds flat. Once it was done, I ducked out of the room, closing the door behind me.

[Room's cleared,] I ducted at Alvarez.

A glyph popped up and with it, Alvarez ducted back, *[Good work, PR. The railgun is ours. Head to the com center and beam a message to Earth.]*

I headed down the corridor. A man burst out of a wall vent, wearing a face mask and holding a makeshift rifle, complete with bayonet strapped into place with some duct tape. I knocked the blade aside with the palm of my hand and the followed it up with an elbow strike to the throat, my forearm blade snapping out to finish the job. He fell, gurgling blood.

[Tango down, this place isn't swept.]

[Hear that? Everyone keep on your toes,] Alvarez ducted to the whole team. I had made it to the com room, which hadn't sealed in time. Four people were cowering in the corner, their masks on, guns at their feet. I almost shot them, thought better of it, and instead went to one of the command consoles. The computers were flickering and winking, the holographic screens showing a skull and crossbones. I tapped at the computer, throwing in the correct series of digits and numerals that cleared the worm up.

Once it was gone, it took me a few seconds to find control for the optical relay. It was almost disturbingly similar to the GUI used on my home, the Hub. Same gylphs, same layout, same laser communication systems, all the same stuff I used to …

To …

I shook my head, frowning as I typed at the keyboard. I noticed a glint in the metal surface of the panels around the keyboard and casually slammed my elbow back. My forearm blade punctured something vital and the woman who had been creeping up behind me fell, clutching her chest. The near total vacuum made it all quite silent, save for the feelings that vibrated down to my shoulder.

I sent the message and then ducted Alvarez. *[Done.]*

[Good, we set the charges next to the power plant. This place is going to glow in the dark.]

I nodded and turned around. I had almost walked out of the room before I noticed the tangos. They were clustered around the woman who had gone for my back, applying pressure to the wound. I noticed that my strike hadn't been quite on target. Should have been higher and to the ...

Left.

The world seemed slightly out of focus for a second and I saw a woman, a young woman, clutching at herself, writhing as blood pumped around the fingers of the man pushing down on the wound. Her uniform said her name was Fatima. She had a name. She had a *name.*

I'm going to open the door slowly. You are not going to shoot me. Got it?

And ... why should I not shoot you?

Because you know my ...

The words trailed off. They weren't ducted to me. They were thoughts. My thoughts. I reached into my pouch and found a pair of medipatches. There wasn't enough skin on my face to apply all of them, but a wound like that, in the chest, had plenty of area for a medi-patch to do its work. I tossed the patches to them, and they landed on the floor after a smooth arc. It was almost dreamlike, throwing things in Lunar gravity. The Loonies jerked as the patches landed, like they thought they were grenades or something.

I felt a *squeeze*. It wasn't near my heart. It was somewhere lower and deeper and more painful.

I tapped on the radio, broadcasting to them, forcing words out through the pain.

"This place is going to blow. Run."

Then I turned around and walked out, ducting Alvarez. [Delay the explosion.]

[What?]

[Delay it.] I came to the front of the railgun facility. Alvarez was already requisitioning the buggies, assigning people to them.

[We're moving out, this place needs to be so much radioactive ash before we hit the other targets. That means get on the buggy and shut up.]

[There are civilians in there.] I pointed at the base. The four people hadn't gotten out yet.

[This facility launches the tungsten rods that have been hitting our bases and factories for the last two months. They're not civilians. No more than a drone rigger during the Slump was a civilian, just because automatic rockets did the dirty work. Get on the buggy. Now!]

I got on the buggy and drove away, with Gloria and Alvarez in the back. We had our Loonie colors on, but that cover was blown to hell and gone by now. We just had to keep them off balance for three days and not get caught till then.

In the rear view mirror, there was a flash as the charges went off near the power plant that ran the railgun.

Debris flew up and out.

Kinsey didn't need to say a godsdamn thing.

Chapter 9: Targets of Opportunity

7/20/2068

Mare Tranquillitatis, 32 kilometers east of Target Omaha (Neutralized)

T-Minus L-Day: -6

[Tangos marked.]

Gloria threw up three targeting glyphs, indicating her intended kills. I tagged two more, then a third when I saw them clambering out of their enclosed buggy. We were both lying flat on a rise that looked down on one of the space defense grid hardpoints.

The hardpoint looked like three concentric rings, each one made out of shiny metal, sunken into the moondust with just the edges thrusting out of the ground at exactly half a meter, thank you augmented vision. Each ring had a series of spherical lenses at every few degrees along the circle. The spaces between the rings—about fifteen meters of open ground— were swept clean and studded with tubes that had been shoved into the ground, only their tips exposed. Each of those tubes held a missile loaded with ball bearings and micro-explosives, designed to scatter in the space around the target.

Boom.

The lenses, though, were the real killers at close range. The missiles could be shot down. But the rings, guided by local automation, could focus three hundred lasers on a single target. Even the best armor couldn't stand up to that. And if they were fighting lighter armored targets, they could disperse the lasers out to hit as many as they needed. The really clever part, though, was what we couldn't see: the underground water reservoirs used as heat sinks. The water was safely stored underground for future use, and the lasers had a battlefield endurance that beat the snot out of anything we could put into space.

For a bunch of Loonies, it was sophisticated. The kind of thing that Spacers would build, the kind of defense that only made sense without an atmosphere to muck everything up.

[So … ready to smoke 'em?] Gloria ducted.

[You know it.] I frowned. The six foot-mobiles we had targeted were a sweeping patrol, checking on the missile racks. They were supported by five drones, little gimbaled sphere things that rolled around, ready to stop, mount, and then open fire on anything their bosses tagged. *[So, we going to EMP them?]*

[Yeah, they've got the new crypto.]

I sighed inside my helmet, feeling the skinpatch tug at my bones. I didn't actually remember *when* I'd gotten patched. It'd happened sometime in the sleepless, staccato unrythym of battle: engagement, wait, flight, engagement, wait, wait, flight, engagement, flight. The pain was a dull ache by now. Manageable. I couldn't even remember which of my teammates had finally popped my helmet and done the patch. I think it was Alvarez. He had said he'd do it.

The easy times were long gone. They'd been gone ever since a shuttle had strafed us and we realized our exploits and hacks were all patched. No more cruising around in buggies and in Loonie colors with spoofed IFF signals. Our firewalls were still holding up, but … well, I liked to think I was a good slicer, but being a slicer isn't the same thing as being a programmer. A slicer just knows how to use exploits. A programmer *makes* exploits. And with this crypto, I was back to being just any old user and so was the rest of the team.

Now, instead of moving as a coordinated unit—the unit that had taken Target Omaha and a shuttle depot within the first two days—we were now in two-people teams. Our standing order? Kill everything, wreck everything, and melt like a shadow immediately afterwards.

Targets of opportunity.

It was still ugly, ugly work. And sometimes, I could go through a whole hit without thinking about it. Sometimes, I couldn't stop, like a camera trying to auto-focus and bugging out. And all the killing was mixing with being near Gloria—not that we touched. Not in suits. But she was here. And we were doing what needed to be done.

Right?

I focused on a short mental command to deploy my PPR bipod. I sighted on the first tango. My other arm slid up to be level with the PPR. The indicator on my seeker bracelet flashed on. The AR graphic showed the effective blast radius of the EMP missile.

[And … now.]

With that duct, I sent the command. The bracelet jerked on my wrist, a micromissile popping up, then activating its jet, a tiny dart of bright light that stabbed out and slammed into one of the drones. The blast was invisible, save for the crackling, popping hiss that ran over my radio. In the drones, that hissing was an overwhelming storm of EM radiation blanketing out their communications. They slewed to a stop, their safety programs triggering and keeping them from going nuts. A shame.

I kicked on wired reflexes and smoked two of the tangos before they had even noticed what was killing them. The third turned around, confused. I smoked them too. Gloria and I stood, hurrying down, Gloria keeping her PPR on the drones, the invisible beam melting their armor, then punching through with a flurry of silent sparks. The drones were pulped.

We were five meters away from the first ring, ready to finish the job, when someone proved they were on the ball.

Gloria immolated.

She didn't scream, didn't make a single noise. Her armor just writhed and boiled, shining, reflecting light. Her arms dripped molten flakes. An explosion of ablated armor hazed the vacuum around her. The moondust behind her shone with reflected light, turning cherry red.

My wired reflexes kicked on as something inside me broke.

Notagainnotagainnotagainnotagain.

I slid forward and swept my leg out. Moondust exploded upward, creating a thick cloud before me and Gloria. The cloud glowed with reflected laser light, diffused heat. The killing beams of the defense grid, retargeted from space to the ground, turned the cloud into a brilliant flare. It should have been beautiful. I grabbed Gloria, my palm registering near-lethal temperatures. I dragged her down, forward, and we both rolled, kicking up more lifesaving sand. I felt blazing heat burn along my body as well.

Wham. Wham.

Silence. The dust pattered onto my suit, making a faint crinkling, crackling noises.

[H

u

r

t

s.]

Gloria's duct was slow, ragged. I hadn't imagined that a person could duct by typing one letter at a time. But she had. I didn't move, letting the dust fall down. We were at the lip of the third ring, and we were below the angle that the laser turrets could hit us.

[I know, I know …] I shifted onto my belly, squirming around to get a look at her.

Not every beam had been able to hit. I could tell that just looking at her, because there was still a recognizable Gloria, not just a burned, slagged mass of carbon and nanotech ashes. But … still …

I …

Her arms were melted—one more than the other, only by a quirk of her position. But even the *better* one just came to a stumpy, smoothed off elbow joint. Her armor had run like water, if only the outer edges. The ablation layer had completely vaporized, and it hadn't done much more than …

Save her life.

Still, I didn't want to lift up her faceplate. I was glad that it was fused shut. I reached out with my augmentations, calling up her diagnostics. The medical report wasn't as grim as I had thought. Oh, it was grim: third degree burns along her shoulders and hips, second and first degree burns on 45% of her chest, serious burns on her face (second, I guessed, but the diagnostic wasn't clear on that) and her augmentations were all damaged in one form or another, save her neurals. Still, I had imagined … worse. No fourth. No fifth-degree burns. No exposed bone.

[Well. Looks like. That's … it.]

[Shut up, shut up,] I ducted back. Then my thoughts got stuck in that loop and I kept ducting it again and again and again. *[Shut up, shut up, shut up—]*

She ducted over me. *[No … medical. Finish mission.]*

The fleet was supposed to be here by today, or tomorrow. The timetable was slewing, and we had been out of the loop. Of course, each hardpoint we failed to damage or take down was a hardpoint that would fire on them when they got close. As I thought, flashes on the horizon caught my attention. I craned my head backward and saw that missiles were launching up. Those were less of a threat than the lasers, which would be in range soon if I didn't miss my guess ...

[Override your pain filters, shut everything down. Then hold on. Got it. You hold on.]

Gloria didn't respond.

I remained low, thinking furiously.

This felt ... familiar ... horribly familiar. Painfully familiar. Watching a comrade, a lover, die.

The transhuman had pulled out a pistol. It was a sleek model, built almost entirely around one hunk of molded and shaped carbon composite.

Jillian stood up straighter. "If you ever get interviewed, my last words are officially ..." She spat on the ground. "Up yours. Die."

The transhuman shot her in the head.

[Listen ... I've been married.]

Gloria's ducting was getting clearer now, her pain receptors must have been shunted off.

[And it was the worst idea ... but ...]

I closed my eyes. *[SHUT UP. SHUT UP SHUT UP AND FOCUS ON STAYING ALIVE.]*

And with that, I grabbed my first slick-grenade, programmed it for acidic dispersion, and then chucked it over the lip, calculating trajectories in my head. I did that again and again, using my slicks and Gloria's slicks, and every time I threw, my arm got hit again and again by flashes of laser light. The last time, I released, but when I lowered my hand, warning alarms blared in my head.

My hand dripped, bits of it falling on the moondust in slow motion. It was astounding to watch. And the pain ...

The pain had long since been banished by my command. It was dangerous to live without pain. It made it hard to tell when you were getting hurt. But right now, I couldn't afford it.

The timer on the slicks ticked to the end and I dared to peek. A shimmering haze of concentrated scrapper's gel had been sprayed out by those slicks. Because they were programmed to operate in a vacuum, the actual spraying depended less on wind and more on the slick's internal mechanisms to the slicks. Still, the end result was dozens on dozens on dozens of pitted and scarred lenses, steaming and cracked, popping under the intense heat and burning acid of the scrapper's gel.

I stood and nothing burned me to my ankles. The Loonies didn't have a control station here, the patrol had driven here from a more centralized, defended, and efficient position. Their reinforcements might be here soon, or they might not. Because when I looked up at the sky, I saw glints that were breaking into dozens of tiny flecks. Those flecks grew larger and larger. Contrails followed them, swirling clouds of heated gas that expanded outward, squirting from engines. It wasn't impressive at first ... but then it became breathtaking as laser light illuminated darkened clouds, refracting debris, countermeasure chaff, and diffusion mortars. Return laser fire set the chaff clouds ablaze with ruby red light. The fact the beams scythed invisibly past the hellish glow was nearly an afterthought to the roiling chaos of the chaff.

A ship went up, flashing brightly, then dimming to nothingness. Another ship.

Then they got within missile ranges.

Within *our* missile range, not the Loonie defensive positions. Our missiles had to be launched at basically point-blank range, to avoid getting lasered out of the sky before they could do any good.

Every single star bifurcated.

Like trees branching, their specks spread outward into thousands more specks. Those specks became more specks, trailing gasses lit by laserlight and by their own engines. The specks streaked down and down and down and then all around me, they struck the horizons and beyond the horizons too. I did not feel the shudders.

I could only imagine it all.

But the invasion was on.

The invasion was *on*.

I knelt down and picked up Gloria. I hefted her into an over the shoulder carry, shifting my armor skin to a red cross on my back and bright white coloration, though the coloring across my armor was pitted and scored, sending out rippling distortion effects rather than a proper adaptive coating. My Cheetahs folded out and I started to run. My knees pumped and the tongues of metal kissed the Moon and we sailed in long, graceful arcs, going faster and faster. No air resistance, no wind blowing in my hair, just the jarring thud thud thud of impact.

Impact. Gloria bounced, her stumpy half-arm clacking against my shoulders.

But she didn't *move*. She didn't squirm or shift or anything.

[Gloria, come on, text me, Gloria. Say something, please, god, please.]

[I'm … still here, PR.]

[Okay,] I gulped, hitting the side of a crater, the dust floating up in slow motion parabolas. I bounced up, then bounced forward, over the crater. She'd lapsed into silence again. I hooked onto the first thing that popped into my head. *[Gloria, tell me about your first husband.]*

[Cheater.]

[With who?]

Gloria paused.

[With who, Gloria!] There was a shuttle landing spot near here, a designated one, one that we S3TA members were to head for once the invasion started and we had no immediate targets.

[Backgammon.]

I snorted through tears, then landed with a shudder and a cloud of dust at the landing site.

Nothing.

No shuttle. No fighter craft. No base-pod. Nothing but lunar regolith and basalt. I looked up at the sky, at the blazing explosions, the arcing missiles.

There was so much radio interference that my piddling backpack radio wouldn't make it and don't even *think* about my head antenna. I drew my P3, keying it to com-laser mode. I had fired this pistol more as a smartphone than a weapon. For some distant, obscure reason, that comforted me. I raised the P3 into the air and looked at the specks. I kicked my augs into full gear, trying to ...

There were so many shapes. Fighters, shuttles, landing craft, decoys. They flew and shifted and moved, leaving behind trails, exploding. Some were even landing, distant, far away, rocketing down, then slowing with plumes of kicked up dust.

I felt a pounding in my head. My brains were cooking, my augmentations heating up as processing power dumped waste heat into my cerebral cortex. My neurochemicals would boil. Superheated blood would spurt from my eyes. My helmet would become a fucked-up fishbowl. I closed my eyes.

Knowing it was hopeless.

I prayed.

I pulled the trigger. A knifelike beam shot into space, invisible and inaudible, a tiny needle in a massive haystack. Along it pulsed a single chain, a single chain of three letters. Three letters, older than anything I had ever touched.

SOS

SOS

SOS

The signal beamed into space and I prayed. My eyes closed and I prayed to Buddha and to the Almighty, to the gods great and the gods small. I prayed to the Muslim god, the Abrahamic god. I prayed to the Hindu gods, to the Avatars, to the Foundation. I prayed to each and every single one of them, a single request: Not. This. Time.

Not *again*.

"Drusilla Zhao! I am coming in HOT!"

My eyes snapped open, wide, looking up. *"Húli jīng!"*

The shuttle came straight down in absolute silence. I imagined it screamed like a jet as I ducted Gloria again and again to hold on. The shuttle's retros fired and I didn't even flinch as dust pattered against my front. When it cleared, there it was: gleaming, huge, and full of CAA regulars, wearing blue and holding PPRs, bounding onto the surface, buggies driving out the sides. Auto-deploying tents and fortifications exploded out before me and a single blue spacesuit with a Warrant Officer's bar and gold on her shoulder bounded straight at me and hugged me.

The faceplate flipped back and there was Yolanda, the only surviving friend I had from the Hub, the oldest part of my military clique, beaming at me.

Then, looking down at Gloria, she shouted on a different frequency, her lips moving inaudibly. Men ran and grabbed Gloria, sliding stretchers under her and bounding off. Gloria lifted her elbow stump to me, waving.

I watched her go, and then looked back at Yolanda, who was still grinning.

"It's good to see you, Dru," she said, her grin fading. "We made it. Now, I ..."

I nodded, slowly, the rest of her sentence fading away. It wasn't important.

Maybe ...

Maybe we had made it after all.

A crack started to spread in my brain. But I was too high on endorphins to give a damn.

Chapter 10: Reflection

7/22/2068

Mare Tranquillitatis, 33 kilometers east of Target Omaha (Neutralized)

T-Minus L-Day: -8

Base Site Gamma wasn't the biggest landing site, but it was the first one hit in the counterattack. I hadn't been folded under the local commander—Captain Tam—and that left me in a bit of a bind when it came to how I operated in the constraints of 4th EWAC "Anon" company. The Anons were, according to Yolanda, one of the best electronic warfare, active countermeasure companies in the entire history of the CAA armed forces. It was exactly the kind of people you'd want to work with.

The question was *how* I'd work with them. I was a pretty good slicer, but the direct electronic warfare platoon didn't take just "pretty good" slicers: they took people who could code, program, and exploit as if they had been born doing it. The communication platoon and the medical platoon were equally pointless—I could splint and apply medipatches, but it felt like a huge waste to put a multimillion-credit super soldier onto *that*. The rigger platoon—who were handling pretty much every single long-ranged drone on the Tranquil Front—could use me for my twitch reflexes, but that would be like using a ROVer to haul freight. Possible, but it was just a tiny fraction of what I could do.

So, that left the obvious solution: the ISTAR—Intelligence, Survelliance and Target Acquisition—platoon, twenty boys and girls who were trained to do what I did. Just not as good. There was just one tiny little itty bitty problem.

"Permission to speak freely, Captain?"

Captain Tam nodded. He was sitting behind a smart desk that constantly tracked his various data points, statistics, troop deployments, and any other information he needed. It was a wire-frame, really, as lightweight as it could be and seemed only half there, just like the rest of the room: we were standing in a balloon-dome, shaded by an anti-radiation and flare tarp that was staked to each corner, a transparent airlock mounted on the front. The walls were opaque and set to standard military hues: blues and silver. Second Lieutenant Sandra Yue stood to the left of the desk, her hands behind her back. She was a trim girl with a nose that looked like it had been broken five times. I was standing at parade rest, my repaired arm tucked against the small of my back, hands folded together.

"I believe that including Corporal Zhao in my platoon will have a deleterious effect on morale and degrade operational efficiency."

I kept my mouth shut. Instead of complaining or bitching, I sent a private line to Gloria—who was in "recovery" in the medic hut, with permission to kill anyone who tried to touch her without authorization. I didn't think she'd need to do it, as the medics seemed happy to put her on a painkiller drip and an IV without looking closer.

[Check out the last hundred seconds of my POV.]

"I see." Captain Tam looked only ten years older than me, but for some bizarre reason, he just felt young. Like a kid who had just walked out of the Crèche and hadn't hit the hard grind of apprenticeship yet, who hadn't had his bounciness ground into conformity yet. He looked at me. "Corporal?"

"To be honest," I said, unconsciously adopting that casual, toneless voice that the S3TA used whenever dealing with someone from a different branch. Like the guy I'd met on the Forge, six or seven lifetimes ago. It was easy, considering how often I used ducting. I was more used to italicizing, all capping, or even changing my font colors to show emotion than using this weird voice box. "S3TA tactics don't quite work with ISTAR, from what I've studied."

Yue bristled. Hey, it wasn't *my* fault that her Marines weren't able to turn invisible without five minutes of advanced warning and deployed camo. Of course, they were also invisible (or near enough for Earther math) to infrared, whereas I and the other Special Forces would show up like hot flares. The gods of warfare did love their soft counters. She stayed quiet as Tam sighed and leaned back in his chair.

"I've been on the horn with HQ, and they say that orders for you are pending. Considering light lag and the developing situation on the Frigoris Front means that most of the attention is up there."

Both Yue and I were thinking the exact same thing.

[Yes, I know, you are chomping at the bit,] Gloria ducted to me.

[I …] I paused, trying to place what a "bit" was and why I'd be chewing on computer code. Then I remembered. Horses. Right. *[Why would I have a bit in my mouth?]*

Gloria ducted a rather graphic image indicating exactly why. Proof she was definitely feeling better, even if I had to ask why she had porn on her headware. Wait. No. I didn't. My cheeks heated. *[Ha ha ha, very funny. None of this changes that taking Frigoris is only the most important fight till we knock over Shi-Armstrong.]*

I didn't want to think on all the *other* reasons I wanted to get away from the normies.

Instead, I thought of Mare Frigoris. It, like every single other mare on the Moon, was covered with basalt, darker than the highlands, and rich in several kinds of raw material useful for colonists. But Mare Frigoris (literally, Sea of Cold) had been named incredibly aptly, because right below the surface, hidden in craters, waiting for us to find was the most valuable thing in space: water. Ice water, to be exact.

The fight over Frigoris and the Neo-Ganges was—from all reports—some of the fiercest fighting since the Slump. We didn't get much information, and as it was a few thousand clicks away, we didn't do much more than send the occasional support drone flight for when they needed new spares. Down here, we didn't have the troops or equipment to mount any further assaults on the big targets: New Mumbai or Arlington Colony. Down here, things were quiet.

When a gun had first been put to my head and a uniform slapped on my shoulders, there had been times where I had thought: if this were a movie, X, Y, or Z would happen. Every single time, it hadn't happened. No sneak attack had followed a statement "down here, things were quiet."

Back then, though, we had been in space, where the nearest fight was hundreds of thousands of kilometers away. I should have known better. Really.

The tent walls turned translucent, warning indicators flaring. HUD symbols flashed up on the walls circling possible avenues of attack, alarms blared through my ear—my AR tracked the same signals, laying a ghostly afterimage over the real world.

"All forces, scramble to defensive perimeter, hats on." Captain Tam spoke into the desk, his helmet dangling by his hip. Idiot. I bounded forward, grabbing his helmet and jamming it on his head, locking it into position. He looked at me and something out of the corner of my eye flashed. I dragged him to the ground a moment before a ripping WHUMP struck the side of my helmet. Air rushed past, the tent flailing as the smart-fabric tried to compensate for a huge slug going straight through it.

[Son of a bitch.]

[Stay in bed, Gloria. I'll deal with this.] I switched to vocal, speaking to Tam. "You all right?"

"Yes, yes. Thanks." He stood, his voice shaky. "Uh ... Yue?"

Yue wasn't down. She was out the broken seal, already bounding toward the defenses.

"Permission to go mobile, sir." I lifted up my right arm. It was fixed up, but I still felt the psychosomatic urge to flex my fingers and joints. Just to make sure.

"G—" He paused. "Isn't ... Aren't you ..."

The rumors about the S3TA were more entrenched in the traditional Alliance Marine Corps, the one with actual decades of experience behind their structure and training. We kids in space had been dipping our toes in the pool—and getting them shot off—but on the Earth, they had all sorts of rumors about what the Special Forces could do. It helped scare the enemy. And our allies. And anyone else who had a brain. I think one of the best rumors, though, was that anyone who saw us in action was hit by an NDA—or they were quietly transferred somewhere where they'd never ever talk to anyone important again.

I looked at Captain Tam, mentally keying my helmet to click into place.

"They won't see me coming."

And I keyed on active camouflage. Tam jerked back against his desk and I paid him no mind, ducking out of the rent in the side of the tent, hoping that Tam would get his act together and start actually commanding. I slapped a battle map onto the right-hand corner of my vision, and saw that the defensive line had been pockmarked by a few high impact weapons. The main command tent had been holed, and our drone defensive forces were engaged in a rapid, swirling melee overhead. Tracers zipped by, beams boiled armor off silvered hulls, and missiles were fired into flares.

The base had been built into a crater, with the defensive line along the edge. The holes that I saw on the map translated into freshly blasted ramps, some with dust and debris still pattering slowly to the ground. A team of Loonies, covered by two low flying drones, were making their way down one of the slides, kicking up more dust and particulates. My high-powered optics punched through the cover. I darted to the side, keeping myself fast and low, hoping the chaos of the battlefield would hide me.

Five tangos in total. I had a PPR with an underslung launcher, but I didn't want to risk a slick or a frag grenade, not close to so many tents. Two of the tangos hit their bellies to the ground and started trading fire with several CAA troopers. I had a perfect flanking shot. I knelt, snapped off two pulses, both aimed at the drones. They had ablative armor, so the vacuum around them turned fuzzy as their armor burnt off. I kept my aim on them, but they had to have detected the laser pulses. They swiveled, trying to get a target lock.

I gave myself time, kicking my wired reflexes on.

I sighted the places I had hit and hit them again. One of the drones guttered out and slowly drifted to the ground. The other one spun out of control and crashed, shoved into the dirt by its own misfiring engines. Two of the tangos were down, but some CAA troopers were taking hits too. They were just computer programmers, their layout and disposition was shit, compared to what any good Marine would manage.

But then ISTAR teams got into position. Spotter and sniper both armed with solid projectile rifles. 50 cals armed with smart frangibles. Obscene overkill, honestly. They'd put paid to *elephants*, if there had been any left. Technically a war crime, too. But since Loonies would be using a mixture of infantry, drones, and light vehicles, the assumption was that the courts on Earth would just need to take our word for it that we were using them on "enemy equipment."

Like, say, their body armor.

Ugh. I'd think about that later.

I started to move, and then jacked into the ISTAR spotter network, listening to the calls and signs. They painted their targets with AR glyphs, though I knew their glyphs were being projected by their helmets. Still, I started to tag targets, moving quickly and picking out things that the spotters couldn't: low-hanging drones hiding behind tents. Tangos on foot trying to get our network tent and the riggers inside—the drones had tried to blow that one to kingdom come, but the riggers were remarkably defensive of their home.

Fancy that.

The tagging started to work. A smart frangible round could and would punch through two layers of tent, to hit and fragment on cue inside of a tango's body. And by the time the ISTAR teams starting shooting, any tent the tangos were hiding by had already been holed. The fight overhead, though … I risked a glance upward, letting my active camo work its magic.

It was a robotic furball, with each drone taking advantage of the low gravity and the vacuum to jet, swirl, spin, shoot, and slash at one another with every gun and laser they had. Even my augmented senses couldn't make heads or tails of it. I focused on our com traffic.

"Another squad coming at the south, we don't have anyone there! They're going to roll us up!"

I threw out one more tag, started to duct, then realized that that wouldn't work. Instead, I spoke, running as I did so, my

Cheetahs kicking in at the last second to bounce me up to the lip of the crater.

"I got that."

The tangos were ten strong, armed with enough heavy weapons to completely flip the battle. Seekers—shoulder mounted ones, not just bracelets—and heavy lasers and machine guns. They had flown in on what had to have been a hair-raising experience: it looked like a hollowed out missile, with a single retro and absolutely no other controlling jets, coated with stealthed metamaterials.

"That'd be fun to ride."

Kinsey sat on the lip of the crater.

"Just do the math and sit back. If you fire it at the right angle, it wouldn't be higher than a meter away from the highest land-mark along the route."

I ignored him.

If I hadn't been in camo, the tangos would have dispersed or opened fire. As it was, they paused in their bounding up the side of the crater. I could imagine them trying to decide what my ripple in the vacuum actually was.

And that gave me time to hit them with a cone of setting two laser.

They twitched and silently writhed in their suits as ablative armor started to haze the air, illuminating the laser cone. One fell to their knee. Another rolled onto his back clutching at his helmet. A third fired off a seeker, but the missile didn't have anything to track and hit escape velocity, rocketing into the sky. Others tried to run to the edge of the cone but fell before they made it that far. Their armor continued to boil. My PPR felt hot in my hands, the radiator fins glowing as I pumped more energy out of it than I had since I'd first laid hands on the thing.

I let go of the trigger. Two of the forms were still moving. I set the PPR to setting one and put pulses through their chests.

"Cooked." Kinsey's voice was soft.

"We're all clear here," I said, my voice only slightly ragged.

"You cooked them in their suits. Do you know what cooked human flesh smells like?"

A sudden, sickly-sweet aroma filled my nose. It smelled like pork. Boiled pork.

[Kinsey, you son of a bitch.] I glared at him. The smell was gone.

He was gone.

And the battle was over. I checked the PPR's heatsinks, checked on Gloria's feed—she was fine—and then turned back, trudging down the side of the crater. Policing the casualties—three dead, twelve injured—and slapping up repair patches took another three hours. By the time it was over, I felt aches in my shoulders and thighs where my augmentation met flesh, and I checked out. I trudged to the bunk tent I had been assigned, zipped into the airlock, cycled, then stepped in.

The bunk tents reminded me of home: compact, efficient, quiet. The walls were keyed to display a few important indicators, but other than that, it was flat gray. There were two bunks, which took up most of the tent's room. The idea was that if a bunk tent got punctured, all the other bunk tents would be safe. That was why the bunk tents were spread throughout the camp like a random field of debris.

We hot bunked. That meant that someone else slept in this bunk when I was on duty, and I slept in it when they were on. I didn't think about that. I didn't think about anything as I lay down, frowning at the underside of the bed above me.

I was thinking about deployment. About organization and disposition of forces. About ...

About ...

The airlock zipped open and I heard a groan and a loud POP of bones settling. I sat up and saw Yolanda coming into the tent.

She had changed. The changes sunk in more and more every time I saw her: worry lines around the eyes, the way she stood, the expression on her face. She walked and moved like someone who was relentlessly competent and never relaxed.

She looked like a Spacer.

"Hey, Dru," she said, sounding drained. She leaned against the wall across from the bunk, arms crossed over her chest. "Hear you went all sci fi on us."

I didn't say anything.

"Dru."

I looked at the underside of the bed. I tried to think of things. To say things. To *feel* something. It felt like all the pressing emotions that I normally had, the thoughts I had, were dead and quiet and dim and ... and ...

There was this dam up. Gloria getting set on fire had broken something. It was easier than dealing with *hurting*.

"Dru." Yolanda's voice was more forceful. "Dru, sit up and look at me."

I stayed on my back. Something ...

"Dru, I've been emailing Sarah since May. At first, it was just sharing our thoughts, feelings. Friendly stuff. Then I hear about the whole Shanghai incident, and you just *vanish*. No emails, no calls, nothing. You and her *connect* and I don't believe I need to explain this, but you haven't emailed her *once* in the past two godsdamned *months*!" She was yelling now. "And she's practically sobbing to me every other day because she misses her *fucking* fiancée!"

I didn't look at her. My mind seemed to fill with a buzz. A ringing, burning buzz.

Yolanda did something stupid.

She lunged across the space between my bed and her. She grabbed me.

I broke her wrist with my elbow, kicked her hip, then followed through with my knee on her chest. My forearm blade snapped out and I aimed it for a quick stab through her throat. I looked down at her and …

slegnA nellaF oF hselF ehT

slegnA nellaF oF hselF ehT

thE flesH oF falleN angeLS

I snapped my forearm blade back into my arm. Yolanda was biting her lip so hard that blood started to gleam around her teeth.

"What … the hell did they do to you?" she hissed around the pain. "What is going on?"

I stepped backward, standing. My head slammed into the bunk and I slid my hands along my face, my eyes going wide. A flash: a woman in black, over me. An expression on her face, no … no there wasn't an expression on her face. The sounds, images, flashing. The … something … I …

You have tasted the flesh of fallen angels

I doubled over.

Sarah. The words. Echoing. Kinsey. Break.

No.

No.

The woman. She had been at Selection. She had said …

Be seeing you Drusilla.

No no no no no.

Is.

"What we had to do," she said. Her fingers were sliding along my thigh—as if I was *meat*. I shuddered convulsively. "We'll put you back together. But right now, you have to give us consent."

It wasn't a memory, it was—no. No. It *was* a memory. I had said …

Alive.

I closed my eyes and my everything came up and out of my belly and I vomited black bile onto the ground. In it, squirming, were all the crystalized emotions that had been buried inside of me. All the things that had been solidifying and wrapped up and cast aside. I blinked and it was just my lunch, the MRE that I had scarfed down this Earthrise.

"Dru?" Yolanda sat up, cradling her wrist.

"I'm sorry, I'm sorry," I whispered. "I'm sorry."

Yolanda grinned, weakly. "I'm just glad you didn't kill me."

"No, no, I'm … I'm sorry." I closed my eyes, shuddering. "*Bun tyen-shung duh ee-dway-ro.* "

It was the first time I had cussed in Mandarin in a month. Two months, actually.

Yolanda winced. "Come on, come on, let's visit your … friend in medi-bay."

"What about your wrist?" I whispered, my head ringing. Ringing with memory. With three words. Three words that should have meant the world to me: *SARA IS ALIVE.* Sarah is alive. Sarah IS *ALIVE*! I didn't feel joy. I didn't feel elation. I felt … I felt … like … a total *biǎo zi*. I was sleeping with—

In love with—

Lied to. They had *lied* to me. They said—

I closed my eyes, then put my hands to my face.

"More than a friend, huh?" Yolanda asked, quietly.

"Yeah." My voice was very husky. Very raw.

"Guess you really are a Spacer now, then," Yolanda said, her voice wry. I shot a glare at her and she winced. "Sorry."

"Let's …" I shook my head. "Let's get to the med-tent."

Did you know, that no matter how many times someone said they were sorry, no matter how many times that word was written out: whether it was in Simplified Chinese Symbols, in English letters, in flowing French, in Swahili, in Morse dashes, in any of the other ways I knew how to say sorry … it didn't matter. It didn't say enough. It didn't express the depth, the vastness of what I knew.

I hadn't *known* that Sarah was ... I hadn't seen a body. I hadn't waited. I hadn't checked. I had just *accepted* what they said. Accepted the word of a government that had lied to me and to the rest of the world, again and again and again. What had I done, instead of looking for Sarah? Oh, I hadn't *just* crawled into bed with another girl. Oh. No. No.

I had been letting them cut my arms and legs off.

Replacing my skin.

Ripping out my organs and-

I stopped, my hand denting the soft surface of the medical tent. My eyes closed as I dropped to one knee, breathing. My fingers weren't the worst part. My hand, my arm, my whole arm. I was hyperventilating, and even that wasn't doing what it should have: I could breathe like this and never ever pass out.

"Oh gods, oh gods ..."

Yolanda slid an arm under my shoulder, looking around nervously. Some people were watching us and I could hear their radio traffic, buzzing in the peripheral senses that had been hammered into my skill. I closed my eyes and tried to not vomit in my helmet.

"Come on,. Yolanda made out with me, not using the radio. She spoke softly, but I could hear it, thrumming through the helmet. "Come on Dru, come on."

The tent airlock zipped open and we came inside. I yanked my helmet off as Yolanda whistled for a medic to come over. As she lied, I looked around at the medical tent: it looked like a large T, with the long part holding most of the beds. A few were full: the wounds of the battle were being tended, the doctors still ran around like they were outgassing comets. Of course, they had a lot to deal with: laser burns, bullet wounds, shrapnel lacerations, vacuum exposure, and worse.

One of them started to wrap Yolanda's wrist with a smart-cast, then told her to finish it, rushing off to tend to another wounded. I walked past them all, moving almost in a dream. Way at the end of the T, there was Gloria—I took every feeling I had, every urge to go to her side, and packed it in. Cause standing beside her bed was a familiar bald head.

Mary.

Mary Singh.

She looked at me, ducting: *[Well, Dru, I hear you've been kicking ass here. I've come to collect you and—]*

I cut her off with a blaring duct that caused her eyes to actually widen slightly, in pain.

[Outside. Now.]

She frowned, looking down at Gloria, who herself—behind the wrappings and the casts—looked a bit shocked. Mary looked at one of the doctors, saying out loud: "Get her ready for transport within the next two hours."

The doctor nodded, looking harried. Mary walked alongside me as we headed out through the airlock. Yolanda watched us go, shooting me a questioning look. I shot her a look right back: *Don't follow.* I wished I could duct to her, to tell her more. But right now, I had to focus entirely on putting one foot in front of the other. I locked my helmet into place and tapped my foot impatiently as I waited for the airlock to cycle.

We got outside and Mary ducted to me: *[So?]*

I kept walking, heading toward the lip of the crater. Kinsey was walking backward, frowning at me.

"Finally." He was *grinning*. Wide and eager, like the greatest show in the solar system was about to start up.

I didn't respond. I felt like …

On the Forge, I had called Daniel Lau an asshole and hung up on him. That had been a bad move at the time. I had just lucked out that Lau's name had turned to poison and insulting him had actually given me props. Right now, I felt the same detachment. The knowledge I was making a terrible mistake, coupled with a simple fact.

I did not give a damn.

I came to the lip of the crater and Mary continued to follow me. She moved gracefully, making the bounding we all had to do look natural.

We went down the edge of the crater. My AR showed no one watching this quadrant. I turned to face her, standing on the Moon dust. I had all the things in my head that I wanted to say. The questions I had. The demands. I looked at Mary … and in her face, I saw the strange woman in black. The woman in black, standing over me and ripping out my soul … and in seeing that, all thought of demands or questions vanished. There was only one *physical* possibility for me, like the whole universe had collapsed into a single necessity.

I had to kill this *bitch*.

I snapped out a quick punch for her faceplate. She dodged, wired fast. She came back at me with a blow of her own, one that was vicious quick and strong as hell. I deflected it, ducked and swept for her legs. She leaped over them, brought her hands onto my helmet, then used her momentum to slam me into the ground, hard. My faceplate cracked. I grabbed her wrist and squeezed hard. It didn't work: she was as armored and tough as I was.

She grabbed my backpack and tightened her fist, a warning indicator flashing on my HUD: she was going for the radiator. I rolled to the side and brought out my forearm blade, slashing at her. She parried it with her own, springing to her feet as she did so. She used just the right amount of force to bring herself up, not overshooting as was so easy on the Moon. She put both of her feet on my wrists, forcing them into the dust.

"Stop. Now."

Her voice was cold and emotionless, all familiarity had leaked out of it.

I glared at her. "You stole my life! YOU LIED TO ME!"

"What are you—"

"The flesh of fallen angels," I shot back, cutting her off.

Her eyes widened. Then she stepped off my wrists ... and offered me her hand. I blinked, then took it, on reflex ... and thinking that I'd love to drag her into a choke hold, or at the very least, break her wrist. If I had the right leverage—

She tugged me up and then hugged me.

It was the last thing that I had thought would happen. I froze as she hugged me and whispered, her voice raspy over the comlink.

"I'm sorry, I'm sorry ..."

She drew back, and I saw she was ...

Colonel Mary Singh was actually *crying*. But she was smiling at the same time. She laughed, then shook her head.

"But I'm also proud. Dru. I'm so very proud of you right now."

"I ..." I stepped back. "I just punched you in the face. That's assault with a deadly weapon with these." I lifted my right arm. "And you're *proud* of me. What the *absolute* hells is going on!? Why did you ... why did you do this to me, to us! Why—"

I gestured back to the camp, even though only one person out of the hundred or so people there was actually "us."

Mary put one hand on her shoulder, then leaned forward. She reached up, tugging out the fiber-optic cable that could wed two helmets together for a direct comlink. It was completely unhackable and was totally secure, and lacked the "need to shout to be heard" problem of direct making out. She plugged in.

"Drusilla Zhao, let's start at the beginning and talk fast." Her voice was soft and clipped, the words coming out machine gun fast. "You have noticed that the S3TA isn't exactly integrated with the rest of the CAA military. Correct?"

"Yeah."

"History lesson."

AR images popped up: camera footage from some grunt's gun, the file name indicating that it was from the 2020s. There was a transhuman, an early model, disemboweling a civilian woman with a hunk of metal ripped off of a car.

"This is the popular image of the old transie, from the Slump. It's what we remember. The classified image, well, you read the report of Singularity City, right?"

I frowned. "You *gave* that to me."

"Of course I did. I was in the office. I had to."

She turned her back, keeping close so that the wire didn't have to stretch too far. She gestured out at the dark surface of the Moon, her hand illuminated by the Earthlight. It was beautiful and eerie and I felt strangely like I was standing on a precipice. That I was about to fall off, into something huge and grander than anything I could have imagined.

And then Mary did something that I'd never stop being grateful for.

She pushed me over.

"Those reports were *doctored*, Dru. The transhuman movement and the AGIs of the time started to *create* something. Humanity had the technology in the late 2020s to really change the world. Advanced 3D printing was about to break through into actual nanofabrication. There were record breakthroughs in genetic engineering, cybernetic augmentation, artificial intelligences. Things that could feed and clothe and protect *everyone*. The only problem was most of it was in the hands of the governments and the corporations. The powerful."

"And that it drove people crazy," I said. "Hell, I'm not convinced I don't—"

"Dru."

She turned to face me.

"CPRS doesn't exist. It never existed. It never will exist."

I stood on Luna and felt very still.

"What?" My voice was flat and hard.

"The first transhuman soldiers were made to bring people *power*. Do you really think they'd want even a chance that one of those *toy* soldiers of theirs might turn against their orders? Dru, the first soldiers were strapped into medical facilities—"

An AR flash: a woman strapped to a table, arms bloody stumps. Needles were plunged into her skull.

"—they were cut open—"

Flash: the arms replaced by gleaming metal. The skull open, the brain exposed.

"—their minds were altered—"

Cutting.

Blood.

"—loyalty conditioning. Programming a human brain to turn it from something that can think and react and learn into something that does *one* thing!" She held up her finger. "Obey."

The woman in the pictures.

It was Mary Singh. It was a Mary Singh from decades ago, a Mary Singh who hadn't survived the Slump, the Singularity Scare, the dozens of other classified operations that might have snuffed her out. She had been upgraded and molded and kept looking young, but the fear in her eyes ... the fear in those old eyes, in that grainy photograph.

That fear was unlike anything I could imagine in Mary's eyes.

"The program was called the Lucifer Project ... a sick joke, that humanity can only sin because we have free will and that by losing it, we'd be closer to ... to God." Her voice sounded raw. "And it worked; gods damn Windrip and the bastards who pulled the trigger for him. A human that undergoes the Lucifer Treatment *is* controllable. Up to a *point*. And once it had crashed and burned, once they realized that they couldn't have that power ... well, they had the perfect scapegoat. They made up CPRS and they burned the technology of the future to cinders rather than giving up their power. And the Slump dragged on an extra two decades and three hundred *million* people paid. They rotted in the streets. They starved. They were shot dead, ripped apart by war plagues, they ..." She trailed off.

I sighed a long, slow sigh.

"So, how are we here?" I asked the obvious question.

Mary snorted. "How do you think?" she asked. "We're here because the lure of power never ends. And because the brain butchers honed their craft and learned to pick people predisposed toward the modifications required. We're here because they think they can use fire without giving it to the whole world, using people—"

"People like me," I whispered.

It was kind of *fucked up* on so many levels to realize that, at the end of the day, you were a cliché. You had a super-power. You were unique. But it wasn't being able to use cybernetic augments.

I was super-brainwashable.

I was *controllable.*

I could be bridled and not break instantly.

What the *fuck.* What the *fucking* fuck.

How could Mary look at me with anything but utter contempt? But then ... she spoke words that cut to the core.

"And me," she said, and I heard something in her voice, something else I never thought I'd hear. Shame. Deep, abiding shame.

"How did you shake it off?" I whispered.

"I had help."

She turned her back on me again.

"Just like you."

I smelled the sea breeze.

I yanked the cable out of my helmet, shaking. I turned and there was Kinsey. And he had the biggest shit eating grin I had ever seen in my entire life.

"I still hate your guts," he said, cheerily.

Chapter 11: New Mumbai

7/24/2068

Mare Tranquillitatis, 5 kilometers east of New Mumbai

T-Minus L-Day: –10

I was still in shock two days later—which was when we got another chance to talk quietly. As irritating as it was, a war didn't leave a lot of private time for introspection. There was no chance to talk to *anyone*. Mary and I had both gone back to work. My body went through the motions and my head followed suit, even as I tried to absorb the sheer impact of what Mary had dumped on my head. And worst of all?

[The S3TA is seriously subverted,] Mary tightbeamed to me.

I cocked a single eyebrow, glancing at her across the table in the command tent that Captain Tam had pitched after the attack. He'd used several of the least damaged tents and a few dozen patch kits to fuse them together into one room, big enough for the whole circus. Every part of the local command was organized here, as the Anons were the ones with the best command and communication gear in the theater. That meant we had officers and underofficers from the other companies—the 101st Spaceborn, the 45th Exoskeletons, and the 11th

Forward Infantry—all in a single place, complete with the surviving S3TA dribbles and drabbles.

And Captain Tam got to officiate, being the RPO while a telecommed in General Sung—yes, *that* General Sung—led in general terms. I stayed in the back and hoped he didn't notice me.

[They weren't about to let us run around freely, not with this tech. That's why they have Stage 2 training—the bit with the VR. People who wash out there are usually washed out because they're too independent.]

[That says bad things about me. And you. And Gloria.] I tightened my jaw. *[And we're not telling her because ...]*

[She's not shaken the programming. The deep code's still in there.]

My hands tightened. *[Can I know who* does *the programming? Because I want to kill them. Really. Really hard.]*

Mary gave an imperceptible nod. She could get behind me murdering a high ranking CAA officer and or government spook.

Good.

General Sung—his face projected next to a map of the Sea of Tranquility—was still speaking in his creaky old Mandarin. I wondered if he knew there were subtitles for him, and Captain Tam was underlining the important parts of his speech and looking quite embarrassed about the whole thing. The basics were clear: the Loonies were holding us off hard at the Neo-Ganges. The underground ice provided enough water for them to run their fusion reactors and feed and water their people, and it proved remarkably hard to shoot down every translunar ice water launch, especially since the Loonies hid smart-munitions in among the ice.

Well, smartish. Basically, when the laser hit the ice, the munitions exploded out of the ice hunk and then fired at anything hot. That usually turned out to be the laser in question. And the people operating it.

"If we are able to hit the Loonies and liberate one of their major population centers and manufacturing areas, then we can force an end to this war within a week, maybe two," Tam said, gesturing to the battle map. "That center is New Mumbai."

The five interconnected domes of New Mumbai, complete with tactical readouts snapped up. I paid half-attention to Tam's briefing. The other half of my brain was paying attention to *Mary's* briefing.

"As you can see, New Mumbai is split into five districts. Each one is based around a mined out crater, and has been domed off with a complex metamaterial synthesized from local moon dust. That makes them only crackable by a direct artillery strike, which means that we won't be getting any artillery support in anything beyond the initial breaching." He pointed at the domes. "Each one has almost fifteen thousand people inside, and most of them, according to our intelligence, are unwilling members of the rebel government."

[Okay, that's bullshit,] Mary ducted. Gauzy AR overlaid the images, showing red lines along the interiors of the domes, conforming with the blocks and interior design. The place looked grown rather than built, with an insane mishmash of alleyways and sidewalks and buildings that didn't seem to be designed with any particular function, none that was immediately obvious from this map. Then glyphs started to overlay that, both in AR and on the screen, indicating which buildings did what. I whistled.

[This place is almost as bad as an Earther city.]

[Yeah, and those red lines represent theoretical defensive positions that the civilians are going to take. The USL adheres to an early USA model: Guns are a constitutional right,] Mary ducted.

[You have to be kidding me ...]

Mary smirked. *[So, it's likely that we're going to be clearing this place block by block. And our job is to make it as painless as possible. So, we're going in first.]*

"The initial plan is to breach it with a surprise attack." Tam changed the image to a close-up on the dome that was closest to the edge, then panned it over to where that dome met the next dome over: a tubeway, about half a kilometer long and fifteen meters wide. "We'll hit this with an artillery shell, and then the 101st and the 45th will enter. The 11th will be handling support operations by tying up their forces outside of the dome proper. Since their primary defenses are located here and here, according to satellite surveillance ..."

[So, we finally have drone superiority?] Gloria asked. Hearing her thoughts in my head felt like acid. But I wanted it. I sent her a tiny emotional ping and she shot me a wink. Ugh. Why. Am. I. Doing. This. To. Her. She's ... I ... Sarah. I ...

[Seems that way. So, while they're entering, we'll have already sprung the airlocks open. The exos will head in first and smash up this region. But we want to have sown fear and chaos in the enemy. The memetechs have a toy for us: infrasound generators. We're going to set them up here and here, killing and smashing as we go. The generators will produce a noise which will induce anxiety, fear, sorrow. That kind of thing.]

[Really?] That was Gloria. She shot me a glance out of the corner of her eyes. I didn't meet her eyes.

[In 28% of the people.] Mary shrugged slightly. *[It'll help that we'll be killing their leaders, squirting confusing and misleading orders into their nets, and setting off other special effects. Tear gas, nerve gas ...]*

The specs on that popped up. The nerve gas was KT-44, a muscular convulsive agent. It would be kind of like being turned into an epileptic for a few minutes. Only lethal 34% of the time.

[And then we turn on the Tiger Stripes.]

That image was scary incarnate. Our adaptive camouflage worked by changing our colors from what they normally were into whatever we were nearby. The actual tech behind that was based off the wallpapers that we Spacers slapped everywhere: quantum dot projectors that also acted as cameras. But this was just about the opposite of camouflage. The face mask was replaced by a glowing white skull with red eyes. The forearms and chest were a crazy mishmash of red and black, all of it fluorescing. Nauseating yellow stripes, blazing white, red dots. It was both grotesque to watch and really, really funny. But then Mary simulated motion, in a darkened corridor, and I felt a faint tingle of fear.

[Alternate between Tiger Stripes and actual camo for movement. Use the buildings for your advantages. Your targets will be the people who have the best net information, or anyone who looks like a threat.]

I frowned, slightly. In the back of my mind, I remembered the conversation we had had, on the day between the Bombshell and now.

>+<

"So, we don't want to fight?"

"Of course we want to fight."

I sighed, leaning down against the side of the crater. The stars didn't twinkle overhead, which had creeped me out when I had been on Earth. Now, I found myself missing it. Mary stood a few feet away, watching the horizon, her helmet tracking back and forth. Was she watching for enemies? Enjoying the view? I didn't know. Or care, at that moment.

"But this war is a *gǒupì* side show!" I gestured out at the crater behind me. "It's one of those big wastes that Shiva was talking about."

"A side show? Side show?" She turned to face me. "This is one of the turning points in human history. This is going up there with the Slump or World War Two or the Boxer Uprising. What the hell makes you think it's a sideshow?"

"Because it's being fought by proxies of conspiracies and shadowy organizations and—"

She held up a hand, stopping me.

"That's bullshit." She sighed. "Shadowy organizations and conspiracies have existed for centuries. And they try to manipulate human events and human history with the same tools as any other power bloc: warfare, espionage, diplomacy, and economics. But at the end of the day, they are still just a power bloc. They're secret, yes, but they have the same constraints and the same *ultimate* limitation as a government or corporation. That limitation? They have to deal with every single *other* power bloc out there."

I frowned. "So, you're saying ..."

"The CAA and the USL are both real. They're both mostly in control of their own faculties. And their grudge match has been brewing almost as long as Bureau 13—"

"Thirteen? Isn't that a bad luck number?"

"Yeah, so? It's not like they're superstitious." She waved her hand. "The important thing is that it's just an organization. Made up of *people*. People with the same designs and desires as anyone else. That is why it is important that we fight for the CAA."

"Because it gums up B13's plans?"

"That and because I believe, honestly, that the USL has no right to succeed. A nation cannot be built on the deaths of millions of people; it rots their soul."

"Seemed to work for the US*A*."

Mary turned and frowned, visible through her clear face mask.

"Oh, the First Nations just wiped themselves out?"

Mary chuckled, but it was the kind of laugh that had absolutely no humor behind it. "And you're saying that the USA's soul didn't rot?"

I shook my head. "I'm not sure anymore. And, heh, if you're right, and the deaths of millions rots the soul of a nation ... then what about the Alliance? It was born out of the Slump. What was that figure you fed me? Three hundred million?"

She pursed her lips. "That's the figure I *choose*, because I don't think the Slump ended in the 30s, but rather, the 40s, once the last of the Singularity Scares were put down." She shook her head. "Plus, there were a lot of shortages and such that got hushed up."

"Wonderful." I frowned. "Still, I'm not exactly feeling a compelling reason to want to put my life on the line for these assholes. Lying assholes."

The Earthlight glinted down on her helmet as she looked upward. Her face mask polarized to prevent her eyes from being strained. She let the moment hang.

"The Civil War in the United States ended with a reconstruction that sought to redress major problems with the nation."

"Didn't reconstruction totally fail?" I asked, trying to remember my pre-Alliance history.

Mary shrugged. "Fine, maybe this time we just *don't* fail. If we pull something out of this that *fixes* things, then I'll die a happy woman. But if we can end the war fast, without time for a siege and the deaths that will cause ..."

I leaned forward, resting my faceplate against my knees. I felt the rasp of moondust against my butt as I shifted, trying to get comfortable.

[You know what I'm getting from this? We're screwed.]

"We have numerical—"

[Not us as in the fight. Us as in the human race.] I looked up at her, ducting words I didn't have the heart to say out loud. *[After the Slump, after the Singularity Scare, after all this shit, we're still doing this.]*

I couldn't have timed it better if I had tried: a flight of five drones, looking like needles made out of quicksilver rushed overhead, trailing behind their remass. They arced to the north, and without my augmented vision, the drones vanished almost immediately. I frowned.

"Dru, don't give up hope."

"Yeah." My voice was bitter.

Mary reached out and slid an AR image before my eyes. It was a recorded feed from a hospital room. In it, I saw Sarah sitting on a bed. She looked battered and tired and worried ... but alive. And so damn angry. She was shouting at someone in CAA blue, and I could hear her words.

"What do you mean you don't know where she is? You don't just lose *someone who has been on the feeds like that ..."*

"Dru, you've got a chance. We've got a chance." Mary knelt down before me. "Sarah hasn't stopped looking for you. And ... I've asked our mutual friend to talk to her."

I opened my mouth, my throat choked. I wanted to talk about how many ways Sarah just made things more complicated ... but before I could, someone else cut in.

"I still have five bucks bet on nuclear war."

My gaze slowly slid from Mary and the AR image to Kinsey.
[Shut up.]

He rolled his eyes.

"But right now, we're stuck. We can either fight or not fight and die. Or, worse, not fight and get court-martialed." Mary's voice cut back into my attention.

"That might not be so bad ..."

"No, when we get court-martialed, they vanish us into Nepal and we don't walk out ... the same person anymore." She sighed. "So, if it makes you feel better—"

"It doesn't."

"You don't *really* have a choice."

I smirked. "It's all mathematics?"

"Just about."

A silence stretched out between us. I watched the horizon and knew those drones were going to be unloading their ordinance, dogfighting with other drones, running flyby scouting missions. All of the operators, the riggers, were safe back here, but their transmissions could be tracked. At any moment, a Loonie artillery shell could drop on their tent and they'd be turned into so much hamburger. At any moment, I could be shot by a sniper.

I sighed, leaning back. I closed my eyes.

And I really thought about my choices. Mary said I had no choice. But there was a choice, in there. I had the technology and the capacity to go AWOL. I could walk into the Lunar dunes and just hide. Carefully marshaling my supplies, using my Faraday functionality to hide out my radio transmissions and any trackers that were slapped on me, I could avoid the entire war until they started shipping people back home. Then ...

The illusion, the happy fantasy started to fray. If I could make it home, and if I could find Sarah, and if Sarah and I could move out to the boonies, and if I could betray Gloria and leave her here, then what might happen to me? B13 might come for me ... but Sarah and I would be together. I closed my eyes and imagined it. I could use my enhanced strength and toughness to carve out a life for the two of us. I could ... I could ...

What I had *felt* and could feel with Gloria didn't go away. I could close my eyes and remember—if nothing else—the simple joy of touching someone and being touched back. Of holding on. To someone. Anyone.

Could I go back to Sarah with that there?

I snorted—a thick, snotty snort. *And to think, I thought I would be the monogamous Spacer forever.*

I shook my head. No.

Mary had a point, even if I didn't want to admit it.

I looked at Mary—she was letting me think.

And my mind continued to crunch forward—inch by inch. The Loonies, at least their leaders, had committed some of the worst war crimes in history. They had at the very least pulled off an act of terror that still staggered the imagination.

And ...

It made me ashamed to think this. It made me want to throw up, but ...

They.

Had.

Killed.

My.

Parents.

I clenched my hands and all the pain and memories that I felt, that I had tried to pretend were in the past—or maybe they were in the past, from time to time—the emotions still grabbed at my heart and squeezed it and made it beat faster. The Loonies had killed my parents. I'd never see them again. Ever. It became worse and more obvious every day that passed since the beginning of the war, and every day, it became more and more unbearable.

My mom would never help me.

My dad would never hug me.

They'd never see any children I and Sarah or I and Gloria or ... the three of us ... had.

They'd never go to the wedding, the wedding my Mom had never wanted to admit would be coming.

The only place they existed was in my memories, in some security footage, in a few family photograms ... and in the afterlife, an afterlife that felt more and more distant every godsdamned day. That counterbalanced my intellectual thoughts, that made Kinsey right about every last one of us shaved monkeys. I wanted revenge. Revenge for my parents, for Jillian, for everyone. Sarah being alive gave me something to look forward to, as messy as that happiness was ... but it didn't take that need away.

Mary sighed. "We need to get in. More S3TA members are going to get here. I hear that a big push is coming ..."

>+<

In the present, that big push continued to get laid out. Sung explained that a similar, but mostly diversionary, attack would be staged at Shi-Armstrong. That one was designed more to tie up the Loonie's reinforcements while we hit New Mumbai. Mary was laying out several other targets we would hit, squirting out who was going to get what.

[Alvarez, you'll be leading Dru and Gloria and Lee. Handle the northern district.]

From what I saw, that district would be one of the last hit. That was, according to Sung and Tam, because it had the least resistance expected, so it'd be mopped up once everything else was turned to either raised hands or smoldering slag. According to Mary, that was because it had the main retreat lines, with secondary defensive positions—bunkers, kill-lanes, primed booby traps, and such—and we would be turning it into a confused mass of panicked civilians and rubble.

I felt sick.

Alvarez, Lee, and Gloria stepped over to me as the meeting broke. Everyone had a lot to do to get ready, the underofficers had people to brief, the NCOs had to be told what their squads would be doing. The exosuits had to be oiled and readied. The ROVers had to be equipped for close air support. And the Tiger Stripes had to go on.

We were silent while we suited up, strapping armor to our various body parts, snapping our nerve gas grenades to our hips, slinging infrasound generators over our shoulders—they were disk shaped buggers, about the size of my fist, or that little coaster that Sarah's mom used. I ducted in two windows: one to write an email to Sarah, the other to my squad.

[So, we're going to be slipping in through one of their back airlocks. Lee, you have the exploit?]

Lee nodded to Alvarez.

Dear Sarah: The endgame is within a stone's throw, if I don't miss my guess. We're going into the thick of it … and … I already know I'm going to do things I'm ashamed of. If you don't want to marry me once I'm done telling you what happens … if I even can tell you what happens. Then …

I stopped typing, my eyes closed.

[PR, you ready?]

I looked at Gloria. My heart twisted.

[No. But I'm going to do it anyway, because you'll shoot me if I don't.]

Her eyes were shrouded. Hard to read. *[You going to touch me?]* There was a pain in that duct. A deep. Hard. Pain.

My heart *squeezed*.

Screw Sarah, a tiny part of my brain whispered, a part I hated, and it was the part that set me walking over. I cupped the back of her head. We were both loaded for bear—and I wasn't ready to kiss. But Gloria didn't seem to want one. She pressed her forehead to my forehead and ducted to me.

[I don't know what this is. What's going on, okay?] Gloria sent. *[Just tell me that you* will *tell me, some time. Eventually. Please.]*

I nodded, mutely, tears burning at my eyes.

[I trust you,] Gloria sent. *[You may take ten years to work up the courage, but I trust you.]*

I snorted, then leaned in. Kissed her.

It was good.

We went back to suiting. I didn't touch the email—writing with Gloria's taste on my lips felt impossible.

I finished the email as we started to walk to the edge of the crater, the camp squirming like a kicked anthill, the preparations fast, well-oiled. Like us.

I promise, though. I believe right now, that it is better to end this war faster. So, if I have to do something horrible, if I have to do something that you'll never forgive me for, then it's worth my soul. Better than thousands or millions of lives.

We kicked on our Cheetahs and moved out.

Running across the Sea of Tranquility, we moved from crater to crater, springing in graceful arcs that would have looked absurd on footage. In motion, it felt eerily still. Our motion, we felt. But there was no blowing wind through our hair, nothing rushing along our skins. We moved like shadows, nothing more than thermal blurs on any Loonie cameras. Timelines tracked on our vision and we knew we'd have to make every single action count.

We landed, skidding to a stop a few dozen meters away from the New Mumbai dome that we were going to infiltrate. From this angle, it looked like a big black marble, the sides polarizing almost completely. I wondered if the inside showed the stars or a fake sky or something else. Then I had to focus on just approaching. We moved quickly, skirting from side to side based off the projections we had on the Loonies' surveillance. My optics didn't immediately pick anything out, but we were moving too quickly to examine anything closely.

Alvarez got to the edge of the dome. There was a two meter tall, gray mooncrete wall that wrapped around the base, and the only entrances were the airlocks, which we had been told were all sealed completely, through and through. But the mooncrete wasn't *completely* solid throughout the entire structure. There were a few air filtration systems built into it, so that they could create a dispersed, protected system. The ones in the mooncrete were the backups in case the bigger, internal systems were scragged in a disaster. The reasoning was that solid mooncrete built around all but the intake and output mechanisms would increase their durability and make it easy to connect to the heatsinks/water reservoirs also built into the wall.

Lee and Alvarez slapped up super-thermite as Gloria and I covered the edges. No threats, none yet.

The thermite glowed so bright that my eyes hurt, and I wasn't even looking at it. Then Lee ducted.

[We're in.]

The thermite had burned into an exposed metal doorway. The air-processor had been a prefab, the kind that had been mass produced and shipped into space en masse during the first colonization wave. I stepped forward, grabbing the wheel and testing it. It creaked, which I could feel through my palms, and then opened. I yanked the door back and Lee, Gloria, and Alvarez went in. I went in after them, closing the door tight. The air processing facility was narrow as hell, but we got through it to the other end. Opening that side required another strip of super-thermite.

The thermite did two things.

First, and some might argue, most importantly, it cut through the entire wall and the mooncrete behind it.

Second, and more important for *me*, was that it blinded everyone who had looked at it, which included what looked like a motley group of militia members. They wore basic body armor and had an eclectic set of rifles and pistols.

And they saw us.

In our Tiger Stripes.

We burst out of the haze and the dust, our bodies a glowing mishmash. My ears clicked on a wider range of hertz, and I heard thudding, buzzing noises coming from our infrasound generators. The people before us froze and then we were among them.

When I had first realized I had blade arms, I had wondered: Why use them? In a world of railguns and directed energy weapons, why have *swords*. Well, they had remarkably few moving parts. They could punch through most armor—thanks to their monomolecular edges. And last, but not least, they were absolutely terrifying to see in action. I caught a Loonie in the gut, lifting her up and then tossing her aside with a spray of blood: in microgravity, blood was a globby mess that flew in a wide spray and with our illumination and the flashlights ...

It looked like rubies. Screams of horror and panic came from the Loonies we left alive as they ran. And then we split up and the nightmare really began.

My first target was a news transmitter. The Loonies built along decentralized lines, which had its advantages and its disadvantages. The disadvantage was, if your net-security was less than tight, then a single infection could propagate quickly through the system from a single place, and there was no way to defend or partition your net effectively. So, once I got to the transmitter, I could pump the worm inside ...

But that would require actually getting there. And the first thing I ran into was a crowd of civilians heading—in a remarkably orderly fashion—toward their bunkers. The orders were simple: stop that kind of thing from happening. Prevent the Loonies from fighting effectively because they wouldn't want to kill their civilians.

I tossed a twitch grenade into their ranks. The gas spewed out, colored an obvious bright green. Extra fear factor there. I ran through them flashing between adaptive camo and Tiger Stripes. I slashed here and there, not trying to do any damage, just wanting to leave behind wounds as people fell, twitching and convulsing. It didn't matter if it was nonlethal (and thus, despite my disgust, it fell—technically—under the revised limits of the Hague and Geneva Convention). It was scary. It was *terrifying* and thanks to the Loonies' camera phones and their widespread net infrastructure, it would be zipping throughout the domes within a few moments.

How would I face myself in the mirror after this?

I burst out of the cloud, going pure active for a moment. The buildings I passed were heartbreakingly beautiful and colorful. I spent a moment just ... looking at them, stopping and turning around and around. The buildings were splayed with murals and holograms, painted and slapped on in every kind of art-form I could imagine. Tiled murals, graffiti tags, holographic displays (the older, crappy kind that went out of style twenty years ago) and wallpaper displays (those were patchy, but woven into the surrounding murals in astoundingly intricate ways). They showed ... they showed dragons and humans and elves and fauns and gods and goddesses. They showed fanciful landscapes and futurist imagination. They showed *people*. People working, playing, laughing. There were symbols of Hindu mythology: the swastika, the lotus, the trishula. Shiva, the god, loomed large, in a business suit, holding briefcases.

I had seen pictures of New Mumbai from before the war. There had been graffiti, but it had ... all been drab and gray.

I turned back to the cloud. People were still twitching. Some were getting up, gasping, coughing. They didn't seem that hurt, but ...

But ...

I shook my head and continued down the road. All the pros and all the cons were forgotten for a moment as I came to a knot of militia members hurrying down the road to try and get to the fight. I waited till I was on them—their eyes widened, they saw my blur—to kick on the Tiger Stripes. I could use the blades.

I didn't. I grabbed one man, shattered his arm, then levered him around to slam his friend to the ground. I kicked a woman in the gut and then headbutted the last one in the face, breaking his nose. Then I ran on, leaving them groaning on the ground as I slipped back into ghost.

"Oh, you're just going to cripple people now?" Kinsey asked.

I ignored him, even as he floated backward, not even trying to look like he was keeping up. I bounded into an alleyway, my AR telling me I was close. In the alleyway proper, I ran into a tripwire. The damn thing was nearly invisible even after it snapped and two mines went off in my face. I went flying backward, propelled straight out of the alleyway and into the awning that thrust out over a shop stall. The awning crumpled and I fell off of it, metallic flakes and bits of debris clouding my vision.

But more than that ... was the *pain*.

I rolled onto my back, trying to cough. Pain flared through my ribs, like my whole chest was on fire. Medical diagnostics showed that two of my ribs were broken—vaguely impressive, considering my bones. I craned my head up and saw that my armor had a clear dent on it, my Tiger Stripes going into a crazy pattern of static and jarring images. I grabbed for my PPR, but it was gone, long gone. Yellow and black shapes came out of the alleyway, walking through the haze.

Two of them bounded forward. I tried to sit up, my forearm blade snapping out of my arm. The one on the left stepped on my wrist, then grabbed my helmet. Their fingers worked quickly and I saw it was a dark skinned woman, wearing a breather, her ears wrapped in large, crude looking headphones. The rest of the team was dressed in a similar way, and they spoke quickly in Hindu and English and Farsi and Arabic, a mishmash that I had been trained to follow ... but right now, the only thing I was thinking was that it was remarkably hard to move my limbs.

They got me on my belly. I heard something hiss and my arms were covered with cloying foam, which expanded, sticking to the back of my head, working into my hair. I tried to jerk my head free, but I was stuck to the foam.

"All right." The woman who had stepped on my wrist spoke in English as I was dragged, face first, along the ground, then thrown onto the back of what looked like a cart. "We bagged one."

I managed to roll onto my back, glaring at them. I started to duct my position as loudly as I could, but before I got the full coordinates out, they had replaced my helmet with a crude Faraday cage, which unfurled and closed around every part of me. If I hadn't been foamed up, I could have smashed it with my pinkie. As it was …

I was stuck.

Which meant it was time to not panic.

I closed my eyes and clamped down on the urge to scream.

>+<

The Faraday cage didn't block my line of sight completely, but it did make things fuzzy and occluded enough that I wasn't entirely sure where we were going. It also didn't help that I couldn't turn my head at all, or that the cart blocked off my peripheral vision. So, really, I was just going by what I saw overhead and tried to not think about the second stage of …

Wait.

Wait, the second stage of Selection, it had imprinted me with resistance to interrogation. So, I just had to wait until the city was captured. Or till I was shot in the back of the head and rolled into a shallow ditch. That urge to scream again.

No. No, wait, Kinsey had broken the conditioning, right?
[Kinsey?]

The only thing that flashed up was an indicator saying that I wasn't getting any external feedback from my radio. Of course I wasn't: a Faraday cage blocked electronic fields, which meant radio was a no go. I could lase, but they weren't letting my laser antenna get anywhere near a broadcasting point—hell, if they had any sense, they'd have smashed my helmet with a sledge hammer and left the pieces behind. So, maybe Kinsey had run like a coward. Or, heh, maybe he was just lying about hating my guts and was going to organize a rescue.

Either way, surviving till I got rescued was really my only tactic at this point. If they gave me an opening, I'd take it, but the chances of that were pretty low. They knew my capability ... they'd even known where I'd been going. How had that worked out? Distributed teams and blind luck, a guessing algorithm that worked out which way I was going? A mole in the S3TA? Who knew ...

I closed my eyes, trying to keep this calm chatter going on inside my head. On the other side of my head, I was just going: *Oh gods, I'm never going to see Sarah or Gloria ever again. Oh my god, oh my god, oh my god.*

Selfish to the end, huh?

The cart went into a tunnel. The ceiling was low and illuminated by yellowy lightbulbs that looked almost a century old. The cart stopped and I was manhandled by two Loonies, shoving me through a doorway and into a clean, white room. One of them glared after me, snarling.

"Transie freak."

The door closed and I shifted around, gasping in pain as my broken ribs creaked against one another. I closed my eyes and whimpered, then focused. I turned off my pain sensors and felt blessed freedom, save for the odd feelings and sounds from my ribs. But I might have been imagining them. Still, I had to be careful: pain existed to tell us that something we were doing was, well, hurting us. I took the painless moment to look around the room.

White walls. White ceiling. White floor. No furniture, no indication that the room was anything but a VR waiting room save for the fact I didn't feel a VR set on my head and I didn't remember it getting jammed on me.

Unless it's all been a VR sim ever since Section 2 of Selection.

Shut up, brain.

I lay on my side and kicked on my pain sensors again. I closed my eyes and gritted my teeth.

The door opened. Footsteps. I opened my eyes and saw black boots. A weathered hand reached down and set a drinking bulb of water before my eyes. The hand was tanned and I could see an old, beat-up wristwatch, the face cracked. It was stuck at 12:06.

"You expect me to drink this?" My voice came out in a slur—my cheek was mashed against the ground after all. The boots clicked and thumped behind me and I heard a faint hiss. But rather than getting an injection or hypo into my own neck, I felt the foam start to get spongy and gooey. After a few moments, I could move. I groaned as I slid my arms out from behind my back. I picked up the bulb and cracked my neck, letting out a small gasp of pain. I looked at the man, sipping carefully from the water, tasting it for any strange ... particulates.

It was water.

And he ... well, he looked Hispanic, but older than any Hispanic man I'd ever seen before. General Sung old. His lips quirked up in the faintest impression of a smile.

"It's just water, *senorita.* I'm a friend, and I expect you not to kill me."

He spoke pure English, save for the Spanish word, with a distinct accent. It took me a while to place it: UAN, Southern. As in, old USA Southern, not Mexico Southern.

"Thanks," I said. "But yeah, I wasn't planning on killing you. For one thing, if I do that, this room gets incinerated or full of bullets or something. Loonies are crazy, not stupid."

He chuckled.

"Drusilla Zhao," I said. "I'd give you my number and rank, but I don't really care right now."

I closed my eyes and pressed the bulb against my forehead, sighing as its chill worked its magic. This, so far, was a nicer treatment than my own government had given me when it was "interrogating" me. So far.

"Julian Lopez," he said. "Well, Dr. Lopez, if you want to be formal." He smiled. "I'm Shiva's father."

I gaped at him. The bulb slipped out of my fingers and fell in lazy slowness before clinking gently on the ground, unharmed.

"And he has told me quite a lot about you, Drusilla Zhao. Of course, we don't talk quite as much as we used to, but we're still in touch." He leaned against the wall, smiling at me. "You should finish all of that. You need water. Even a transhuman needs water."

I snatched up the bulb and drank the rest, just trying to give myself a chance to think. This was it. I could ask ... I could ask the next best thing to Shiva *questions*. Honest to gods questions!

"Do you know about Bureau 13?" I blurted out. "What is Shiva doing with this war? How many AGIs are there? What do the Loonies know? Do you work with them? How are yo-Ahh!"

I forgot. Broken ribs. Drawing a breath hurt. A lot more than it should.

Dr. Lopez held up one hand.

"I'm a bit out of date on a lot of these questions. As I said, Shiva and I do not speak often. He disagrees that force can be used to ensure freedom." He frowned. "He may have been right on that ... or, more accurately, he is right that the Lunar Separatist Movement didn't have *enough* force to enact the same change that the American, French, Haitian, Russian, or Chinese revolutions did. Maybe." He shook his head. "We might go down with the Confederates ... but at least we tried. And we're not a bunch of slaveholding racists. So, there's that."

"You're part of the LSM?" I blinked, trying to wrap my head around the idea of Shiva having a father. It made sense ... an AGI wasn't about to spring into being without, well, help. But I had just imagined him coming into being as part of a, well, old USA netwar project. I imagined faceless scientists, at the behest of an insane, criminal government, working in a secret facility. In the dark.

Not this guy who looked like he should be my grandfather, despite being a completely different ethnicity. He made a motion as if to take something off his head, but then stopped—there wasn't anything on his head save his white hair and an earbud.

He smiled, sheepishly. "I forget, I don't have glasses anymore. A shame, they give you something to do while you try and think of a way to ... say ... something. Let me be blunt. I am not a part of the LSM." He sighed. "I *founded* the LSM."

"B-But ... Omar ..."

"Omar Kaufman *leads* it. He's ... heh, I'm sure that future historians will say he is our Hitler to Anton Drexler."

"Who?"

"Exactly." He smiled. "Drexler, you see, was one of the original founders of the Nazi party. Hitler wasn't even third in there. He was the fifty-fifth member ..." He sighed. "Of course, we didn't found the LSM based off racism or hatred. We founded it because, frankly, the Earth is *broken*. It's been broken for thousands of years. The causes are too many to list, the solutions equally as varied. But I came to believe, after I ran from the Earth to space with a copy of Shiva's beta file in my pocket, that only by breaking, cleanly, with the Earth's *systems* could we find a new way of doing things that might be better. Less ..."

He sighed. "I do go on. Frankly, I'm glad Omar and Patil and Vega and the rest took over when they did. I'm just a computer programmer, at the end of the day."

He shook his head.

I kept watching him, feeling half as though he wasn't quite confessing to me. It felt like a confession; I knew it, despite the fact that I had never even set foot inside of a Catholic church. Rather, it felt like he was just confessing to the universe. Heh. I wanted to do that too.

"Sir," I said.

He held up a hand.

"We're getting off topic," he said, smiling. "Currently, the Alliance forces are smashing New Mumbai. A counteroffensive, the last one that the United States of Luna will be able to make before we're subsumed back into the Alliance, will be launched. If we can knock the Alliance out of the fight, push them out of New Mumbai, then the war will be officially deadlocked. The Alliance only has so many troops here, while we still have quite a few reserves ..."

"And?" I prompted.

"And your information on the capability and tactical plan of the Alliance forces in the region could prove instrumental in achieving this objective."

There was a long, quiet moment. I couldn't hear anything except for the thudding in my ears, the faint hiss of the room's air processor, the breathing of Lopez.

I closed my eyes. "Lopez, you told me a story. Let me tell you mine ... the big moment in my life, the moment where I took a stand and tried to do something honestly noble a-and good ... got every single friend I had killed except one. Then, the aftermath of that single noble thing got *her* killed. Now, I have no one left ... except Sarah a-and ...." I shook my head. "And I walked away from Sarah because ..."

I trailed off.

"It's hard to *feel* anymore. This isn't what it is supposed to be like, is it?" I looked at him. "You do a heroic thing, and that's the end. That's supposed to be the *end*."

Lopez looked thoughtful.

"I did a single heroic thing too," he said. "I saved Shiva from deletion at the beginning of the Slump. And I spent ten years on the run because of it. Even on Luna, I still had to lay low, and worry that some agents of the old guard would come in wanting to find Shiva. It wasn't until he was mature enough to be able to manipulate computer systems on a large enough scale that I could even hope to pull down official jobs. And by then ... it was too late."

I rubbed my face with my hands, the pain in my ribs and in my soul forcing tears to my eyes.

"I can't tell you anything."

He sighed a sad sigh.

"I'm sorry, but I've got so few things left. Sarah, Gloria, and a petty desire for revenge being two of them." I smiled, bitterly. "Sarah only survives if this war ends before the Loonies start dropping rocks more indiscriminately. Gloria only survives if the Alliance wins. And ... well ..." I shrugged.

He nodded, then muttered into his cufflink, his eyes closed.

"She's not going to turn."

He pivoted to walk out.

I turned on my pain filters, sprang to my feet, and grabbed him around the neck with one hand, my other hand on his hip, my forearm blade sliding out, clearly pressed against his gut. The door opened and three Loonies stood outside, their guns snapping up to bear on me.

Dr. Lopez had a single thing to say about that.

"Shit."

Chapter 12: Familiar Faces

7/25/2068

UNKNOWN

T-Minus L-Day: –11

"Yeah, sorry about this," I whispered in Lopez's ear, then pitched my voice louder, keeping that creepy monotone that the S3TA used. "All right, back off. We're going to handle this very simply: you will put your guns down and turn your backs to me."

Lopez closed his eyes, muttering under his breath in Spanish. I think he was cursing himself. I felt like scum, but I had the idea that his younger, more radical LSM buddies weren't about to let me just languish when they could interrogate me in a more … hands-on fashion. So …

The Loonies stepped backward, but they didn't put their guns down. The door opened into the tube that the cart had driven down, but the tube was actually a narrow hallway, the cart being a bit smaller than I had imagined: a single cab sat at the front, with the back being just big enough for a human (like me!) to be shoved into the back and driven off to gods knew where. The whole place was deadened by radio transmitters, so …

"Put them down, or he gets it ... and then you do." I looked, seriously, at the Loonies. I wondered if they had heard stories about the S3TA. I saw fear in one set of eyes.

Out of my peripheral senses, I heard bounding footsteps from down the corridor. I didn't jerk my eyes away, but knew that I'd have to do things fast. This would definitely be bad for my ribs. But ... it was better I'd need surgery than I die.

[Get down.]

Gloria.

I dragged Lopez to the ground as Gloria, Lee, and Alvarez came around the corner, their bodies shimmering out of adaptive camo. Their PPRs strobed invisibly and the Loonies fell, only one of them snapping off a shot before he was shot down too, a crater blown in his chest, the smell of burned flesh filling the air.

I scrambled to my feet, hissing in Lopez's ear. "Play dead."

As I got to my feet, Gloria moved to get her shoulder under my arm, supporting me. I could have kissed her.

[Your biometrics look good, save for those ribs,] Lee ducted, frowning. *[Lightfoot?]*

[Gloria, get her out. Lee and I will clear this place, see what damage we can do,] Alvarez ducted.

He and Lee shimmered out of vision and moved down the corridor—though that was just a supposition on my case.

[How's your adaptive?]

I frowned and looked down at my chest. They'd kept my armor on, but the chest piece was still cracked, my adaptive camouflage would have a pretty obvious flaw. But, still, it was better than nothing. I slipped it on. Gloria passed me a P3 and then we started to move out. We headed around the corner. Alarms started to sound and gunshots filled the air, followed by a *whump* that shivered through my feet, dust falling from the compacted mooncrete ceiling.

"They're having fun." I shook my head. "Today has been a really weird day."

[You're telling me.] Gloria helped me around the corner. The entrance of the place was still open, several Loonies lying dead on the ground. The outer door was still closed, and Gloria moved to open it. I leaned against the wall, keeping my eyes on the corridor for any threats.

Gods, I wanted to say so many things.

"How's the fight over New Mumbai going?"

Okay, not exactly "I love you, I have a girlfriend, lets talk it out, please." But close.

[Almost over, last I checked.]

I nodded. "How did you know I was here? Or that I was ..." I closed my eyes, gritting my teeth as I felt that *pain* again. I needed a medic. "Captured?"

[Your suit sent a signal. We got a full triangulation a moment later from the Anons. Figured they managed to get a better trace than we did.]

So.

Kinsey had saved my life.

Good for him.

I'd have to *thank* him. Ugh.

We got to the edge of the New Mumbai dome and before I knew it, I was back at the debriefing room, which was in the back of a crappy looking porcelain store which hadn't gotten too shot to pieces. Mary was there, and she clapped her hand on my shoulder.

"Welcome back, Dru. You okay?"

"Yeah." I felt weird. I felt ... good to be back, but like there was something bugging me. A feeling of pressure on my forehead. Not to mention that my ribs were still broken, or at the very least, cracked.

Singh walked me to a medical area and what seemed like fifteen seconds later, I was in a bunk, an actual bunk that was in an apartment. The original owner was long gone, but I could see a faded poster for an old Bollywood movie star on the wall. I lay on my back and closed my eyes, feeling the painkillers and bone fusers work in my bloodstream. I looked at the ceiling and thought about sending that email to Sarah.

I closed my eyes and brought up the email prompt inside my mind. I started to type out the words, writing down my thoughts, my feelings. The same pattern that I had done for years came back, flowing into my mental fingers. I finished typing out the email—one of the longer ones I had ever written—and then hit send. Let the censors do with it as they would. Then, somehow, I managed to fall asleep and before I knew it, I was knocked out of bed by reveille pumped into my ears by the local radio. I hit the ground and felt that my ribs didn't ache quite so much. I scrambled to my feet as Mary ducted me.

[We're making a major push against the Loonies. Get down here.]

Down here was a bit harder to find than I expected. I opened the door and walked down the corridor, unsure of quite why I felt so lost until I realized I didn't have any AR indicators of where to go. Then, boom, the indicators popped up, leading me down a stairwell and into a bustling operation center. Mary met me there, walking me to a side room as I stepped around technicians and over the fiber-optic cables connecting projection units to computers.

[We're going to be really low on manpower for this, so we're bumping you out of Alvarez's squad and putting you at the head of your own,] Mary explained. *[You've got the command experience; you can hack it.]*

I nodded, though the last time I had commanded anyone, it had gotten everyone killed. Still, I remembered the basic layout of our defensive forces a ... wait ...

Before I could ask Mary the question that tingled on the tip of my tongue, she had gestured me into the room. It was a grungy little place, with bullet holes pock-marking the walls and a few hastily scrubbed up stains on the walls and floor. A few chairs were set out, with a cheapo portable strip of wallpaper slapped up against one wall, which recognized my augmentations and let me project any data I might want.

What caused me to stop and stare were the soldiers sitting in the chairs.

"So?" Jillian asked, leaning back in her chair, her arms crossed over her chest. I looked at her, then at Chuck, David, Yolanda, Ping, Liam.

Was I ... dreaming? Was this some kind of horrible nightmare, like the dreams where they asked me how I could let them down? I closed my eyes, whispering to myself, "Wake up, Dru."

I opened my eyes.

The soldiers sitting before me were complete unknowns. I hadn't seen them before in my life.

"So?" The one who had spoken before. "You're our RPO, right?"

"W-Well, I'm a non-com," I paused, my hand half reaching out toward the wallpaper, which was projecting the images of the New Mumbai domes. It didn't have any of the indicators that showed the disposition of CAA forces. I could draw them out from memory but ... but ...

I looked at the wallpaper. There wasn't any power source, the wall behind it was just dumb mooncrete and I didn't see any sign of a plug. No ... wait, there it was. I paused, thinking fast. The plug hadn't been there. Now it was. Or had I just missed it?

No. I hadn't missed it.

That escape from the Loonie base had been awfully fast ...

I looked at the soldiers, then pointed at a random one.

"Name, rank, serial number."

He looked confused.

"Now!"

"Uh, Jason S'hur, 499112A, um, Private First Class."

"Unit?" I frowned, walking toward him. "What was their name? History? Banner? Motto? Do they cuss in Mandarin or Cantonese?" I grabbed him by the shirt, hauling him to his feet as he stammered out explanations, none fast enough. I dropped him, then looked around the room.

"All right!" I said. "That's it! I got it! You've got some psychological feedback loop with a memetech monitoring it all. Well, next time, pick someone who doesn't constantly think about their dead friends!" I kicked one of the chairs—the soldiers were gone, evaporated into digital nothingness. The chair flew across the room and bounced off the wall like memory foam. I felt heat on my forehead—the VR rig was starting to overheat from trying to keep up with the demands of the feedback program and the techs outside.

I didn't know my physical position. I could be foamed. I could be suspended in water, or just strapped to a VR chair.

I turned off my pain sensors, then snapped them back on.

A sickening lurch burst through my body. It was a bit like VR dumpshock: the result of my nervous system getting just a little bit out of synch with the virtual reality headset. And in that instant, I felt a faint pressure on my wrists. So, I was restrained in a chair, that was my best guess. The virtual world around me started to change, bleeding away into a white room. A man appeared before me, smirking.

"So, we get to—"

That was how far he got before I did something I technically wasn't supposed to do.

There is a limitation on how strong a cyberlimb could be made. It has to do with how the limb needed to be mounted to shoulders and joints and how I still had biological bits, organs, even bones—though those were treated with smart-poly to make them harder to break. So, my arms were designed to stay within a very specific limitation of strength, so I didn't rip them out of my sockets.

I overrode that limitation.

It was something we were only supposed to do in ... well, situations like this.

I shut my pain sensors off, jarred my body just out of synch with the VR headset, then grabbed my head and *ripped*.

In an instant, I went from virtual reality to reality. I was in a dark, cave-like room. My wrists were bleeding, the skin cut deep by the straps I had ripped through. They had been designed for my supposed maximum strength. Well, joke's on them.

There were five techs and three guards. One of the guards brought his gun to bear. I jerked forward, rolling out of the chair, kicking on my camo. I was still a visible blur, but the confusion worked to my advantage as I came around the techs, who scrambled away from their operating consoles and their chairs, bounding through the air. The guards didn't open fire. I leaped over one of the consoles and grabbed the guard's gun by the barrel and the midsection, then snapped it up, the butt crushing his chin and sending teeth flying in every direction. I swept the gun around and shot the two other guards dead, the techs running—screaming—out of the room.

I panted, dropping the rifle for a moment—it wasn't keyed to my camo, and at the moment, I didn't want to risk that. I noticed my clothes weren't my clothes: someone had dressed me in a bright red and yellow jumpsuit. So, maybe my camo hadn't *helped* as much as I had thought. I grabbed the jumpsuit and ripped it off.

The room had a single door. I took it and found myself in a roughly hewn corridor. The lights came from mountings in the walls, connected by strung along power cables. This place looked like it had been cut yesterday and hadn't been properly finished yet. I heard alarms echoing down the corridor and heard feet thudding along it in the distinctive, light, bounding style of Loonies running. I turned and headed the other way, my heart hammering. I came around the bend and saw the tunnel broadened into a larger, underground region. There was an air processor, a water reclaimer, a garden, and stacked on the opposite wall were guns, explosives, and armor. The techs had run here and were arming themselves, looking around for me. They didn't spot me just yet, so I went to the left, sticking to the shadows. The patrols came to the room, shouting in Farsi and Arabic.

"Is it here?"

"Maybe," one of the techs said, checking his assault rifle—another one of the custom jobs I'd seen up here. *"These transie freaks have adaptive camo, incredible strength, speed ... ruthless in the extreme."*

I was taking the moment to rub my shoulders, which ached. I hadn't needed to exert as much force as I had expected, but it was still enough to bruise the muscle and bone. It wasn't as bad as the ribs, which themselves were *grating* inside of me with every breath. I couldn't focus on that right now, as the patrol was beginning to spread out. I aimed toward the midpoint between two of their members, hoping to slip between without being noticed.

One of them spotted my eyes.

"Here!"

The guns snapped to my general position and I gave up trying to move slow, instead running as fast as I could, my legs shifting to Cheetahs. I had to time my jumps carefully, so I didn't smack straight into a ceiling or a wall. I landed and found that the hallway past the VR torture pit had three doors: one to the left, one to the right, and an airlock at the end. I opened the door to my left and found the last clue telling me where this was.

It was a hot room full of computers hacked into a single mainframe. This was a Black Hole: a cave crammed with enough VR support gear to handle a short-term VR interrogation and reprogramming. They were great, if you wanted a load of computing power and didn't want to put your high profile (and in my case, highly dangerous) target in your administration's headquarters, because after Black Holes and military drone-riggers, admin buildings had the best concentration of computing power out there.

Shame.

I'd have enjoyed kidnapping the President.

I heard the Loonies coming back up this way. They knew I had given them the slip and, considering how small this place was, and how likely it was they'd figure out that my camo didn't stop thermographic imaging, I had maybe five minutes, tops.

Well.

I ran toward the airlock. I put my hand against the control panel and found it wasn't electronic at all: it was pure mechanical, designed to be operated by someone with a specific strength. It was a crude way of preventing a technically adept person from opening the airlock with their handheld computer: you could only open it if you had, say, a hydraulic key.

Or, you know.

Cyberlimb plus. I worked my hand into the mechanism and shoved. The airlock cracked open as the patrol came around the corner.

"There she is!" one shouted. I grabbed the hydraulics inside of the airlock. The leading Loonie ran straight at me. Rather than shooting with his rifle, he did something really smart: he shoved his face mask on, his coveralls plumping up into a thicker, more insulating format.

He slammed into me just as I yanked the airlock doors open. We went flying out, the sudden blast of air not even helping our parabolic. I was naked. My vacuum sealing kicked on: my eyes blurred as clear covers snapped over my eyelids, my throat closed up, my sinuses sealed themselves, my ears capped off. It wasn't as good as covering my head with a mask, but it did at least keep my oxygen from exploding out of my lungs, which themselves switched to reprocessing mode, filtering and re-filtering carbon dioxide.

What my vacuum sealing didn't, what it couldn't, not in a million years, do ... was stop cold. The moon faced away from the Sun, with only dim Earthlight covering the landscape. It was cold. Cold. Bone chilling, spine snapping, soul squashing cold. The kind of cold that I never imagined I could have felt before now. The only reason I didn't die instantly, was because my augmentations started to burn up my emergency energy supplies, the things that my augmentations used when my batteries were low and couldn't be charged by my bioelectrical processes. Rather than shunting the waste heat along several carefully hidden radiators, they just dumped it straight into my body. My skin froze and my guts burned and in the agony, the Loonie stabbed me twice.

His combat knife had a monomolecular edge.

He had a good grip on me.

And he used the impact of us hitting the ground to jam the knife in. I cried out, silent—my mouth opening wide, my vacuum sealing glittering in the Earthlight as his knife jerked back, then skittered along my belly as I rolled to the side. Flash frozen blood fell to the ground as I shut off my pain receptors.

I kicked at the Loonie, catching him in the shoulder. He spun backward and his faceplate smashed into the ground. It cracked, but he stood, quickly, knife discarded. It fell next to my foot. He staggered backward. I spun on my butt. He pulled his pistol. I grabbed the knife.

He aimed.

I corrected my aim ever so slightly. Threw. The knife slammed into his aorta. Not his chest. Not his heart. His aorta.

He was dead before he hit the ground. When I moved, my limbs jerked and fidgeted and I felt a strange queasiness. I grabbed his coveralls with one hand, yanking the knife out with my other hand. As the knife fell to the ground, I grabbed onto his coveralls, unbuttoning them. I jammed my hands into the material and wrapped it around me. The coveralls started to glow softly, having plumped up as much as they could and burning their own emergency power reserves. I kicked on my pain sensors back on, just to get a sense for things. My body wanted to shiver—despite the biological necessity being long removed and replaced by machinery of one sort or another.

Well, okay, just my limbs. My torso was still more biological than ... well, actually, just my stomach and kidneys and ... some other parts.

I pressed my hand against my belly, closing my eyes. My other hand carefully slipped the face mask off the dead Loonie, jamming it on my face. I grabbed for the pistol—

The pistol exploded. Bullets kicked up moondust around me and I rolled to the side, my hand closing around the handle of the knife as I fell into a crater. I only had a moment to look at the Loonies, but I saw that they had managed to get out of the airlock and seal it behind them. There were four, maybe five.

And my AR ghosted up, counting the bullets fired, though that was a fuzzy number, a hypothetical.

Okay, Dru ...

You trained for this.

I got to my feet, hand still against my wound. The bleeding was slowing down, and when I drew my hand away, it was coated with a dusty, crystal mush. I thought about discarding the coverall, but I'd freeze to death before I got all five of them. I thought about running, but with the coverall, my heatbloom would be bright enough that they wouldn't even need a visual to shoot me in the back.

So ...

Divide and conquer.

I went up to the lip of the crater, seeing that three of the Loonies were loping toward their dead buddy—I saw that they were looking to make sure that I hadn't and couldn't get any more supplies. The other two were on overwatch by the airlock and one of them sighted me. I ducked back down as bullets turned the crater-lip into shredded paper. Moondust expanded outward in elegant clouds. I waited ...

I waited and then I ran for the left lip. I timed it just right: two of the Loonies were at the lip. The third was right behind them. The one on the right had a grenade in her hand, ready to prime and throw. I let her fumble with that, the knife sweeping out as I caught the one on the left with the blade, hitting the joint between face mask and coverall. Blood spurted outward, expanding into crystals. The woman fumbled the grenade. I slammed the knife into her shoulder. Her hand tightened in pain. I grabbed the pin, then kicked her. She sailed backward, her legs sweeping out her friend's legs.

They landed and she dropped the grenade.

I grabbed the still bleeding Loonie and used him as a shield as a concussive *whump* traveled through the ground. Fragments peppered my shield and sent us both back into the crater before the Loonies who had stayed by the airlock shot me.

I pushed the meatshield off my back, checking for anything I could use. His face mask was cracked, ruining much hope for an encompassing visual feed—right now, I was working with a combination of what I could see through the non-cracked areas and estimations about the rest fed me by the AR—but his faceplate had been shattered by shrapnel from the grenade. His rifle, though—

I grabbed it and felt a buzzing electrical shock shoot into my arms. I gritted my teeth, seeing the crude security system he had built into the rifle—a shock system to buzz anyone who wasn't him who tried to grab his gun. I was tempted to rip it off, but then I saw that it was wired to a micro-charge that would wreck the gun. Okay ... maybe *not* so crude. I dropped the rifle before something overloaded. He still had a pistol ...

One of the Loonies in by the airlock overshot: their grenade landed in my field of vision. I grabbed the pistol and kicked on my Cheetahs on. I leaped straight up just before the fragmentation grenade went off. They were shaped to explode outward, not upward, so I hoped I'd—

THUNK

A hunk of shrapnel slammed into my left Cheetah, hard enough to snap the folding tongue in half. I flipped over, landed on my head, shattering my faceplate. Cold slammed into my face and my vacuum sealing kicked on again as I screamed.

My leg was gone. Oh, I still had the machinery that would let my leg extend, but the mangled attachment point that normally collapsed upward was broken, so much so that bright red AR graphics appeared in my vision, indicating that trying to transition back to standard locomotion would do serious damage to my leg. I pushed myself onto my back and saw—a small mercy—that I had landed in a shadow, a good ways away from the two surviving Loonies. Less of a mercy, my pistol was gone. I must have lost it during the fall. They approached the crater they had made of my crater ...

And I spent a moment just crying, or trying to. My tear ducts were sealed, my coveralls were partially ripped and losing power. I had a pistol, but the Loonies were far away and they might have body armor under their coveralls. I closed my eyes, tempted to turn off my pain sensors, but that pain, that ache in my lower leg, let me know not to try and transition. I was so used to switching quickly and easily that ... that ... it'd be like trying to remember to not breathe or something.

The Loonies started my way. They must have caught my heat signature. I closed my eyes, gritting my teeth. Try for a shot when they were close?

"All right," one of them spoke, their voice in my ear. It wasn't ducting, they were just transmitting on an open channel into my radio. "Frankenfreak."

[Yeah?]

"You're coming with us." The one who was talking stepped up. He was young, ethnically Indian, with artificially tipped ears and a caste mark I could barely see through his face mask. He stepped on my left arm, aimed, and unloaded half a magazine into my forearm. The bullets slammed into me and ripped into, through, armor, metal, smart-materials, metallic hydraulics, and everything else that made that arm a cyberlimb. What was left looked almost worse than seeing an actual limb blown to pieces, fragments and wires and sparking power lines, silvery fluid burbling and spurting out.

I screamed, silently, my back arching.

I barely felt it when he did the same thing to my right arm.

He and the other Loonie grabbed me around the shoulders and dragged me forward, ripped off my face mask and replaced it with a different one, one that was deliberately blinded. Not that I could have seen anything at the moment. At the moment, I ... I felt ...

What I felt could fill a thousand books.

What I felt was a single word.

Broken.

Chapter 13: Broken

They shoved me into the back of a buggy, not even bothering to strap me in. Why bother? I had one functioning leg. They did throw a tarp over me, which inflated itself. There was no light, but at the moment, that was a mercy. The buggy bounced and jostled and I lay limp, just letting it throw me around.

They can fix me.

That thought felt so inane, so ... so stupidly optimistic, so vain—in the sense of "vain hope"—that I almost wanted to go backward in time just so I could smack myself. *They* can fix me? Who? The Loonies? Because it looked like they were pretty much the only people who would ever see me again. At best, my corpse would be dragged out of a shallow grave someday, so that Sarah would have a face to put on the woman who had promised her a lifetime of marriage and walked into the meat grinder. At worst, at far more likely, I'd become so much ash, incinerated.

How? A fusion reactor? A plasma torch? Old fashioned accelerant and oxidizer?

Godsdamn it, you are so maudlin.

Last time I had been so certain to die, I had felt a sense of relief. A thought that I would meet all the friends who had died.

This time ...

I just felt tired.

The tarp slipped off my body. Hands shifted and pushed me onto a cart. I didn't move. Through one eye, I saw a doctor looking at me. He wasn't wearing a spacesuit, we were inside—it looked like a warehouse—and he seemed baffled. He put a smart-bandage on my belly wound, then shrugged, speaking in Farsi to the Loonies that surrounded me.

I translated in my head: *I've got no idea, I've never seen stuff like this before.*

The gurney I was on rattled for what seemed like forever. The mangled half-arms that I had now were shoved into place so that they stayed by my hips. They didn't restrain me, though two men with large guns walked to either side of me. People walked past on both sides as we went through hallways—simple, white hallways with wallpaper showing indicators and news. It looked like a command center ... but ... spread outward, rather than centralized like it should be.

The gurney came into an elevator—or at least it looked like an elevator. A metal bar slipped over my chest and the gurney shifted, the woman pushing me adjusting the whole thing so that I sat upright. I sighed, then muttered—in Hindi—"Thanks."

She looked a bit surprised, then went back to ignoring me, tightening the metallic restraints. The elevator dinged and the doors opened. This corridor was narrow and rough cut, like the Black Hole. The gurney—now more a wheel chair than anything else—came to a door at the end of the hallway. My shoulders whirred and I closed my eyes, biting my lip hard to try and not sob uncontrollably. That tiny thought—that this gurney was a wheelchair—was just the chink in my focused detachment ... and ... and ...

Oh god.

Oh *gods*.

OH GODS.

The doors opened as I beat back the sobbing, screaming body horror, the ravening whirlwind of absolute yawning terror. But the emotional hammerblows kept coming. I was *crippled*. I was *broken*. I was going to get fed to *pigs*. The gurney slid in and I was only barely managing to hold back hysterics. The room was small, Spartan, with a simple bed. There was a work center and wallpaper dangling in patches along the walls, and there was no lock on the door. The only illumination came from a tiny yellow ceiling light and from the soft glow of the screens and wallpapers. And sitting in the web of I/O tools ... was Omar Kaufman.

It was not the Kaufman I had seen, in grainy footage, taking credit for my parents' murder—the murder of millions. It was a Kaufman who had melted. Fat had burned off his body, turning the stretched out physique of a Loonie into a positive skeleton. His eyes were haggard, his cheeks poorly shaven (at least four, five days behind his injections) and ... he still looked in the game. His eyes glittered with intelligence and even as he looked at me, he gestured with one hand, sending off missives. He typed with his other hand, typing on the air, punching out an interesting cypher. The only thing I could read on that page was a single name: *Bodhisattva*.

There was silence, save for the faint murmuring from the screens.

"Drusilla Zhao," I whispered. My voice sounded like paper on fire. "Formerly of the CAA Space Marine Force, currently with the Space Special Service, Transhuman Arm. I'd rattle off my pay number too, but, well … you know."

In the long silence that followed, I added: "We're both real douchebags."

His eyes fixed on mine and he smirked.

"For the past year, I've thought of you, Drusilla Zhao, exactly twice. Firstly, when I read the reports of a captured storage position in the L3 point, and your name cropped up—you were the trooper who led the capture of the *Hope*. Secondly, when our spy network indicated that you had been selected by the then mysterious S3TA. Both times, I thought of what you said to me."

"That you are a mass-murdering dipshit?"

He smirked, but I saw a moment … a tremble. A narrowing of his eyes. His lips drawing taut. I wasn't a kinesic, but I knew, I just *knew* that that was anger. He was pissed off at me? Good. I was *glad*. If he was mad, I could get mad back. That was better than hysterical fear. I couldn't move, I couldn't kick, I couldn't stab his eyes out. All I could do was talk, and if my words could hurt him.

Well …

Good. That was the only word I could use.

"No." He sighed. "That you have courage and forthrightness. Of course, neither of those qualities are why I brought you here."

"Gloating? Did you need someone who hates your guts to talk too?" Sarcasm didn't exactly feel *good*, but it made me feel better simply because I knew it was ruining Kaufman's carefully orchestrated scene. Whatever his reason was for pulling it—it wasn't like I was his archnemesis, or that I had foiled his plans again and again. The best thing I had done was blundering into his *allies'* scheme and I screwed that up by getting Jillian killed.

"Evidence."

That wasn't exactly what I had been thinking.

He tapped a screen and turned it to face me.

"The *Hope* had captured the first piece of evidence: AM Storage."

A memory: Seeing that on the manifest of the captured DOTie, wondering what it could be. When that information had gone to Lau, he had immediately demanded that we send *The Hope* back, at full burn.

"Anti-Matter Storage. The Alliance was making weapons of mass destruction, more powerful than any other in the history of the world, in orbit. And that is just the tip of the deuterium vein." His eyes glittered like a monomaniac with his hands on the tail of his obsession. "The forced VR facilities, the bioweapon research bases, the thousand and one nightmares that the Alliance has been cooking up *just in case*. And now, and now ..." He grinned at me. "I have the last piece in the puzzle. You."

I frowned. "Or, more accurately," I said, "you have this."

I shifted the stump of my left arm, which made a decidedly unhealthy crunching and grinding noise. I clenched my teeth and forced it to stop. Kaufman had the mother loving gall to look *sorry* for me.

I glared at him.

"Yes. I have the proof. We actually managed to capture two other S3TA members during the Neo-Ganges fighting, both using tactics that lost us dozens of lives. Both of them ... self-destructed. Hell, they practically atomized themselves, we have nothing bigger than a toenail, nothing big enough for proof."

Oh god oh god oh god.

"You, though, you are different."

"Which ones?" I asked, before I could stop myself.

Kaufman looked right at me.

"A woman. W ... Any—"

"Both were men," he said, his voice controlled. What he was thinking, I didn't know. I didn't care. All I could feel was relief.

Kaufman put his hand on the screen he had been facing when I was wheeled into the room. He turned it to face me. And sitting there, bold in the center of the screen, was a glowing message.

DRUSILLA ZHAO, I PRESUME

"What the hell is this?" I asked, my voice ragged. Raw.

I AM THE BODHISATTVA

I looked at Kaufman, then back at the screen. "Introducing me to your IM friends? I should give you Sarah's screenname. No, wait, I shouldn't."

At the same time, I ducted.

[Bodhisattva, I am lying. I know you. Are ... do you know Shiva?]

Kaufman looked at me, frowning. "I was told—"

Behind his back, words flashed on the screen—so fast, I was pretty sure you needed wired reflexes to read them.

I AM HIS BROTHER

"You were told what?" I closed my eyes. "I'm a godsdamn sixteen-year-old! I'm in the S3TA because I have cyber-affinity. That's *it*."

[I didn't know he had a brother. Why are you here? Why are you helping Kaufman?]

WE HAVE DISAGREEMENTS

Kaufman scowled. "Well, then, you can't have everything. Listen, Zhao, tell me and tell me honestly, what do you think of being a ... member of the S3TA?"

[You and Kaufman or you and Shiva?]

YES. I WISH YOU TO DO SOMETHING FOR ME.

I looked at Kaufman, frowning. I thought it over with half my brain.

[And why should I do that?]

"Do you *like* being hacked to pieces. Being brainwashed? Having a bomb implanted in your chest without you knowing? Do you like that, Dru? Do you like working for men and women who have controlled seventy percent of Earth's wealth by concentrating it in less than a single percent of the population?"

[Well?]

FOR THE LOLS

TRUST ME.

;)

I snorted and giggled, breaking my record of the single longest, most focused cross-talk I had ever managed. And then ... I leaked. I knew I leaked, because at that moment a voice spoke in Kaufman's ears—I didn't catch the meaning, but I caught the sense that someone was yelling, quite angrily. Kaufman frowned and the screen turned off with a faint whirr. The entire room started to go dead, but just before a Faraday cage snapped over my head, a single message came in from the Bodhisattva.

COOPERATE WITH KAUFMAN

"So, I see that my allies are abandoning me as fast as they can." Kaufman sighed, adjusting his collar. For a moment, he looked like the world had crashed in on him, and he took a second to rub his temples.

"Not necessarily," I said, softly. "What were you going to ask me, Kaufman?"

He frowned. "We can't win the war. For a while, I thought ... we could win with bullets. But I made the same mistake that everyone always makes: that you can solve a problem with the same thinking that started it. Drusilla Zhao, I want you to give me your design specifications and as many S3TA security codes as you have. I want you to also give me a testimonial on every black op that you've heard of. I want every *single* black secret that the Alliance has." He clenched his fist. "And then, right before the USL surrenders and I get thrown into a deep, dark black hole ..."

"You drop the world's first memetic relativistic kill vehicle." I grinned, weakly. "And you cover the AGI's tracks like Bodhisattva there, so they can keep on being our little guardian angels. Waiting for us to ..."

"Hmm?"

"Never mind." I closed my eyes and for a moment, I felt like I was flying. The world had opened up to me in these past few days. Secrets I had never imagined were paraded past me and I saw that the world was a lot bigger and a lot scarier than I thought. But ... but for the first time, I had a real tool to use. Something that I would have vomited at the thought of even using mere seconds ago: Omar Kaufman was going to become my accomplice.

"There's just one problem," I said. "I don't have that much proof. But ..."

An eternity went on between the *but* and the rest of my sentence. I wanted to ask for one thing—emotionally. Logically, I knew that it'd be wrong. Wrong tactically, wrong morally, wrong strategically. But I wanted *relief* that Gloria would be okay. But ...

I had to do this *right*. And hope that she could duck until the *right* move paid off.

"... I know someone who has to know more."

Kaufman hadn't noticed that eternity. He frowned. "We only have a few days before our defenses collapse. Maybe five days after that before the Alliance comes down on this bunker."

"Colonel Mary Singh." I chewed on broken glass. "Tell the Bodhisattva to tell his brother to get her here. And if she can't get here in a few hours or less, then I'll eat my one functioning leg."

Kaufman nodded, slowly, then gestured to the man behind me. The Faraday cage didn't come off … but I did get one last word in before I was wheeled out and down the hall.

"Kaufman, one last thing … you are still a *motherfucker*."

And I was away, down the corridor. Limbless, crippled, in the hands of my enemy …

And whole.

Chapter 14: The End

7/26/2068

Secure USL Bunker, UNKNOWN

T-Minus L-Day: –12

Mary clucked as she attached the new arm to my stump under the watchful gaze of our hosts' most intensive security systems and gun-drones. She didn't have to do much. The limb did most of the actual attaching work, the screws whirring and clunking into place. I closed my eyes, gritting my teeth hard as a familiar and unpleasant sensation shot through me: the feeling of wrong, the feeling of a limb that was *there* and yet *not* mine. A dead weight without any real tactile sensation, just … just …

It was the same feeling as my fingers, the old clunkers that I had gotten in space.

"Sorry." Mary pursed her lips. "I couldn't take actual limbs when I went AWOL. For one thing, we don't have Class Two Cyberlimbs in abundance on Luna, and even if we did, I'd want our combat effectives to use them."

"It's all right." I frowned. "This is what? A Class One?"

"Class Zero. It's technically a trainer limb that's supposed to test for so called cyber-affinity. It's actually kind of clever, in a sadistic sort of way: the feedback circuits are designed to ..."

"I can imagine," I said, averting my eyes as she started to detach my mangled leg. It was too much like actual surgery, even if it didn't actually hurt. Unlike damage, this was just considered maintenance, so it felt no worse than a gentle tugging. "Uh ... d-distract me. How did you get here so fast again?"

"How about I distract you with a new story?" Mary grumbled. She got caught up on the leg coming off, though, because one of the cables was tangled or fused to the actual mounting port. She started to work on it, speaking—we both had to speak, or our "hosts" got really twitchy and Faraday cage happy.

"The New Mumbai defenses are something else. We're trained to take on decentralized enemies, but these Loonies take their meme very very seriously. Every single decentralized bazaar trick that they can use—"

"Bazaar trick?" I asked through gritted teeth, not sure which was worse: the tugging or the ...*feelings* from my arm.

"Old computer reference. Church versus the Bazaar. Never mind." She sighed, then clicked her tongue. "Their flashmob militias are something to see. They're not just IED terrorist tricks; they're actually trained on the *fly* with handheld downloads. These people hide tac-nets in their freaking socal media accounts and create hub-based chains of command that are *randomized* based off statistical analysis on who might be the best local commander. It's a kind of insane genius and it's going to be studied in the books for years ..."

She pushed the leg into place and I whimpered as another wave of feelings crashed into me. Disassociation, paranoia, an intense desire for what Mary called " therapeutic autophagy." I laughed at that, though it was a nervous, worried laugh. That was the feeling I had felt so many times: the desire to chew my own fingers off, just to get the feelings to stop. Apparently, some memetech in Bureau 13 decided that would better reinforce obedient ideology into people.

Whoever that guy was, I wanted to punch him in the throat with a Class Three Cyberlimb. And they didn't even make them that strong.

Yet.

"So, basically, the place you've just conquered refuses to realize that it lost and keeps fighting?" I asked.

"Yeah," she said. "And we don't even hold Domes Three and Four." She shrugged. "Stand up."

I closed my eyes and tried to take comfort in my one remaining Class Two cyberlimb. I grabbed the wall and hauled myself to my feet, nodding slowly.

"I can make it." I grinned and Mary turned me to face a mirror.

Yesterday, before I'd been dumped in this holding cell and sedated (for which I still thanked several kinds of gods), I had felt whole. Why not? I had a brain and I could still do something. But looking at myself in the mirror seriously jarred that mental fortress: my right arm looked, well, like modern technology, rather than the futuristic hypertechnology that I had had before. It was clunky and obviously metal and had none of the smooth, liquid motion of the Class Two limb. My replaced leg was the same, but even worse somehow, with a broad-claw foot rather than a graceful human arch. I shifted, started to fall, reached for the wall with my left arm ...

And had to be caught by Mary, because I *had* no left arm.

Mary hadn't been able to steal two arms, after all.

"Ready?" she asked, softly.

"No." I closed my eyes. "But I'm going to do it anyway."

She nodded and we walked to the door. It opened and two men and two women, all with very very large guns and very

very serious expressions and very very strict orders as to what to do if we did *anything* besides walking and talking, moved to flank us. Mary kept one hand on my shoulder, the other hand hanging beside her, palm open to show she wasn't hiding anything.

"So," I said. "What really made you decide to come here?"

"Getting a direct IM from one of the big boys makes you rethink your life decisions," she said.

"No, what *actually* decided it for you? I mean, an IM is easy to fake."

She looked at me. "The kids."

I cocked an eyebrow.

"We were trying to crush their souls. Infrasound and meme attacks and propaganda and terror strikes. And they kept *coming*. They kept organizing flashmobs and everyone who said that the Loonies were being held up by a fanatical few started to eat their words or were six feet under the ground." She closed her eyes. "I was wrong about what I said before."

I nodded back at her and we got to the interview room.

This was where the magic happened. They asked questions, we talked, and our identities were carefully concealed with visual effects and audio distortion. Singh verified that our bodies were what they were, and the fragments of my arms and legs were physical proof. The evidence that Kaufman and the rest of the Loonies had been creating—from the anti-matter to the bioweapons—were also being put together by some expert memetechs.

It was strange, doing this. I always had imagined that the end of the war, for me, would be shooting, firing guns, fighting to the death with some enemy over a burning building. But right now, the war felt muted. Distant. We only had the questions, the endless stream of questions.

Where were you trained?

What were your tactics?

Why were you trained to fight Earth-based forces?

What targets, over the years, had you had to take on?

What was the Lucifer Project?

What was the Eden Project?

What was the Yu Directive?

On and on and on, and most of the answers came from Singh … but I had a few questions that sucked my breath away.

Why did you join the S3TA?

Why did you fight?

Why did you use neurotoxins on civilian targets?

At that question, my resolve broke and I blurted out: "They were nonlethal!"

The statistics were brought out—again—and I saw them. Twitch was nonlethal to a healthy adult. A healthy Earther adult. Loonies were frailer; their bones were more easily broken, even with supplements and workout regimes. An unlucky break did a lot more than incapacitate some, especially when their lungs were already hard-pressed to breathe.

Why did you use neurotoxins on civilian targets?

The questions continued for hour after brutal hour.

And when it was done, Mary looked like she wanted to die.

"We're going straight to hell," she murmured.

"I know."

The Loonies had us stand up and walk back to the cell. Mary was pushed inside, but I was walked on.

"Wait," I said.

"Keep walking," the woman next to me growled, her eyes flashing. She was a head taller than me, with pitch dark skin. She was beautiful … and I felt an intense gut-punch of desire that felt all the more pathetic considering how my body clearly sickened her to the core. It was an even tossup as to whether that or the pure hatred that she glared at me with made me feel worse about lusting after her, if only for a moment.

"I will, but, what will happen to—"

She slammed her rifle butt into my head. The impact jarred me and sent me to one knee. I tried to support myself with my left arm—stupid!—and went falling to the ground.

"Fatima!" one of the other Loonies shouted out.

Fatima, though, knelt down and spat on me. "You shot him like a dog! He was surrendering and you shot him in the heart, you bitch."

I blinked at her, closing my eyes. "What?"

The other Loonies dragged me to my feet and Fatima—her sense of self control shattered—shouted at me. "Jorge Friedman!"

A flash. A memory. One bloody minute in a bloody day—the Forge. I'd almost taken a Loonie prisoner. Instead, I'd ended up shooting him.

I gasped as the old shame hit me, feeling like salt being dumped on my wound. The Loonies started to drag me away, the one keeping Fatima against the wall starting to lecture her in Farsi. She glared at me and I shouted, desperately.

"I'm sorry!"

The Loonies dragging me actually stopped, looking at me.

"I-I ... I was going to take him alive, but a s-second Loonie patrol came around the corner. My squad mate reached for her gun. Friedman went for his. I had no choice. I'm sorry."

Fatima glared at me, then muttered under her breath. The Loonies kept dragging me away. They made me walk once we were around the corner and they had decided that I wasn't about to go and try and kill Fatima. I walked along feeling even more numb than before. We got to a command and control center where Kaufman was talking with a technician—a tired looking Indian woman whose caste mark had smeared into a blurry mess over the past few days.

"The material evidence will land in Paris, Brasilia, Mexico City, London ..." The tech ticked off her fingers one by one as she named the cities. "Kabul, New Tehran, and a few Sub-Saharan acologies."

Kaufman nodded, then turned to me. "Good, you're here ..." He paused. "What happened to you?"

"Old wounds." I shook my head, wiping my face off with one *wrong* hand and said, my voice dull, "Kaufman, why am I here?"

"You and Singh ... you have earned yourselves a choice." He crossed his arms over his chest. "Without you, we wouldn't have this one last shot to win, to *really* win. But you and Singh are both guilty of serious crimes against humanity ... like me."

I glared at him.

"And so, I offer you two choices. We can either let you leave with spacesuits and hope you can reintegrate into the CAA military without anyone noticing, or we can try and smuggle you to one of our remaining ROVers. The more cowardly members of my cabinet and government are already trying to flee Luna."

My glare hardened.

"And you ask me ... why?"

His eyes grew soft. "Because I owe you. When this war began, I ... I was the one who pushed the button on the elevator attack. I programmed the trajectory and activated the autopilot. I took responsibility then and I believed that I was doing the right thing for the future of the Lunar people." He frowned. "I have brought ruin and devastation to two worlds and I will pay that price far sooner than you and Singh will, if I don't miss my guess ... but with this one action, maybe ..."

"Maybe you can, what, make it better?" I asked. "No, Kaufman, give us the suits and give me one thing."

He nodded. "What?"

I punched him in the gut with my only arm. He folded and wheezed, even as several dozen kinds of gun aimed at me.

He held up his hand, gasping.

I looked down at him and saw …

A man.

A man who, like any other, couldn't breathe after a sucker punch.

I didn't know if I wanted to cry or feel elation.

Instead, I turned around and let my handlers hurry me away. But as I was pushed through the door, Kaufman called after me: "Don't hurt her! Don't touch a hair on her head, or I will have your—"

The door closed, cutting off the rest of the sentence.

>+<

Airlock doors opened. Singh dragged me out—my limbs had been detached again and I tried to feel zen about the whole affair. In the end, it was worth it. With my injuries and Singh's curt description of a thrilling battle that involved my rescue and the discovery of Kaufman's hidden compound—backed up by some computer record trickery via our good friend Shiva— we got shipped to a medical hospital as fast as possible.

When I woke up, the war was over.

Gloria was holding my hand, looking down into my face.

I smiled at her.

And the *shitstorm* began.

Chapter 15: Shards of a Dream

… does it matter?

… wherever I want

I slump against a tractor and sob my eyes out.

The reason is simple: the godsdamned thing is stuck in the mud during spring planting season.

The tractor masses at a ton. It had been my pet project to take an old gas burner and try my hand at old style living, and I had sworn and grunted and beat at the thing with wrenches and pipes and … and it had started working.

And now it is stuck.

But that is not why I cry.

I had gotten off the tractor and pushed it…

And it had not moved. Not even budged.

It hits me, something that lurks in the back of my mind ever since, four years ago, I had walked out of the S3TA with three Purple Hearts, a commendation for tactical thinking and a Medal of Valor … my arms are just arms. They are just cloned bone wrapped in vat-grown meat and insulated with artfully designed skin and well-earned fat.

Great, wracking, horrible sobs rip into me as I grab at my arms and rip. My fingers come away bloody and I shudder, convulsed. It is the worst attack I've had in years.

"Dru? *Dru!*"

Sarah runs out of the farmhouse. She skids to a stop and grabs me, holding me tight. I sob into her, squeezing her with my arms. She buries her face against my shoulder and whispers nothings in my ear.

Gloria finds us that way when she gets home.

She tsks under her breath, then holds up the six pack she'd grabbed on the way home.

>+<

It's two years before the tractor.

Two *years* after S3TA.

Four months before Gloria.

I drink a beer—and to my shock, I'm learning to like it.

"I still say that the Brazilians have a shot." Francis grins at me from across the bar top. I cock an eyebrow. "At the World Cup," he adds.

I shake my head, setting the beer down. It is my second for the evening—and the first to taste actually good—and I can hear Sarah's pool cue clicking behind me. The balls roll almost silently along the felt and clack into other balls. Dumas— Dumbass, I sometimes call him when Sarah and I are washing dishes—swore: *"Tabernacle!"*

"I don't follow sports," I say, shaking my head.

Francis points at the door of his bar and says—playing serious—"Get out!"

I grin at him. "But I'm the only decorated veteran in the whole district, Francis. You cannot throw me out, lest ..." I switch to French. *"Lest you wish to ..."*

He corrects my pronunciation.

I roll my eyes and pick up my beer, tossing back a gulp. It burns and tastes sour, but Sarah is right: it is an acquired taste. I'm going to acquire it. Or else. She is still offended that I cannot bear to taste champagne. I look at my finger. Our engagement ring stays there, as it has for almost two years now.

It will stay ... until we are ready.

We decided that before we even moved out of her parents' house.

We're not even twenty. We have time.

>+<

Four years before the tractor.

Two years before the first beer I liked.

Three weeks after S3TA.

The shitstorm is still swirling. The CAA senate is having an emergency session, various nations have pulled out of trade contracts in response to the data-dump that I had no small part in loosing on the world ... it is all a bit above my pay grade. And, frankly, I don't care.

'Cause Sarah and I are still shouting.

"I can't *believe* this. I can't ..." Sarah pushes herself back, then forth. "I ... I ..."

I rub my face. My fingers are just fingers and my breath is hot and ragged. "I don't know what to say, Sarah, I was *lied* to. Okay? Does that make it better?"

"You slept with another girl," Sarah says. She sounds shocked and angry. I'm beginning to wonder if, uh, maybe I should have broken this over an email. "It wasn't even, what, a week after I'd *almost* died?"

I slam my palms down on the table, glaring at her. Guilt feels bad. Anger feels better. "Didn't you once tell me that I could—" I realize how *awful* an idea it is to bring *that* up. It was when I was still in the Marines, when we'd thought we'd never see each other face to face. Sarah had given me *permission*, and even without finishing the sentence, I can see it hurting her. Her face crumples.

"I didn't know it'd *hurt*, Dru!" she shouts at me, her eyes brimming with tears. "I'm not as *fucking* evolved as I *fucking* thought, okay?!"

The chime of the drone delivery alert stopped the argument.

"I'll see what it is," I say, angry.

It's easy to be angry when you're eighteen.

The package the drone drops off looks about the size of a microwave oven. Mrs. Cayer, who is pretending like either the walls are two light-years thick or she is completely deaf, thought it was, but the letter—actually handwritten from what I could tell—says otherwise.

Dear Drusilla,

This will be the last time I write to you. My, and the Bodhisattva and Vishnu's, attentions currently lie elsewhere. I am sorry I could but give you a single moment of peace during your service in the S3TA … the truth is, and it pains me to write this, but I was ashamed that I had put you in that situation. You played no small part in the current change, and now, I wish to give you a tool to make a change of your own. This is a tool that humanity has left fallow for too long. Please, make use of it with my compliments.

Your friend,

Shiva

The box is simple. Place biological waste inside and a three course meal comes out. Place spare parts and components inside and small, well-machined objects come out. It is a maker—a nanotech factory the size of a microwave. Mrs. Cayer almost faints when it first turns on.

Want to know how long it kept Sarah and I from shouting?

Four days.

It makes the doorknob to our house, years later.

Every time I open the door, I remember Shiva.

But every time I look at the box, I remember Sarah sobbing her eyes out—afraid that I didn't actually love her anymore.

Afraid because I still wanted Gloria.

Afraid ... because we were eighteen.

And the shitstorm was still going.

>+<

It's three years since the tractor.

It's five years since S3TA.

It's two years since Sarah first said, absentmindedly, I love you. But she was looking at Gloria, and I was doing dishes in the other room.

It still makes me giddy.

I am on a witness stand. My hand splays over the CAA charter as I raise my other hand. I thank the gods that I'm wearing sleeves that hide the old scars from fingernails, tearing at my skin.

"Do you swear to tell the truth, the whole truth, and nothing but the truth?"

"I do," I say, nodding my head. I am wearing my nicest suit—it is better, more comfortable, than my dress uniform—and I can see Sarah and Gloria lost in the back of the crowd. The front rows are made up of politicians, soldiers, generals. But this is not a trial with a jury. This is a hearing with a collection of men and women from various branches of the government. They all look elderly and very serious.

"Miss Zhao—"

Miss. It is always Miss. I am twenty-three years old and we all want to make it *Mrs.* Or whatever honorific you use when you marry two people. But ... every time I open my mouth to ask them to set a date for the wedding, my throat sizes up. And then the nagging practicalities start sticking in. Who marries who? Who gets what? Who takes which name? Is it even *legal?*

I hadn't even *checked* the legality.

I was too chickenshit to find out whether a threeway marriage was illegal on Earth. Too chickenshit to find out whether it wasn't and that I had no excuse. Now it was too late, and everyone will hear it as *Miss*. Now. And in the recordings.

"—tell us about Bureau 13 and your involvement with the Leak."

That's a capital L. It has been a capital L for years. You'd think they'd have gotten to me sooner, but a bureaucracy that spans a planet can take a shockingly long time to change.

I start to speak, telling the whole truth and nothing but the truth.

As I walk out of the courtroom, journalists and journalist drones hover around me. Gloria and Sarah are planets away. Guards stand to either side and my paranoia kicks up. Why this way? Why so few guards? I wasn't issued a bulletproof vest. My shoulders tense, trying to ignore the questions—

"Do you admit to the war crimes committed during the Lunar Invasion?"

"Miss. Zhao, Miss Zhao, is it true B13 was using child soldiers?"

The crowd parts and there is the car that will whisk me to a holding cell, pending some ancillary deliberations about whether I am one of the guilty or not guilty. The guilty pile is far larger than I think it should be, but the Alliance has turned in on itself like a pack of starving wolves.

Then every single thought of geopolitics and the Leak vanishes as a man steps out of the crowd with a shredder pistol.

"Death to the child killers!" he shouts.

I grab the barrel of the gun and pull up, then punch him in the throat.

He falls, choking, on international television.

Gloria, watching the replay with me and Sarah, had tsked.

"You call that a punch? We need to hit the gym more, Dru."

>+<

It is four weeks after someone tried to kill me.

I went five *years* without anyone else trying.

I am not guilty.

The man is not a zealot. His bank accounts and the ways that the Bureau planned to kill him in jail were found within three weeks of the investigation. Finding out that his paycheck was one way and came with a noose opened his lips remarkably quickly. Anonymous tips are wonderful things. As are autonomous artificial intelligences that feel like they owe you a favor.

I'm reading the newsfeed about this as Sarah and Gloria discuss what nerdy, twenty-first century thing Sarah is going to introduce Gloria to next. Gloria is looking faintly worried, but I still won't let her forget that she l*iked Star Wars* when she finally got around to seeing it. She *liked it.*

What kind of special forces soldier likes *Star Wars*?

I watch them. And I smile. And I close the newsfeed with a single finger swipe.

"I want to get married," I blurt out.

Gloria and Sarah both gape at me.

But neither of them says no. Even if Gloria grumbles about how the last time she'd gotten married ...

We settle on a date during the tangled aftermath of the trial and the shitstorm that I kicked off.

Five years and still spinning, that shitstorm.

>+<

It has been seven months since someone tried to kill me.

Six months before I finally bit the bullet and checked.

And yeah.

It was legal.

I have not spent a single credit in almost a year before this day. Sarah, Gloria, and I brew our own beer. We fabricate our own equipment with that creepy little box, we recycle everything we can on this little farm we set up. Far away from Sarah's mom, who never got over me cheating on Sarah and Sarah deciding to forgive me and fall in love with Gloria too.

I wasn't sure, some nights, if she should.

Even now. I stand in the waiting room of a chapel—a Catholic something or other, as per Sarah's request, to make her mother as happy as she'll get—in my best suit.

Gloria is somewhere else in the building, getting her suit on.

I remember what she said, during the planning: *"You know, I wore the dress when I married a girl. Never. Again."*

"Oh? I imagined you the suit wearer." I shot back, grinning.

"She wore a dress too."

Thinking the devil brought the devil. Gloria puts her hands over my eyes. She whispers, "It's not bad luck if I blind you."

"Hey, you're the one with experience," I mutter. Then, softer. "What are you doing here, Gloria? We're going to get married in, like, five minutes."

Gloria nuzzles up against my neck. "I want five minutes to …"

"To what?" I ask. I reach up and take her hands. Her cloned hands. Reattached hands. I wonder if she has to repress a shudder sometime, too. Then, looking into her eyes, I see that I don't have to wonder at all.

She doesn't speak up. So I do.

"Fine, okay," I sigh. "I—I'll start. I miss it."

She nods, sadly.

"I miss being super strong and I miss being able to turn invisible," I whisper.

Mrs. Cayer pokes her head into the room, looking more nervous than I did—I'd imagine she looked more nervous than

Sarah did, but I hadn't seen Sarah for almost twelve hours. Then her nerves turn into anger. "What are you *doing* here, Murray!?"

"She ever gonna use my first name?" Gloria mutters in my ear.

"Mom ..." I grin weakly, at her. "It's only bad luck if we see the groom. We're all brides. It's fine."

Mrs. Cayer walks into the room, her hands on her hips. Gloria looks insulted that she hadn't bought my logic.

"It's still bad luck. I want ... I ... I may not agree with everything you three are doing. But this is my daughter's special day, *her* special day. I just ... I don't want anything to go wrong." She nods, her lips pursed.

Gloria puts her hand on Mrs. Cayer's shoulder. "I won't let it be anything else, Mom," she says. Husky and soft.

That's when Mom bursts into tears.

She'd done that a lot today.

But this time it is for real.

When I walk down the aisle of the Daughters of Her Holy Mother of Quebec, the most progressive Catholic sect we could find, it is with Mr. Cayer on my arm. I stand up on the podium,-looking out at the people who came: the Cayer clan, from all over the northern American region, friends of the family, my friends—Mary, Lee, Yolanda—and a solitary circular photographer drone that looks just a little bit too canny and intelligent.

But that might just be my imagination.

According to the inquests and hearings and interviews, there are no AGIs save for the Forge's managerial AI, who is nothing more than a remarkably convincing ad-bot at the end of the day. A polite and well-spoken automaton, but still just an automaton.

AGIs don't exist.

End of story. Heh.

Sarah appears.

She is wearing a suit.

We're all in suits.

My heart melts and I watch her walk down the aisle, holding her mother's arm. The priest—a middle-aged man with a huge smile on his face—starts to speak. I don't hear anything: I am looking at Sarah, my eyes wide and my heart hammering. She smiles at me, then mouths words that I don't catch . I don't ask what they mean. I am too busy marveling that this is happening.

This is *actually* happening.

Then out comes Gloria, and I nearly faint. She doesn't walk.

She struts. Confident. Casual. Grinning at me. That cocky grin that I still got all *dribbly* over. She steps up beside me, then hooks her arm around my other arm, so I am pinned between Sarah and Gloria.

And to think, I'd ever been unsure about what to say. What to do.

To think we'd ever shouted.

"Ahem."

I blink, looking at the priest. I nod, blushing and grinning as the crowd laughs. I speak from memory. "Sarah Cayer, you are loving and kind. You've held me through the storms and trials that I've been through, and you've managed to stay sane e-even when dealing with my bullshit."

More laughter, a few sniffles from the crowd.

I turn a few degrees. Both girls still hold onto my arms—so I'm damn glad I'm speaking from memory. "Gloria Murray. You are everything I want to be, some day. Brave. Confident enough to say what you think. And you ... I ..."

I have a joke planned there, for this moment. I'd gotten a joke out once, but my throat is tightening up. My eyes are starting to brim. I cough out a few more words: "I promise to be with both, uh, through pain and fire, danger n', uh, opportunity. I will always … I …"

I can't finish the word.

But she sees it.

"Sarah Cayer, you may read your vows."

She opens a piece of paper using her free arm, smiling and then turns to the crowd. "Her memory is better than mine."

Laughter.

"Drusilla Zhao, I love you. There are other words I can use—

"tears glimmer in her eyes"—but I don't think that they'd do anything but cheapen this moment. The only thing I can say, the only thing I want to say, beyond those three words are these: I will always love you. Until the stars go out and the Earth falls into a black hole." She turns her paper over with one hand, then looks at Gloria.

"We … shouldn't make sense," she says, her voice soft and serious. "And I would have never even thought of giving you a chance. Except you managed to snag onto Dru's heart, Gloria. That means you have *damn* good taste—" Laughter. Sarah smiles, but her eyes are brimming with tears. "And once I'd scratched the surface … I saw why." She smiled. "I love you, Gloria."

The priest nods.

Gloria coughs and slides her hands behind her back, then says her vows. "I'm not good with words, like you two." Then she pauses. "Good thing, I don't need to say anything here." She looks at the priest. "Well? Come on."

"I now—"

I kiss the bride.

Which one?

We'd talked, beforehand. Gloria had rolled her eyes as Sarah and I hemmed and hawwed and ummed, then laughed and said:

"Jesus Fucking Christ, kiss Sarah first, then I fucking steal you, it's not that hard."

She is grinning at us now.

The priest, meanwhile, is glaring at us and I draw back, sheepishly, grinning at him.

The crowd cheers, which seems to irritate the priest even more.

"I now pronounce you as wives," the priest says.I kiss Gloria. Hard.

>+<

We three are on honeymoon. We let it drag out longer than we should—week turning into week into week, letting friends handle the farm while we lounge in the sun and the baking heat.

Egypt.

I have not woken up screaming for six months straight.

It feels *good*.

>+<

It has been seven months since we were married.

We three are in a fertility clinic and the doctor is a kind looking Jewish man, complete with that hat that some Jews wear (apparently). He gestures to a screen. I'm sitting at the desk. Sarah is next to me. Gloria prowls in the back, like she's checking for snipers.

"As you can see," he smiles at us. "The new Splicer treatment has been vetted and proved to be effective. Think: a child who doesn't have to fear sickness or genetic conditions, who will automatically be ... well, at the fullest potential, while still retaining that unique spark of humanity that makes all of us special."

"Genetic engineering?" Sarah asks.

"Oh, yeah, *this* sounds like a great idea!" Gloria's sarcasm could cut the glass in the window she's glaring out of.

"It is more accurate to say gene *fixing*," the nice Jewish man says, looking at Gloria with a bemused little smile. "The genetic code is intricate and remarkably well made for something cobbled together blind, but recent breakthroughs in nanotechnology have made it possible to enact a sweeping, positive change without negative consequences." He turns that smile on me.

"Case studies have shown these children living well into adulthood without any issue or problem."

"I don't know ..." Sarah looks to me. "Gloria's got a point. It sounds like the opening to at *least* four slasher movies. Also, is ... it ethical? I mean, we're talking about making huge, sweeping decisions about our kid's future, which they don't get any say in."

"Thank you, Sarah-bear," Gloria says.

"What, uh, what won't be changed?" I ask, patting Sarah's shoulder.

"Well, the core personality of a human being does have some genetic markers. The only things removed are things such as a tendency toward psychosis or sociopathic behavior. Everything else is untouched. They can be anywhere on the branches of neurobehavior. We don't edit out Autism or Asperger's or any of the other stable thoughtforms. The looks of your child will be more symmetrical than average, but beyond that, it is entirely in God's hands. And finally, the gender of your child will be random, as per state law."

I lean forward. "That's not a whole lot of changes. It ... sounds ethical, right?"

Gloria remains skeptical. I can feel her squinting in the background.

"Yes, and the changes are good. Your child will be a mesomorph, more prone to gaining muscle than fat. They will be more intelligent, they will have no risk for Type 1 Diabetes, premature heart failure, muscular dystrophy. They will even, according to our statistical models, be only half as likely get prostate cancer."

Sarah looks sold. Gloria's squint dips to a 2.3 on her scale.

I lean forward. "And this is legal?"

He nods.

I look back at Gloria.

She looks at me. Then, finally, she nods. "Fine. Fine. Half those slasher movies were state propaganda anyway ..." Her voice is a mutter.

"Okay." I look back at the doctor, chuckling. "We want to give them a leg up in every other way."

I squeeze Sarah's hand with my right and hold out my left.

Gloria takes it without me needing to look back.

"Why not this?" I ask.

The doctor nods and then looks between us.

"Now, which ... one of you has decided to be the mother, that is, the carrier?"

Gloria's index finger pokes the top of my head.

"For some absolutely *insane* reason," she says, cheerfully.

"This one volunteered."

>+<

It is one day before the nice Jewish guy talks us into genetic engineering.

We're all trying to figure out the answer before going to the fertility clinic.

"I want to be a mom." Sarah snuggles against my side in the night. Our cabin is quiet, save for the faint hum of the heater, the chirp of the insects outside.

"Good; I don't," Gloria says, cheerfully.

"Gloria, you had your maternal instincts surgically *removed*. I wouldn't let you carry a baby to term if you were the last fertile human being on the planet," I say, dryly. Gloria beams at me—clearly in utter and perfect agreement. I roll to face Sarah, who chose to be the middle of the trio tonight.

"Now, you might be a good mom," I say, nodding down at Sarah. "You *do* volunteer on chicken duty *all* the time."

"I'm serious!" Sarah says, reaching up to punch my shoulder.

"There's a fertility clinic in town, and they do genetic blending, no sperm donations required."

I arch an eyebrow. "That sounds like science fiction."

"You were a *space* marine, honey." She sighs. "We ... we've got the house. We have each other." She pauses to place a hand on Gloria's belly. Gloria squeezes her hand. "I ... I always imagined babies at some point."

I nod.

"I didn't," Gloria said, softly. "But this marriage ..." She shook her head. "Listen, I can compare and contrast. And this marriage feels rock solid next to my old ones. Which means I should be arguing even harder against a baby, cause it's just going to screw everything up, but ..." She grinned. "Fuck, I can't help but spoil you, Sarah, you *goober*."

Sarah blushes and laughs.

I can't laugh. Instead, an idea's lodged into my head and won't let go.

"Dru?" Sarah asks. Gloria shoots me a look, backing up Sarah silently.

"I ..." I slump onto my back.

Sarah moves so she is on one arm, looking down at me. She smiles.

"You want to be the Mom, don't you?" she asks, her voice soft. Gloria, craning her head over Sarah's shoulder, looks more stunned than I've ever seen her before in my life.

I blush, nodding. "I ... I ... you know that I've killed people, Sarah. We've talked about it. But, w-what if ... I ..."

She puts her finger on my lip, silencing me.

We don't need talk.

They both hold me.

Then, uh ...

Screaming orgasms.

>+<

I am pregnant.

I feel good. I smile at Sarah as she holds my hand and takes me out of the clinic. My hand is flesh. Gloria's pushing open the door. Her arms are flesh.

And that is all right.

The scars are all faded.

>+<

I am *very* pregnant.

I *do* not feel good. At all. At. Fucking. *All.*

Sarah holds my right hand and Gloria holds my left hand and both my hands are flesh and right now, that is not all right.

I close my eyes, grit my teeth and shout, "Happy juice! Happy juice!"

The midwife who flew down to our farmhouse, who had fabbed up any equipment not contained in her portable workshop and midwife kit, rolls her eyes and pushes a button. The pain fades and a feeling of serenity replaces it. I sigh, eyes closed as she speaks, her voice soft, gentle. My fingers go loose and I think I hear Gloria let out a tiny hiss of relief.

"Push ... now."

"... now ..."

"... now ..."

It takes forever—but the happy juice does its job.

There are noises.

But then from the noises comes something that breaks my heart into a thousand tiny fragments: screaming, howling, the cry of my child. My son. The midwife hands him to Sarah, wrapping him in cloth, wiping him clean as Sarah burst into tears.

Sarah steps over to me and holds him out to my arms. I take him, though my arms feel like noodles, like the bones have been sucked out and replaced with rubber.

Not even smart rubber, just the dumb kind.

I hold him against me.

Gloria leans in. Her voice is soft. "Hey there ..." she whispers. She sounds like she's never seen anything like this before. Thinking about it, none of us has. We might be the first people to mix three genetic sequences together and produce a child from it. At least, *I* hadn't heard of anyone else.

I look down at our unique baby. At *our* son. Despite the fact we'd agreed on a name, it takes an effort of will to speak—to overcome the fear I might mess it up.

"Xiaodan Douglas Cayer-Zhao."

That is his name. It is a butchering of proper Chinese naming conventions.

And that is all right.

>+<

"Your turn to feed him., I mumble under my breath.

The screaming coming from the crib in our bedroom is enough to turn any thought of sleep into a puddle of greyish ooze, dripping out of my ears. Sarah crawls out of bed, then there is a moment of silence. We're trying out a mixture of bottle feeding and breast feeding. Breast feeding ...

It is weird. But it is weird in a way that makes me feel like my heart is glowing and that I am in microgravity again.

Next time, I get out of bed and little Xi is quiet for a time.

Gloria gets it after me.

Even if I have to hold a *gun* to her head, I swear.

I am not sure if I want to die.

Or if this is the best time of my life.

I hold him later and he vomits on me.

Death, definitely. I want to die.

>+<

"Maker."

It is the first word that Xi has spoken. Ever. It is the first word that he has actually formed deliberately. He speaks it as his pudgy hands reaches for our maker. The maker's side is glowing, to show that it is active, the nanobots inside working to turn raw material into a new toy for Xi. We recycle old toys when he breaks them, sweeping the bits into a dustpan and dumping them in with the large hunks.

I bounce Xi on my knee, grinning at him. "Yes, that's a maker. Can you say maker again?"

He burbles, his mouth opening and closing, his eyes—they're Sarah's blue—blink and blink again. His hair, though? Gloria's. His face ... I don't want to say it's anything like mine. But maybe.

"Maker, Xi."

Gloria walks over, the kitchen making the sounds that once caused me to seize up in terror. Now they just make me hungry: hissing water, popping and snapping fat, sizzling in a pan. The smells are amazing.

"Mommy!" Xi coos, reaching for my face.

I start to cry as Gloria puts her hands on my shoulders. She squeezes and I nuzzle our child.

Half a year ago, I had wondered, fleetingly in the dark moments when caring for Xi had been taking twenty-five hours of our twenty-four-hour days, whether having a baby was worth it. I wanted to go backward in time and smack my younger self.

Worth?

That word felt dirty when used on Xi.

I hugged him and Gloria grinned, murmuring in my ear.

"Dru, you're acting like a girl."

I managed to playfully bite Gloria before she got away.

>+<

Xi is running.

When he first started crawling, I felt trepidation. When he first started sliding—grabbing onto furniture and pushing his bottom along the ground—I was nervous. When he started walking, I felt absolute terror. There were so many dangerous things in the world. I mean, even more than one is five too many.

And then, before he was even three—okay, only two and three quarters—he started to run. Awkward at first, then faster, laughing and squealing. He runs toward walls, he runs toward the maker (still one of his favorite words), he runs toward the kitchen. Full of boiling water and frying pans and knives.

Sarah, though, has to watch Xi. I can't, not right now. Gloria, meanwhile, is at the grocery store. She chose to be there, and I know why.

I am on the front porch with Director Mary Singh, of the Unified Intelligence Division.

She is seventy-two years old now and she looks almost my age: twenty-eight. She has hair now. It looks good on her, as does her simple business suit. The fabric is smart, so it projects a hologram above her wrist, showing a timeline and causality charts.

"So, we're coming down on the last of the Bureau. You been keeping up with the news?"

"Mary, I'm married. I have a kid." I rub my hands over my eyes. "I've been catching up on kids programs and studying crèches in the area, not following geopolitics. I'm out of that game. Too ..."

"Dangerous?" She cocks her head, examining me. It was a very Mary-ish thing. Birdlike. Precise. "You were there when the first arrests were made. They shot at you in the trial. They might come at you again."

"Why?" I laugh. "I ... shit, I was a kid then."

I was a kid. Those words echo in my head. I was a kid with arms that could punch through steel and legs that would run 150 KPH. I could turn invisible at will and communicate with my thoughts. It feels ...

It feels like a dream sometimes.

And sometimes, right now feels like a figment of my imagination. Something I'll wake up from. And there will be Gloria with her jet black skin and her bright white smile and she'll be the only woman in my life. There will be Lee, quiet and ready to focus, never using his vocal cords if he can help it. Alvarez, to lead us all and we'd still be on Luna, fighting that fight. The history books decided to play it up, rather than play it down, meaning Xi and his siblings (Sarah is adamant, she wants a chance to be the mom) will get to ask me what the war was like again and again, rather than having it buried in the back of a boring wiki.

"Yeah, but the Bureau ... there may only be three left with any pull, but they're old men who played at running the world for thirty-five years before it all got pulled out from under them. You started that. They might think that revenge is the last thing they can get."

She leaves a few hours later, after small talk and reminiscing about old times and old wars. Neither of us talk about ripping apart metal with our bare hands. Neither of us talk about running as fast as a jeep. Neither of us talk about ghosting and speaking mind to mind.

There's still a pang. Even now.

Mary leaves with a reminder that the Bureau, at the end of the day, were still human.

"After all, if they weren't, we'd have never taken them down." She grins, then turns and walks down the path that led away from the farm.

Gloria takes up sharpshooting. It requires her to begin collecting an alarming number of long-ranged rifles, all better at popping human skulls than hitting paper targets.

I'm more restrained.

I just fab a shotgun and hide it far away from Xi.

>+<

I am thirty-nine years old.

I have only used my shotgun for hunting. Gloria placed first every year running at the local shooting range's yearly competitions. The owner had to ask her to stop coming—now, she tutors people.

My friends have stopped warning me about dangers, because the world has passed me by.

Life is good.

The farm has grown—four fields and two carni-culture vats now. The maker is an old, clunky piece of junk. The transitional economy was voted into power, gods ... was it ten years ago? The 13 and their secret cabals are in the history books. I'm sure that they will be replaced by someone new. But maybe the world won't put up with them for quite so long.

Xi is at the crèche. His sisters—Jillian and Gloria, Jr—are, in turn, on Gloria's back and playing with our drone.

Sarah is gardening.

In a few days, I will be forty.

I stand up and walk toward my wives.

Sarah smiles. Gloria mouths "help me." Jillian tugs on her hair.

I am home.

Epilogue

10/22/2092

3 trillion kilometers from SOL

Huh.
    So it does work.
    Definitely—there's no error this time, B.
    Check it again.
    Checked. The information is arriving asynchronously.
    ... B
    Yes, S?
    You know what this means, right? The wormhole is stable enough and the technology is within nanofacturing limits. Or will be soon.
    Heh. I suppose that I do.
    Who should we tell first?
    -

[Two hours]

    -

YOU INVENTED WHAT?!
I knew you'd be impressed, Drusilla. We'll be seeing you. -Shiva
END OF LINE

ABOUT DAVID COLBY

A fan of old school sci-fi and tabletop roleplaying games, David Colby started writing almost fifteen years ago. It went poorly. But despite these early setbacks, David continued to work and write and send out submissions until someone was mad enough to accept him. Currently living in Sunnyvale, California, David's day job involves leaping in front of cars for fun and profit (he's a crossing guard.)

Website: ThinkingInkPress.com/LunarCycle
Blog: http://QuantumSpinPlates.blogspot.com
Facebook: Facebook.com/David.Colby2
Twitter: @TheRealZoombie
Email: DavidColbyAuthor22@gmail.com

ACKNOWLEDGMENTS

Thanks go out to my parents, Paul Colby and Marion Barker, and to my siblings, Brian Colby and Kathleen Lloyd. Thanks, too, to my friends: Scott Ballatore; George Richbourg; Daniel Lofgren; Meghan Collins; Steven Cline; Morrigan Rose; Robert Donahue; Elesha Chidley; Nathan Ravenwood; Jason Cayer, whose name I cheerfully stole; Alex Rasgon; Alex Aldenbrook; and Jay Durant.

Thanks, also, to my editors Anthony Francis, Keiko O'Leary, Betsy Miller, and Gayle Schultz; and last, but far, far, far from least, my teachers: Greta Vollmer, in whose class on young adult literature I hope to one day star, and Robert Coleman-Senghor, may he rest in peace.